Pangyrus

For information about permission to reproduce selections from this book,
please write to Permissions at info@pangyrus.com

The text of this book is set in Palatino
with display text set in Crimson and Baskerville
Composition by Alex Green
Cover design by Douglas Woodhouse

Editor: Greg Harris
Managing Editor: Alex Green
Fiction Editor: Anne Bernays
Nonfiction Editor: Marie Danziger
Contributing Editors: Kalpana Jain,
Carmen Nobel
Poetry Editor: Gregory Lawless
Associate Poetry Editor: Cheryl Clark Vermeulen
Editorial Assistants: Ahna Wayne Aposhian,
Annie Harvieux, Myles McDonough
Graphic & Web Designers: Erika Rich, Esther Weeks
Copy Editors: Chris Hartman,
Ahna Wayne Aposhian, Rachel Zwiebel
Business Manager: Lakeisha Landrum
Logo Design: Ted Ollier

Pangyrus
79 JFK Street, L103
Cambridge, MA 02138
pangyrus.com

Contents

Motion Harmony #3 by Jennifer Barber 7

Empty Summer Houses by Pamela Painter 8

City of Widows by Kalpana Jain 17

Pastoral by Kiki Petrosino 22

Coming of AIDS by Timothy McCarthy 23

Excellence by David Rivard 39

High Street Park: The Kindness of Boys
      by J.D. Scrimgeour 41

New England February by Elizabeth Moore 46

Cowardice by Mitchell Grabois 48

Crime Shows by Matthew Lippman 50

In the Pocket by Suzanne Bouffard 52

Away from my Dream Desk by Peter Ramos 60

Keepers by Michael Badger 61

David Sedaris is Sick of Himself by Carmen Nobel 74

Istvan by Lauren Haldeman 81

The Memorialist by Kelly Matthews 83

Allen Ginsberg: An Encounter by Harvey Blume 96

The Pain Scale by Julia Story 110

The Tonic of Wildness by Christina Porter 112

Holy Family Holds the Line by Tom Zygiel 118

Goodbye Climate Change, Goodbye Global Poverty?
      by Paul Adler 134

In Praise of Nothing by Eric LeMay 140

Living with Pain by Greta Austin 143

Poem in Film by Jack Christian 157

X-Ray by Anne Bernays 160

Benign Indignities by Kim Stafford 183

The Living Dead by Carol Band 184

Self-Portrait Before by Anna Ross 187

Demolition Trio by Zach Savich 189

Blue by Leslie Anne Mcilroy   192
By the Pool by Julie Monrad   194
Temptation's Crush by Allen M. Price   204
Licensed Outlaws by Sebastian Stockman   216
A Borrowed Copy of Ben Fountain's Brief Encounters
        by Eric Anderson   226
Five-Finger Discount by Dwight Livingstone Curtis   227
Interlude: Yemen by Effie-Michelle Metallidis   238
Young Man Afraid of His Horses by Caryl Pagel   243
Losing Translation to the Marketplace of Ideas
        by Alex Green   244
An End to Impunity? Protests and Hope for Mexico
        by Alfredo Corchado   248
DEAR GRACE by Collier Nogues   252

Contributors   260
About Pangyrus   266
Index   267

Pangyrus

Motion Harmony #3

by Jennifer Barber

His Muse

He undresses her jewel-hard mind
every morning with his brain.

Her Muse

She looks for an unmarked room
down a long corridor

and finds him, warm with sleep,
his soft shirt beside the bed.

Their Muse

The female seahorse loves the male
who carries the pearls of her eggs

inside his pouch
where they hatch as miniatures

he fosters and ejects
by doing a forward, a backward bend.

He's relieved, she stunned.
Soundless, the little fleet sails forth.

Empty Summer Houses

by Pamela Painter

Colten's wife, her blonde ponytail swaying above her jacket, boots crunching on oyster shells, had turned off the sandy lane onto the white path that lead to the house she'd added to her List in August. Three weeks ago, after they'd photographed an improbably pink stucco house on the bay, he'd decided that stalking empty summer houses was getting too strange—not what they saw, but actually doing it. Today, he'd promised himself was the last time. After this, Liz was on her own. He hadn't told her yet. But he would.

"Colt, see that," Liz said. She pointed to a limp garden hose and a wheelbarrow propped against a dilapidated shed with no door. "Eerie, right."

Ignoring 'eerie' Colten said, "No, dumb. Why not put the gardening stuff in the shed." 'Eerie' was Liz's major criterion for the photographs she'd taken for the past two years: broken lawn chairs; rusting grills, rotting chunks of driftwood. Then peering through windows: crooked lamp shades; couches swathed in sheets; paintings of watery landscapes and molten sunsets; a red kayak in the middle of a living room; wind chimes on a table, kids' stuffed animals. To Colten, these houses just looked neglected, empty.

"I'll leave the shed for later," Liz said, patting the camera he'd given her last year for her 30th birthday. Her ponytail beckoned him onward.

"Fine," Colten said.

It was November and most of the summer houses in this Outer Cape town had been closed up for the winter. Water drained, deck furniture dragged inside, plywood nailed over windows facing ocean or bay as the population went from 65,000 to 4,000 in a matter of days. Traffic disappeared and restaurants using white tablecloths and cloth napkins closed. The back roads of Truro and Wellfleet were hidden and lush in summer, but fall pulled down their curtains of leaves and vines, and houses of wildly varying proportions and styles seemed to appear overnight. Many summer residents were now the absentee owners of what was called in real estate parlance "a winter water view."

Colten stopped to assess the compact one-story house ahead, caged in by tall scraggly pines. A spongy carpet of needles rimmed the path to the front door and dry leaves ruffled the edges of the gray shingled walls. Everything gray. Cedar roof, decks. Gray. Mortal.

They'd started photographing empty houses the autumn after Rosie died. She was seven months old, when late one June night she stopped breathing. The ambulance's siren split their world in two. The next day they were childless. Soiled diapers still reeked in the pail; the mobile of circus animals still trembled above Rosie's crib. Colten found himself clasping a throw pillow against his chest. Liz was inconsolable as the languid hours of nursing Rosie were replaced by the whooshing rhythm of a sterile square machine pumping out Liz's milk. That fall, her breasts dry and the baby furniture stored in the attic, they took long walks to get out of the house. Liz began to keep a list of odd, closed-up houses to photograph. She called her collection Empty Summer Houses. If she ever displayed them, which he suspected she would do sometime in the future—maybe in her next Provincetown show, it would be a form of transgressive art.

This morning she'd said, "OK. Let's take a walk. I want to visit that house set back from Ballston Beach." It was her way of getting them past the argument they'd had last night. Colten had started it by saying let's think about having a child. Liz had slammed down her wine glass so hard the stem broke. "How can you say that without adding the word 'another?' Have you forgotten her?" she cried. And he'd said, "Never. But I want to raise a child. I don't want to replace Rosie. I want a different child. Children." Turning away, she said what she always said, that it was too soon. This time he'd countered with, "Then when? It's been two years. We don't have one photograph of Rosie anywhere." He'd never pushed so hard before. Last week in the Stop & Shop, in line behind a harried father with a squalling baby, the smell of Johnson's Baby Powder nearly made him cry. "When?" She'd slept in the guest room.

After a silent breakfast, she'd thrown his barn coat at him and said, "Come on." He'd hesitated—long enough for Liz to ask "what?"—so he put on his coat, telling himself this was his last such walk.

Having declared that the shed was for later, Liz led them to where they were now—peering through the screens of a large screened-in porch, so open that it was the obvious place to start. The Cape hadn't had a first snow, but when it did everything on the porch would be covered in a sifting of white.

They pressed their noses to separate panels, inhaling the fall screen smell, metallic and woodsy. The porch had the sort of clutter that Colten had come to admire, even envy. A round Weber grill missing its lid and filled with pillows of gray ash stood beside a statue of a cement cupid holding cement grapes. In the corner, a dimpled soccer ball. A second green hose, newer, wound around and through various wicker chairs and small wrought-iron tables. An old glider reminded him of the one his grandmother once had, gently sliding back and forth, a movement a swing can never replicate.

Liz took two or three dozen photos. Two trellises leaning against a wall had caught her eye. Dry bits of vines still twisted in and out of the squares. She'd always liked squares, checks, polka dots, clay roof tiles on Italian villas, twenty nude torsos of manikins in the window of a store going out of business—all patterns. He could have predicted her choice for Rosie's wallpaper—tiny pink rosebuds that from a short distance, looked not like rosebuds, but delicate splashes of color. Gone. Stripped away a month later.

Lagging behind, Colten photographed the cupid and red tricycle. The cupid's concrete arms and legs and tummy were all soft gray curves. The tricycle's seat was cracked and crooked. He pictured Rosie's bruised knee and a faded blue tennis shoe doing a left dismount. He longed to pinch the bell and hear its fuzzy ring. Rosie always waved her chubby arms when they set her mobile into musical motion.

"Colt," Liz called. He hurried to catch up.

Methodically, they began to circle the house, looking in every ground floor window that had an interior view. Flimsy curtains covered the windows of the first two narrow rooms, probably bunk rooms for kids, but not the kitchen's. It was circa 1950 with stainless steel counters and a fridge with a rounded top.

Liz pointed to the rotisserie standing on its splayed four legs. "Just like my mother's," she said. Her camera's shutter clicked four times.

To Colt, it looked like a baby's bassinet but he didn't say so. A row of seven coffee pots on a top shelf attested to not much being given away—or moving on to the swap area at the Wellfleet dump.

"Dump"—a word the woman at town hall still used, to Colt's joy, when he got their yearly "Transfer Station" sticker.

"Now, there's a shot," Liz said.

He strained to see what she was seeing. "That space under the sink?" he ventured. A limp curtain covered with perky chickens hatching eggs was pushed to one side, revealing all the household poisons: Lysol, Fantastic, Clorox, Windex, Murphy's Soap Oil. Enough to kill a houseful of kids. What would Liz title it? Rather, why?

As she focused on the lethal collection of cleaning solutions, he moved to the next window and peered into a pantry or mud-room. Two dolls stared from the seat of an old wooden highchair, the counters were piled high with stainless mixing bowls and a bottle warmer. The floor was cluttered with sand toys—plastic pails and shovels, a water mill he would have loved. It wouldn't interest Liz, but he'd loop back after she'd moved on. His thoughts snagged on those words 'moved on' and brought back last night's argument. Could he ever stand to be without her? Here, they were known as year-rounders. They were both teachers at the Truro high school, where he used to think he taught teenagers, but now he affectionately thought of them as somebody's children. As kids themselves, they both had looked forward to a month's summer vacation on the Cape where they stayed in the tiny stand-alone cabins like delicate dolls' houses lining the long shore road to Provincetown. Perched just five to twenty feet from the azure bay depending on the tide, they all had flower names: Petunia, Gold-enrod, Wisteria, Lily. As teenagers, Colten and Liz fell in love with the Cape, and then with each other while working hot summers as fry cooks at The Lobster Pot in Provincetown. Their clothes reeked of oil and both sets of parents insisted they undress outside their cabins. Giggling, they had run into the shimmering surf, declaring this is where they wanted to raise a family. Or was.

"You'll want to skip the pantry," he called out, feeling sad and also mean. Withholding from her the beautifully carved highchair. He rounded a corner, ankle deep in brown leaves. And then he saw it. A narrow wooden door ten feet away was open about an inch. It probably led to a washing machine or hot water heater. The wind must have done that. "Liz," he called. "Come see."

He slowly pulled on the metal handle and the door scraped open about a foot.

In this moment, more than anything, he wanted to go through that door. "Liz," he called again. He needed to push her through into some unknown space.

When she came around the corner, her eyebrows raised in a question, he pulled her forward to stand in front of him. "Our lucky day," he said, and reached around her to tug the door open all the way. Then he firmly placed his hands on her shoulders and propelled her through. She swung around as if to slap him, then stumbled and turned so she wouldn't fall as he continued to push her forward through this narrow damp room and into the kitchen.

"Jesus, Colt," she said. "Are you crazy? Now we're trespassing." Her nose was red. Her ponytail swung in wide arcs of anger.

"We're not doing any harm," he said, shivering. "What? Are the police going to show up?" It was colder in the house than it had been outside. He took his hands from her shoulders to bury them in his pockets.

"You know Charlie does rounds on all the empty houses," she said, peeling back a curtain to peer through the dusty window above the sink.

"Like our friend is going to pull out his handcuffs. Like he's not going to buy our neighborly story about looking after a neighbor's summer place."

Liz swished the curtain down. "Neighbors whose name we don't even know." She moved as if to leave but he caught her arm.

"Just this once," he said. "You can't see everything from the outside." He pointed to a meager collection of salt and pepper shakers on a narrow shelf above the stove—all cutely brazen animals. Then to a potholder with a seriously burned corner.

"Five minutes," Liz said, jerking free. Unable to resist, she raised her camera to take six photographs of the poisons under the sink. Then the kitchen sink itself.

He left her and walked into the next room, a sort of parlor. White bookshelves were filled with *National Geographics* and mostly smart people's books: Hilary Mantel, Robert Caro, Cees Nooteboom, Witold Rybczynski, John Banville, Murakami, Bolano, Krugman, Tolstoy. No mysteries. No "summer books." Every book bristled with a bookmark and when he turned to that page it was also dog-eared as if the reader in the house stopped before the end of each story. Surely it wasn't possible that someone could live with all these unknown endings.

He called out for Liz to join him. "Only another minute," he promised when she appeared. As she scanned the shelves, he said "Notice that every book has a dog-eared page also marked with a bookmark."

When Liz pulled *Anna Karenina* off the shelf, it fell open on its own.

"Maybe we should leave a note, explaining how each story ends?" he said. "We want you to know that Anna (after page 224) leaves her husband of the big ears and her beloved young son for Vronsky who turns out to be a cad, which leads Anna to commit suicide."

"Anna wanted to change her mind in those last moments," Liz said.

He said he didn't remember it that way.

He pulled out *Home*, one of his favorite books, and put it back. "But why did they stop reading?" he wanted to know. All these unfinished stories frozen in place."

As if to ignore what he'd just said, or to confound the house's incurious readers, with a grandiose gesture Liz plucked out the bookmarks from one entire shelf and stuffed them into her windbreaker's pocket.

"Don't," he said.

She took more photographs. "Don't what?" she said. She took more bookmarks. Her pocket bristled with them. "You brought me here."

"That's all I did." Colt retraced his steps to the mudroom to make sure he'd closed the door behind them. Returning, he stumbled over a single two-by-four propped just inside the doorframe. He dragged it over to a tiny window to see it in the light.

On the first four-inch side, unevenly-spaced horizontal lines rose from the bottom. Each line had a name and a number: Sam, age two, age three, four, five, six, up to ten and each age was accompanied by a date. Sam was ten and tall this past summer. Slowly Colt turned the two-by-four. Ben's side was next. He was now eight. Zoe's narrower side was next. She was four last summer. Colt pictured their father holding them still, his hand on their rounded tummies, then using a ruler and pencil to mark how much they had grown in the past year. Each kid would step away, eager to see their progress. It was evidence of a real summer family—now a winter family somewhere else.

"Colt. Colt. Where are you?" Liz's voice rang out. And then she was there, her gaze sweeping up and down the two-by-four, asking what he was holding in his hand.

"A family record," he said. "Here, read it." He toppled it toward her and she was forced to catch it.

"Sam," she read, "age ten," and stricken, stopped.

"And Ben and Zoe," Colt said, pointing to the penciled lines. "Look how fast they are growing."

"Where did you find this?" Liz said, her voice breaking. "We need to leave. Charlie doesn't need to be put to the test."

But the test was for himself. His heart was forever gone from this venture. "Liz, Liz," he said, taking the two-by-four from her, leaning it back in place. "When we're out here photographing other people's houses, our own house is empty." He turned her around and gathered her into his arms, her boxy camera a dark and silent heart between them.

She closed her eyes.

"I won't do this again," he said.

"Don't leave me," she said into his chest. The camera had to be hurting her as it was hurting him. He held her tighter for now.

City of Widows

by Kalpana Jain

*I*n the month of July, when both heat and humidity are at their peak in the holy city of Vrindavan in north India, thousands of devotees stream in to offer prayers to their Lord Krishna on a day that is among the most auspicious in the year. As devotional music blares through loudspeakers, a surge of bodies presses forward towards the temples that have been adorned for the special day. This place of the childhood *leela* (divine play) of Lord Krishna, a Hindu God who is considered to have taken human form to fight off evil, never lacks abundant festivity or throngs of visitors. But a few streets away, where the crowds and the chanting fade away, a row of lime-painted buildings, with freshly washed white cotton sarees strung neatly on a clothesline, offers a glimpse into the daily life of some of the city's residents. Going about their chores are abandoned, widowed women, aged anywhere between 35 to 80 years, who have traveled thousands of miles to find this place of refuge.

In one of the dormitories here, sitting on the edge of her bed, is Geeta Bai. For 60 years Geeta Bai was entirely devoted to her family. She married at thirteen; her family was the only life she knew. Her husband was her Lord, whom she still addresses with deep reverence as her 'swami' (master). After her husband died some fifteen years ago, she had hoped to be looked after by her two adult sons, whose birth she had prayed for. In the patriarchal Hindu tradition, it was expected that the sons would take care of her in her old age and perform her last rites when she died.

But her sons resented her dependence after her husband's death. "I couldn't take the fights anymore. So, I left," she said, as she wiped her tears with a corner of her saree and hugged me tightly. Fifteen years ago, Geeta Bai left her village, traveling hundreds of miles, after hearing stories about a place where "widows like her" could find shelter. "I'm hungry for love," said the 80-year-old widow, casting her glance around the large dormitory, where at least thirty other women are sitting or lying in silence on their beds. Geeta Bai held my hand and let out sobs that shook her frail body. Her family has not visited or ever inquired about her since she left. The story of others is no different. Vrindavan continues to draw thousands of widows, who, within India's patriarchal tradition, lose their sole means of survival and protection after their husbands' death. When abandoned by their surviving family, many women, hearing about this place of shelter, head to Lord Krishna's city, seeking refuge from a male God, who, in the Hindu tradition symbolizes divine love.

Bai and her roommates live side by side on beds arranged closely in two parallel rows. Their few belongings — some clothes, and a few prayer books — are stacked on a corner of their beds. The space under the bed is used for storing a small stove and some items for cooking. The air in the room is thick with an odd mixture of smells: old clothes, disinfectant, and the stench of urine. In many ways, it resembles the bleak wards in India's public hospitals, except that most people in those hospitals would have a home to go back to.

A deep melancholic silence pervades the room. As a way to fill up their day, the caretakers of the home have handed these women slim notebooks, in which they repeatedly write the name of Lord Rama several times a day. As I enter, a few women are trying to write the God's name. Some are chanting it. Most are simply lying on their beds. Chandrawati, who has been living there for the past fifteen years, has occasionally visited her sons. "But I don't like it there," she says. Bankumari came about five years ago and has not heard from her family since then. Gauri Devi left her home about twenty years ago.

Among the throng of devotees in Vrindavan, the widows are easily recognized by their attire; their white cotton sarees are considered traditional dress for a Hindu woman following her husband's death. As evening descends, these women start to fill up the many temples. The *bhajans* (holy songs) that they will sing for the next few hours in praise of the Lord will earn them a few cents' worth of rice and lentils as the day's meal. Those unable to find a place in a temple will beg for food or money from the thousands of devotees who throng the city at all times. As demand for shelter far outstrips the supply, not all who enter the city are fortunate enough to find a bed and shelter.

"I am here for Krishna's love," says Kamala Bai, who is without shelter and begging for food on a narrow street outside Radha Rani temple. Squatting alongside are many others in similar conditions of desperation. They are half covered with their sarees, their upper garments missing, showing visibly starved bodies. Lord Krishna and his consort, Radha, remain their only hope. "The Lord will look after me," says Sharda Bai. In one hand she holds a metal pot, in which some passing devotees may toss a few coins. In the other, she holds a stick, used to scare away the hundreds of monkeys present in the city; unchecked, they will prey on the widows' food. "Take off your glasses," she urges me, while pointing at the monkeys. "If they don't find food on you, they will take whatever else you have." With no place in the widows' homes, these women share the space on the streets, with these simians and others.

Despite India's promising economic development, the condition of widows, who flock to the city, mostly from the eastern state of West Bengal, has not changed in the past several decades. In the absence of any formal social security systems, temples of Vrindavan have become the place of refuge for aging women, once they lose the sole means of their livelihood, which often are their husbands. This is thus the common thread in all life stories here. Each woman has a story to tell of maltreatment or abandonment by her surviving family. Almost all of them tell their stories with remarkable restraint as they choose not to complain. But the pain of abandonment surfaces in their words, tears or even their silence.

In this city of teeming devotees, the women are alone. With no family around them that would give them a purpose to live, the widows spend their living days waiting for their death. Bai keeps a portrait of Krishna by her side and prays to him to call her back to his abode soon. "There is nothing for me to look forward to. All my desires have ended," she says with a sadness that does not speak of renunciation, often believed to be the reason for the women choosing to live in Vrindavan. Their last rites are performed by NGOs.

The dormitories that I visited are among the many that have come up in the city; some are run by NGOs and some by the state government. Despite the shelters, deprivation remains acute. Winnie Singh, who started an NGO, Maitri (Friendship) in 2008, says, while summing up the condition of widows: "I witnessed a near stampede, when we were distributing food, for just half a kilogram of grain. And most of the women were so emaciated, they could not even lift the grain."

At times, the widows try to exchange the food they get for other necessities. "They were extremely malnourished, yet we noticed they were selling the grain to get a little money," said Singh. To Singh, the condition of the widows speaks to the violence against women that has been getting some attention of late. "It is an extension of the same violence against women, that we see in India, but in a different form," says Singh.

In India's patriarchal society, women accused of stepping outside of tradition are often punished in various ways. Ironically, these widows have complied with every tradition known to them, yet they suffer severe poverty. According to Hindu theology, caring for one's parents alone is said to result in accumulation of good karma, the fruits of which are to be enjoyed not only in this life, but in the many to come in the cycle of birth and rebirth. Thus a mother is traditionally given the highest place in a person's life, and cared for after a father's death. But here, in India's sacred town, the presence of desperate widows in large numbers illustrates the necessity of programs towards economic empowerment of women that can address the needs of different generations as well.

Pastoral

by Kiki Petrosino

Where did it start? In a city of gardens & muck.
When I held someone close, in watery light.
We drank & I bled all the way home.

Red-orange light on my legs. *Oh, wow*
that blink-blink of bright, that flip of the pulse.
Where did it start? In the garden, the muck

where insects jumped in starry arcs. My body
took shape, then. A greenhouse I entered alone.
We drank & I bled all the way home.

I wore so many clothes. Cotton, cotton, wool.
I burned in my skin like a stone. How, exactly?
Where did it start? There, in the muck

no one saw how we blazed into poppies.
Light raked through our bellies like combs.
We drank & I bled all the way home.

Now, I put myself to bed. My dreams
are coins to dispense as I like. On water. On light.
In a city of gardens & muck, you can start
to feel rich. You can start to feel right
& tumble for years down the hill of your life. You ask
Where does anything start? In muck. In a garden.
You drink the drinks & bleed. You're foam.

Coming of AIDS

by Timothy McCarthy

Dedicated to every angel in America—then and now.

Coming of age, as I did, during the 1980s meant that I came of age in the midst of the AIDS crisis. I entered middle school the same year Ronald Reagan took over the White House, when the Centers for Disease Control (CDC) reported the first cases of Kaposi's sarcoma among gay men, before "AIDS" got its name. I entered college the same year ACT UP (AIDS Coalition to Unleash Power) took over the New York Stock Exchange and Saint Patrick's Cathedral, when the National Institutes of Health (NIH) finally invited activists to participate in discussions about AIDS research and treatment, before medicine was available to anyone who wasn't rich. By the end of the decade, more than one hundred thousand Americans had died from the disease. At the time, I knew none of them.

But I did know about AIDS. I feared it, probably more than anything else in the world, even nuclear war. I felt it: every time I thought about or had sex; every time I visited New York City (I was from Albany); every time I went to church or watched CNN; every time I got hard flipping through the pages of *Sports Illustrated*. AIDS was everywhere back then. You couldn't escape it, as badly as I wanted to. My closeted adolescence was marked by persistent bouts of terror, the haunting certainty that I, too, would inevitably "get it." This was no way to grow up.

I suppose I could say that I wish I knew then what I know now, but I didn't. Hindsight is only clear because life, as it unfolds, is not. It takes time to make sense of things—especially sex and love and identity, the threat of an early death—but as James Baldwin reminds us, we must "earn our death" with our life. And I thank God I still have time to work on that. I do know more now. I know that the AIDS crisis could have been prevented. I know that it was caused by prejudice and neglect at the highest levels of church and state. I know that the late Ronald Reagan has blood on his hands. I know the extent of the hypocrisy of the Catholic Church. I know that ACT UP was brave, and that AIDS activists were burdened by internal battles over strategy and tactics. I know that women and people of color and trans* people have always been on the front lines. I know that one's access to affordable treatment still depends on one's race, class, nationality, and gender. I know that AIDS is far from over, here at home and everywhere else. I know that HIV rates are still rising in too many communities. I know how beautiful and complicated it can be to love across the color line. I know that my story is just one story, that the full story of AIDS has not yet been told, that certain voices have been left out, and that all stories—heard and unheard—are bound up together in some way. That's what I know now. Back then, all I knew was that AIDS was a death sentence. I knew that I was homosexual. I knew that I couldn't tell anyone. I knew that I was in love with a black boy from New York City. And I knew that I was fucking terrified.

The first time I had sex with another boy I thought I was going to die. I'd been raised very Catholic, and in that world, homosexuality was among the worst of sins. Perhaps not as bad as murder—or abortion, which the Church equated with murder—but definitely worse than "self-fornication," which some of my Catholic "elders" assured me would result in blindness. Despite these dire warnings, I masturbated much of my way through middle school. When I had to get glasses in seventh grade, I saw it as a clear sign that God was already beginning to exact His vengeance upon me for my nightly sins. I then resorted to jerking off under thick blankets, as efficiently as possible, in the hope that He wouldn't catch me. By the time I first encountered a dick other than my own—in July 1985—I was already stroking my way straight (as it were) to Hell.

It was hot as hell that summer—the kind of hot that made adolescent boys smell even funkier than normal. In those pre-deodorant days, no amount of cologne could have spared those around me. But believe me, I gave it my best shot. It didn't help that I had taken up sports—any sport, any time, anywhere. I always carried a bottle of Polo in my gym bag (this should have been another sign, though not from God). After practices and games, I would apply the cologne liberally—the more I sweat, the worse I smelled, the more I spritzed. It wasn't long before my father had enough of this: "Jesus Christ! You smell like a French whore!" he would exclaim. I was confused by this—no one in my family had ever been to France—and I certainly did not appreciate my devout Catholic father's hypocrisy in taking the Lord's name in vain. Then again, Dad was an Irishman, so I learned early on that he could accommodate a certain amount of inconsistency. I also learned to pick my battles.

I rarely say this now, but I was lucky to grow up in the suburbs, where swimming pools abound. It took me years to figure out why my mother so strongly encouraged me to "go for a swim" every time I walked through the front door during summers in middle school. Chlorine probably saved our family back then—from my "natural" fragrance *and* Ralph Lauren's manufactured one. But come fall, she, too, had had enough. I returned from school one day to find a big stick of "fresh scent" Right Guard on my bedroom dresser. Mom was the kinder, subtler parent.

◌

Emmanuel was also an adolescent jock, though I remember that he smelled more like sweet lotion than sweaty cologne. We met for the first time in *Señora* Persico's sixth grade Spanish class. Emmanuel was the new kid, introduced to us all as *Manolo*, which is Spanish for "God is with us." Several kids snickered, partly, I'm sure, because his Spanish name sounded like a mix of cooking oil and the Latin boy band that was popular at the time, but also because it was probably beyond the reach of my mostly white classmates to see the image of God in a fourteen-year-old black kid. I'm sure Emmanuel could sense this. On the first day of school, he seemed distant: quiet, intense, cautious. Who could blame him? He had transferred to our upstate suburban middle school from "the city," a place I had visited many times as a child, where classrooms no doubt looked a lot different from the one he was now sitting in. When he was assigned to the empty desk next to mine, I was never more grateful for alphabetical seating. "*Hola, Manolo!*" I blurted out like some culturally incompetent welcome wagon, "*Yo soy Timoteo!*" Emmanuel looked me up and down with great skepticism, my grey V-neck sweater vest and thin-laced Docksiders clearly no match for his bright-colored sweatshirt and fat-laced Adidas sneakers. I must have seemed so *foreign* to him. "I'm not Spanish, *hombre*." I muttered some awkward defense, in English, about how I knew that, but that *Señora* Persico wanted *nosotros* to *hablamos Español* in class. Eventually, he almost smiled at me, with an equal mix of caution and pity. I fell immediately in love.

Though my attraction to Emmanuel had many sources—he was new and cool, tough and elusive, smart and beautiful—our relationship was forged, initially, by a more specific kind of desire. I needed a Spanish tutor, and Emmanuel, the New Yorker, was pretty fluent. After a bit of pressure, *Señora* Persico let us team up in the language lab. *Manolo y Timoteo.* Together, we'd breeze through the lessons, and then replace the Spanish language cassettes with mixed tapes of rap music his buddies from back home would send him. This was the first time I had ever heard this kind of music, and I fell in love with it, too. Emmanuel and I would write notes back and forth about which songs we liked best, and why, always in a chicken-scratch "Spanglish" to give us cover if we were caught. (We never were.) I spent many hours alone in my basement copying Emmanuel's mixed tapes on my Sony dual cassette boom box, and many more hours in my bedroom, also alone, jerking off to thoughts of the two of us breaking it down as DJs scratched and MCs flowed in the background. I still get horny sometimes when I listen to old-school Hip Hop, especially L.L. Cool J, who at the time looked like a slightly older version of Emmanuel. (It wasn't just the ladies who loved Cool James!)

My relationship with Emmanuel wasn't all language lessons and mixed-tape masturbation. You see, in addition to being a Spanish whiz and a pioneering connoisseur of rap, he was also a spectacular athlete, and my father was the high school basketball coach. I can only imagine how excited my father must have been the first time he saw him play ball: his lightning-quick first step, his long arms and lanky torso, his then oversized feet seemingly made of springs. Turns out they had much more in common than hoops. My father had grown up in and around New York City, and was always eager to talk about the place. Emmanuel had lost

his father at an early age, and was eager for the type of coach-
ing and mentoring my father was famous for giving his players.
My mother loved Emmanuel, too, and his mother me. We were
both only children and "mama's boys," and it wasn't long before
our mamas started referring to each of us as "second sons." Over
those early years—from the fall of 1983 to the spring of 1985—we
became the brothers we never had but always wanted. We would
often joke about this, being "brothers from another mother," and
it felt good to laugh about such things rather than labor over them
for too long.

○

It was no surprise to anyone that when my parents told me I
could invite a friend to come with us on our trip to Disney World
the summer after eighth grade, I asked Emmanuel. My family
didn't have much money—and besides, my mother wouldn't fly—
so we drove from Albany to Orlando. Our white Dodge Aries station wagon had no air conditioning or FM radio, twin disasters
that resulted in two increasingly disgruntled teenagers. Emmanuel
and I spent much of the trip with the windows rolled down and
our Walkmans over our ears. Our gangly legs became entangled as
we searched in vain to make more room in the back seat for bodies
we could barely contain. This was the first time we'd been so close
physically, and it was hard. I mean this quite literally: as we drove
south, we kept getting erections. Anyone who has spent more than
a few minutes in the company of an adolescent boy knows that
this is perfectly normal. Fourteen-year-old boys get hard brushing
their teeth. But this was different: *we were aroused.*

This was not an ideal situation. Emmanuel and me, jammed
into an Aries wagon, broad daylight, my parents positioned com-
fortably in the front seats, perfectly oblivious to the hormonal hell
being experienced in the back seat by two overheated adolescents
with chronic, raging boners. We decided to handle the situation as

best we knew how: by comparing dick size. First, we made sure that my folks, already deep in conversation about something or other, thought we were just playing with our hand-held video games. Then, we put a blanket over our heads and bodies—pitched a tent, as it were—rubbed our crotches aggressively to make sure we would be putting our best dicks forward, and then whipped them out. In retrospect, this was nuts, but it made perfect sense to us right then and there. His was slightly longer and darker. Mine was a bit thicker and pinker. Both had impressive heads, at least for that age. I was pleased, even relieved, to see that I measured up, and I suspect he felt much the same way (this was before either of us learned fully of Black "myths" and Irish "curses"). Boys are funny about their penises: the only thing better than playing with your own is the visible confirmation that yours compares favorably to the others in the room—or in this case, the car. We checked each other out for a couple of minutes, long enough to know we liked what we saw, and then put our junk back in our trunks. We removed the blanket, put our Walkmans on, and stuck our heads out the window like a couple of puppies in heat.

All of this was happening as we entered South Carolina. When my parents stopped to get gas at "South of the Border," the weirdest place I've ever been, Emmanuel and I exploded from the car and ran into the restroom, sat and stroked in separate stalls, and emptied our own tanks. We never talked about it; just a head nod and a smile as we washed our hands. It was either that, or explode. As we got back into the car, we both noticed the sandy-haired, blue-eyed gas station attendant with "Jose" on his nametag. (They all had "Jose" on their nametags, the boys anyway, which is one of the things that made "South of the Border" so weird.) He was frowning at us—not a grumpy, I-hate-my-*job* kind of frown, but the far more menacing, I-hate-*you* kind that naïve Yankees sometimes get when they travel together, white and black, below the

Mason-Dixon. This was probably the first time it really occurred to me that Dixie was different, that *our* difference—our *friendship*—was something *abnormal*. Fortunately, our final destination was Disney, where dreams, evidently, come true.

○

That first night in Florida was the most thrilling and terrifying of my life. Emmanuel and I lay there on the queen-size bed in silence, near darkness. My parents had rented a modest place on the outskirts of Orlando. It had two bedrooms—one for them, the other for us—separated by a long hallway with a shared bathroom in the middle of it. My heart was racing, sweat running down my face and chest and crotch as if my body were a kind of in-house hot spring. I was hard again. I thought Emmanuel might be asleep until he said, "It's too hot for clothes." Then he kicked off the covers, pulled off his shorts and underwear, and took off his shirt. This was the first time I had ever seen another boy totally naked. It was exquisite. His sinewy body was soft and smooth, tight patches of black hair just visible beneath his armpits and around his swelling cock. He was skinny, skinnier than me, which for some reason I found very exciting. I looked at him, awkward and anxious, and slowly removed my clothes as well.

Then I panicked. In something like a postlapsarian spaz attack, I rolled over on my stomach and turned away from him. I couldn't look at Emmanuel any more. Or perhaps I didn't want *him* to look at *me*. "What's wrong?" he whispered. "Nothing," I snapped back, "Good night." Truth is I didn't know what the fuck to do. I had never been this naked, this close, to anyone, boys or girls. Sure, I had kissed a few girls—with tongue, even—and I had copped a feel or two in the movie theater. But only with the good Catholic ones who would never, *ever* (thank God!) let you touch them underneath their clothes, or (God forbid!) without them. Sure, I had bragged about "getting some" to my boys in the locker room, but we all know boys tell the biggest lies about girls when they're in the locker room. I was no different.

But this *was* different: Emmanuel and I were in the *bedroom*. I regretted ever inviting him. I wanted to go home, throw away all those goddam mixed tapes, and forget any of this ever happened. My meltdown was accompanied by several long minutes of silence, the kind that leaves just enough room for sinful thoughts. I lay still. Still hard, hardly breathing. I heard a soft rustle of the sheets. Then the rising heat of Emmanuel's body pressing gently against mine. His right leg over my left one. His penis against my pelvis, moving slowly across my ass. He was on top of me now. My dick was jammed into the mattress beneath us. "Spread 'em," he whispered. "No, you," I whispered back, turning my head to the side so that his lips could touch my ear. He reached down and spread my ass apart, gently, and put his cock where we both wanted it to go. Not in, not yet, but near, next to, up against, as close as it could be without really hurting. Then he began to move his hips, back and forth, up and down, quick as hell. As quiet as he could. The friction felt fantastic. But my parents were in the next room, and the door was barely shut. *Fuck*! I wanted to be asleep, alone. But I was awake, aroused. Back and forth. Up and down. In and out. Even quicker now. As quiet as we could. Breathing in sync. Hands locked. Legs tangled up again. Like in the car. But different this time. Not sure how long it would last. *I loved it*. Then he broke his rhythm, jerked several times, and collapsed onto me, the sticky sweat between his chest and my back sucking us together. Fifteen minutes of fabulous.

When Emmanuel finally rolled over, I escaped to the bathroom. I reached back and felt cum all over my ass. I reached forward and stroked myself with it until I produced a load of my own. As I stood over the toilet—wet, withered, wanked out—I heard my mother's sweet, familiar voice in the hallway: "You OK, honey?"

Fuck! I took a long, deep breath: "I'm fine."

○

I wasn't fine, and I wouldn't be for quite some time. The blood had really freaked me out. That night was the first time I'd ever found blood in my ass (it wouldn't be the last). Not much, but enough. This could only mean one thing: I was going to die. What's more? I felt like I *deserved* to die. As a kid growing up in the Church, you learn three things about sex: first, when married people have sex, they have a child; second, when unmarried people have sex, they commit a sin; and third, when two gay people have sex, they go to Hell. No pleasure. In each case, just a means to an end, predestination by another name. This was the simple "truth" that had been fed to me alongside the wine and wafer for as long as I could remember. And there was no escaping *that* truth.

The other truth—*my* truth, notwithstanding the blood in my ass—is that I *loved* having sex with Emmanuel. And he seemed to enjoy having sex with me, too. That trip to Disney changed my life. Each night, both of us naked, more of the same: back and forth, harder and deeper, top and bottom (it was only later that I learned to call this "versatile"). In terms of quantity, if not quality, it was probably the single best week of sex I've ever had.

But I *really* couldn't get the blood out of my head. Around the time Emmanuel and I began our affair, one that would last nearly ten years, homosexuals were starting to die in droves from AIDS, commonly referred to as the "gay plague"—or worse. At the time, neither of us knew much about AIDS, other than that you could "catch" it through a combination of bodily fluids like blood, saliva, and semen. Fucking and sucking—especially the kind that Emmanuel and I were now doing on a regular basis—was a sure death sentence, but kissing and sneezing and sweating were also considered "risky." None of us were immune to this widespread (and often wrongheaded) public panic. Prejudice and prophylactics were everywhere. Hell, even the cops wore forearm-length rubber gloves when they arrested the activists who were protesting prejudice. But the churches were among the most dire of doomsayers. Many "Christians"—Catholics and evangelicals especially—considered homosexuality a form of "moral depravity"; AIDS was "God's wrath against homosexuals." I heard these morality-mortality plays over and over again from various pulpits, and each time, they penetrated a little harder and hurt a little deeper. It was like a Mass-induced mind-fuck, with President Reagan and his deputies playing a secular, supporting role. They all seemed to be preaching to the same choir—and that choir would *never* include people like me.

There was only one way for me to deal with all of this: fuck the Church and find some other way to figure out what the hell was going on. And that's just what I did. Each Sunday, I would sit in the pews and tune everything out, dead to that world. After my Confirmation—required of me by my parents—I even stopped going to Communion; no more body and blood of Christ for me. All the while, Emmanuel and I continued to build a secret life together even as we denied its many risks. Despite the corrosive fear and shame we both felt in different ways, desire trumped everything else when it came to fucking. And we found every possible way to do so. We would sleep over at each other's houses, room together at summer camps, and eventually shack up in cheap motels. And we would often steal away during school and sports competitions: locker rooms, bathrooms, wooded areas, darkened hallways. In high school, we even arranged our schedules so that we would have gym class during the same period. The football coach was our physical education teacher, and he frequently let us go off on our own to play basketball, which invariably ended with a very different kind of "one-on-one" before our next class. When we both made the varsity basketball team—my father's team—we initiated a new ritual: Emmanuel would come over to our house in the late afternoons on game days so we could take a "nap" and then shower together before catching a ride back to school for the evening's game. In retrospect, it's hard to believe we never got caught, but we were pretty clever and we counted on the fact that it never even occurred to anyone that we were doing anything out of the ordinary. We were just best friends, co-captains, getting ready for the big game.

I suppose it didn't hurt that we had pretty, popular girlfriends for most of high school and college, the perfect "beards" (another term I would learn years later) to hide our increasingly brazen sexual trysts. More and more, our lives were rooted in routine deception. Looking back, my greatest regrets from this period of my life—and there are many—involve all the girls, and then women, I lied to along the way, some of whom I loved, almost as much as I loved Emmanuel. It is to their credit that they found ways to love me properly long before I figured out how to love myself, much less reciprocate. Closeted gay men—especially those, like us, who could easily "pass" or "cover"—are often terrible partners to women. As ashamed as I am to admit it, I see clearly now that this is a form of abuse. But it's probably too late to apologize.

○

All this deception was its own kind of private hell. Throughout those years, I was torn apart by the terrible inner suspicion that I was indeed a homosexual—not just Emmanuel's best friend and lover, but a full-blown *faggot*. I began to check out other boys in the locker room, to fantasize about the athletes I read about in *Sports Illustrated*: Michael Jordan, Brian Bosworth, Bo Jackson, Greg Louganis. But those weren't the only images that stuck with me. I was also quietly obsessed with the increasingly frequent coverage—in newspapers and on television—of those who were dying of AIDS: the gay men, now numbering in the many tens of thousands, with emaciated torsos, sunken cheeks, purple lesions, and wheezing coughs. These people terrified me, precisely because I was still so afraid that I would someday share their fate. I lost count of the number of years *There but for the grace of God go I* played on a torturous feedback loop in my head. Every now and then, I can still hear it.

Therein lies the toxic tautology at the core my adolescent worldview: if you were gay, you got AIDS; if you got AIDS, you would die; and if you died, you deserved it—*because you were gay.* Back then there was no alternative messaging. Nowadays, adults like to tell queer kids "It Gets Better," a no doubt well-intentioned assurance that they will someday, eventually, be free. But there is no such thing as freedom, or a future, when you are sentenced to the solitary confinement of your own self-loathing. And that was the tragic irony of my closeted, Catholic adolescence: I didn't need to die to go to Hell; I was already living it.

For some reason, not sure, I decided to take matters into my own hands during my junior year of high school. Disturbed that our public school's health curriculum made no mention of AIDS— like the Catholic Church, it emphasized abstinence over contraception insofar as it talked about sex at all—I decided to use my position as front-page editor of the school newspaper to write an investigative article on how other schools in the area were dealing with these topics. I wrote a scathing cover story, claiming that these high schools, including my own, were failing their students by not teaching them about the dangers of AIDS and the importance of "safe sex," a relatively new concept that I had yet to adopt in my own private life. The article made quite a splash, and it earned me the kind of praise that probably enhanced my college admissions prospects. Yet another tragic irony of my tortured teenage existence: I was celebrated for writing publicly about the very thing I was incapable of working out privately. Here I was demanding better AIDS education even as I refused to learn its lessons. Here I was challenging the stigmas surrounding homosexuals even as I was hiding my own homosexuality because of internalized stigma. And here I was advocating safe sex practices even as I failed to use condoms during sex. I was a *champion* hypocrite.

College was an even deeper closet. I limited myself to girl-friends, and began using condoms on a more regular basis, but only when they insisted on it. My encounters with Emmanuel were less frequent, mostly holidays and summers, and less satisfying. Sex became more of a macho competition than a team sport. The closet—and the culture—was clearly taking a toll on both of us.

"Coming out" is a long-term process not a one-time procla-mation. On some level, the process started for me when I realized I was in love with Emmanuel, even before we ever had sex. But it be-gan to accelerate, despite my best efforts at resistance, over Christ-mas break during my senior year of college. I met Emmanuel at his place before going out drinking with friends. He had a present for me, a used copy of *Cures: A Gay Man's Odyssey*, the coming-of-age memoir by gay historian Martin Duberman. "He reminds me of you," Emmanuel said, knowing that I had just finished applying to Ph.D. programs in history. He smiled as I opened the book and read the first few paragraphs of the introduction. I had never heard of Duberman, and the thought of reminding anyone of a gay his-torian freaked me out. Still, Emmanuel had clearly read and liked the book—which made me curious—and that was enough for me to devour it the very next night. It was the first "gay" book I ever read. My life hasn't been the same since.

At about 4 a.m., drunk, Emmanuel and I stumbled back to his place. I was horny. He was reluctant. He kept insisting, "I'm not really like that any more." After a big fight—I think I called him a "cocksucker"—we ended up in bed together. As we were fooling around, he stopped me, lifted my head to his, and told me to kiss him. In all those years, now nearly a decade since Disney World, this was the first time we had ever kissed each other. It was also the first time I had kissed another guy. I told him I loved him. This, too, was a first. He smiled, and then asked to suck my dick.

In the morning, Emmanuel's mother cooked us breakfast. He was in the bathroom, and she sat down with me at the table. "I saw you and Emmanuel sleeping this morning." Sensing my shock—this was the first time anyone had said anything about us out loud—she added: "I love you for loving my son. I know he doesn't always show it, but he loves you, too." She stood up from the table, put her hand on my shoulder, and kissed me on the top of the head. I smiled, and then choked down the tears.

In the fall of 1993, shortly after moving to New York City to start graduate school, I went to see the first installment of Tony Kushner's epic two-part play, "Angels in America." I was blown away by what can only be described as a theatrical miracle. It was the first time I could remember seeing homosexuals represented positively in art. What struck me most, however, was not the play itself, as brilliant as it was, but the people in the audience: gays and straights, men and women, who, like the play's main character, Prior Walter, had so far survived the AIDS crisis. That night, sitting by myself in the theater, I began to contemplate what it might be like for someone like me to be part of this kind of *community*. When the house lights in the theater went up, everyone around me was in tears—not the kind that dampen the cheeks but the kind that roll down like waterfalls, the kind of tears I had wanted to shed that morning at breakfast with Emmanuel's mom. I was just now learning how to cry.

At the end of "Perestroika," the second half of "Angels," Prior Walter speaks directly to us: "This disease will be the end of many of us, but not nearly all, and the dead will be commemorated and will struggle on with the living, and we are not going away. We won't die secret deaths anymore. The world only spins forward. We will be citizens. The time has come." The time had certainly come for me—to love Emmanuel, and myself, enough to let go and move on; to stop drowning in that toxic abyss of fear and shame that threatens the lives of far too many queer people; to come out, on my own terms and in my own time; and to start to figure out what it means to *live*.

Coming of age is never easy, for anyone, but AIDS certainly made it far more difficult than it needed to be. It still does. When we were growing up, AIDS seemed like a death sentence. It shaped and shattered a generation, but it did not destroy everyone or everything—not nearly. Emmanuel and I haven't seen each other in years, but we did not get AIDS, and we did not die, and we did not go to Hell. Still, I wonder how things would have turned out for us if we had been born ten years earlier—or later.

Excellence

by David Rivard

Peg says
Luca Signorelli gave even
Michelangelo

ideas, but
exiting from the duomo
in Orvieto

the excellence
of sun still
seems greater to me

than Signorelli.
How great? As great as a cicada
in dry sawgrass

awakened
like a spark; or so it might
feel to you too

if you'd grown up
next door to a casket maker's
storehouse, a Quonset

hut, salvaged
War Department junk—its galvanized
corrugated sheet metal

like chrome rubbed raw & dull
by year of steel wool
and shivering hot at noon—

it would burn you
burn you good & sorry
if you touched

fingers to metal
while peering through
the grimy windows,

all those market-rate
coffins stacked flat inside on sawhorses
and dark as lead doorways.

High Street Park:
The Kindness of Boys

by J.D. Scrimgeour

Two blocks from my house, tucked behind the homeless shelter, is High Street Park. It's an urban playground, with a typical, modest assortment of slides and structures set on an island of woodchips. The woodchips aren't the best material. Some get in children's shoes as they play, and some get scattered around the rest of the park. They litter the small asphalt loop circling the playground where my two boys used to ride their bikes, and they're sprinkled about the basketball court, which is annoying if you want to play basketball—though not as annoying as the broken glass.

When my sons were little, I'd walk them to High Street. It's where they learned to slide down poles, kick and throw balls, and ride bikes. It's where they would swing and I would pretend to be a person walking, unaware, and get bumped by their feet as they swung forward. I'd spin and howl in mock pain, and they'd laugh and demand "Again."

Some years back, before the city cracked down, the park was almost uninhabitable as the weather cooled. People would let their dogs shit in the woodchips, and they wouldn't clean it up. Too cool to decompose, and too warm to freeze and crumble, the turds just sat there for weeks. I spent a few visits frantically hopping in front of poop before my boys stepped in it, circumscribing the "safe" area.

It's not a lovable park, not clean or beautiful. Some might say it's not especially safe, given that it is set in the middle of a block, back from any streets, and that the homeless shelter, with its handful of documented child molesters, borders it.

And yet, it is beautiful. When my youngest son, Guthrie, was an infant, I would wheel him to the park, my other son, Aidan, three years old, walking beside us. When we would arrive, Guthrie would sit in his stroller, watching, as Aidan climbed the jungle gym. There would often be a few older boys about, and one of them, Frankie, would come over, lean down, and talk to Guthrie. He knew to use the high-pitched voice that babies love. Guthrie would listen and smile.

A few years later, when Aidan was into baseball, he and I would go to High Street and I'd pitch him whiffleballs on the basketball court, the park's only open space. He'd try to knock the ball over the chain link fence into a small parking lot. Sometimes Frankie and his friends, Greg and Armando, all young teens, would join us, and we'd play a casual game of home run derby. Those boys would argue among themselves, but they were always kind to Aidan, always would tell him how good he was. The simple, encouraging words from older boys meant a lot to Aidan. I wonder if he even remembers them now.

The boy Greg, a skinny, dark-skinned Latino, was in an awful accident a couple years after those games. He and a friend had been riding a bike together, neither with helmets, and they turned a corner and got hit by a truck. The accident was serious enough to make the local nightly news. Greg got hit especially bad and had to be medevac-ed to Boston. I remember hearing the helicopter whirring over Salem that day and wondering what had happened.

I felt sick when I heard Greg's name and realized who he was. I not only recalled the whiffleball, but a holiday concert at Horace Mann Elementary School. Greg and my boys both attended Horace Mann, and when Aidan was in 2nd grade, Greg was a 5th grader. At the end of one of the 5th grade's songs, Greg scooted off the bleachers where the students were stacked and ran and slid on his knees across the stage, arms flung wide. It was a nice touch to the show by the school's music teacher, and Greg was a perfect choice: graceful and ebullient. The younger children loved it.

Greg had gone on to develop a love for basketball and real skill at playing it. He had made the Salem High varsity as a freshman in the winter before his accident.

His injuries were severe. Greg was in the hospital a long time, and was virtually paralyzed. The basketball program helped raise money so that Greg's family could get a wheelchair, a handicapped van, and a remodeled handicap-friendly bathroom. Now, three years later, Greg is still unable to walk.

I know that Greg is still in a wheelchair because I saw him at High Street Park recently. I had been at that park with Guthrie, now a seventh grader who likes basketball. Guthrie was taking shots and I was rebounding when a car pulled up and parked in the lot. Then another followed. Four stocky, short guys got out, one bouncing a ball, and they started shooting around. Soon, a van pulled in, and two more guys got out and helped maneuver Greg out the side door. They wheeled him over to the court and placed him just behind the basket, next to the pole that held it up.

And then these six guys, all about 20 years old, all a bit overweight, played three-on-three. They played hard, swearing at each other over fouls and the score, but they also played loose, friends who laughed at each other's screw-ups—a stupid, too-fancy pass, a humiliating blocked shot. Greg laughed, too.

They weren't great players, but they weren't bad, their bodies a mix of grace and clunk. A few of them had sweet jump shots. Once or twice they even set picks for each other. I watched them between rebounding for Guthrie, and as I did, two things became clear: they were playing for fun, and they were playing for Greg.

One March day well before Greg's accident, back when Guthrie was still a little boy who liked playgrounds, he put on his coat and red and blue knit cap with the ties that dangled down around his chin, and I took him to High Street. There was a group of young teens, boys and girls, hanging out around the basketball courts. They were noisy—the boys making the girls squeal—and boisterous, shoving and pushing, an occasional swear, tossing woodchips at each other. They were teens, and, like many teens, they were mildly annoying and stupid. One of them, a tall blond boy with a bowl-shaped haircut, had made faces at me a few days earlier when I asked if Aidan and I could shoot at the same basket he and another boy were shooting at. Watching those teens, I thought— grumpily—how this was what Aidan would be enduring in the next few years as he headed into junior high.

Suddenly, there was a flurry of motion in the group, and they all crowded around something under the basketball net. "Oh, he's alive," I heard a girl say.

"Don't touch him," said another, "don't hurt him."

Then there were more squeals, and the crowd parted, and I saw the blond-haired boy with his hands cupped in front of him. He was holding a baby bird that had fallen out of its nest to the concrete. He looked up at the backboard, then stepped to the pole.

"Come here," he said to another boy. "Come here and hold it." The other boy came forward and put his hands out, and the blond boy eased the bird into the other's palms.

Then he climbed the pole, wrapping his arms and legs around it, pulling, and pulling again, until he was near the backboard and the nest that he must have seen somewhere on its back side. "Give him to me," the boy said, reaching one hand down. The other boy raised his cupped hands and the blond boy clutched the bird, lifted it up and placed it in the nest. A girl clapped a little, the boy slid down the pole, and they all went back to being noisy.

Pretty soon Guthrie was ready to go, so we cut across the basketball court. I peeked up at the nest as we passed under the backboard. "Look at that," I said to Guthrie, "the baby bird is back in the nest." Then we ducked under the chain that kept cars from driving onto the playground and walked home. Maybe we even held hands.

New England February

by Elizabeth Moore

This is the month that tests the hidden
frameworks of things: the studs within
the walls of home and body—both of which,
you suspect, are now becoming tenuous at best,
having already seen you through the previous
plagues of winter, and never creaked louder.

Even your faith suffers these days. You
hear "another blizzard" and find yourself
braving the miniature frozen world inside
the fridge, again and again, ensuring that
you have enough milk, even though you know
you already checked it earlier this morning—
the knowledge of this, perhaps, also nagging
at you as you make your way back to the couch,
and sit there, and brood, and start to worry
instead that you might be developing OCD.

You look for ways to distract yourself from
these morbid thoughts. You tell yourself
it's only snow, after all—that another world
will surely come after this—and with
this new boldness to bolster you, you go
to your window, and open the shade, and gaze
into the whirlwind that your front lawn has

inexplicably become, at the acts of creation
and dissolution happening there: a new earth of
frozen milk, it seems, over-layering the old.

"God, why?" you ask the whirlwind, and when
it hurls its white cloud of broken glass at you,
(just like you knew it would), you do the only
thing you know how to do: the only thing
anyone can do in a New England February, when
the lintels of doorways all across the kingdom
are threatening to fail beneath the weight
of the dread angel's passing, its behemoth grey
shadow blotting out sun and color, its leviathan
shoulder nudging at the icy crust of the world.

You go back to your fridge, and open the door,
and face that inner cold once again, re-ensuring
that you have enough milk—re-assuring yourself,
too, that you will paint the studs of your bones
with it, that you will hunker down and wait out
this last rage of winter, this final breaker of king
and subject alike: that it, too, will soon pass
over you in favor of another, less fortunate first-born,
leaving you intact, your own lintel untouched.

Cowardice

by Mitchell Grabois

My thin, barren aunt had twins. God was working through her; God, with his sick sense of humor. They came out of her like fiends in a horror film and, because there was so little of her to devour, they began devouring her husband, my uncle, who was a kosher butcher, and had been emasculated by my aunt. He was a thin, grey man who never walked, but always shuffled.

The twins started by licking the beef blood from his fingers. They gnawed on his cuticles and knuckles. There was so little he could give them, and so little he wanted to give. He'd assumed he was sterile.

Even I was infected by his cowardice. When I was two, I flung a weeding tool in his direction and it embedded itself in the mesh of his garden chair, right between his legs. The garden chair sat on a green lawn that my father mowed every Saturday. The blades of the lawnmower were surrogates for his anger.

My father yanked the tool from the mesh and turned toward me as if I were a weed. I took off running. You'd think he would have caught me easily, but he was portly and smoked unfiltered

Chesterfield Kings, and cigars. I looked back and he was bent over on the sidewalk, his elbows on his knees.

A neighbor invited me in. He was a kindly psychologist who wore plaid berets. He offered me milk and chocolate chip cookies, and I fell asleep at his kitchen table as the sun streaming through the windows melted the chips. Years later, he would be convicted for being a child molester, but I don't remember him touching me. You might say I'd had three close calls in one day.

I returned home. The front door stood open. I gingerly entered, careful to wipe my feet before putting them on my mother's pure white carpet. There was no sign of my father, though I could smell cigar smoke.

The bloodthirsty twins sat on the stairs between the living room and my bedroom. They had made the stairs their rocket ship, and wouldn't let me pass.

Crime Shows

by Matthew Lippman

I watch crime shows from Norway and Sweden.
Wallander and *Salamander* and others with names I can't pronounce.
I watch crime shows from England with American actors.
There are guys who hang out in dark corners and women police detectives
who talk about one night stands
and hang out in closets.
Then, there are killers who seem like nice guys
with sons and daughters that go to fancy schools
and live in apartments by the sea.
It's easy to love them all
and hate them all.
The thing about being a teacher
is that you don't hate your students
when *Light In August* is open to the first page
and you get to talk about Hip-Hop
in Faulkner's diction.
Then, when you get to have them write Hip-Hop
that isn't Faulkner's diction,
it's impossible to do anything but love them.
If Faulkner was a character actor in *Wallander* he would have been an old man
who lived in the tall grass.
The point is there is mystery in the woman's heart
who strides the stroller down the street.
When she gets to the playground,

puts her baby in the babyswing, and looks up at the sky
wondering how her life got to be so crowded
with selflessness
that all she wants to do is cry.
I know this. All I want to do is cry.
I am that woman in the playground sandbox
with my children getting sand in our eyes.
We love it together and then they get to go to summer camp and
play with glue
and watch television.
I watch crime shows in mystery hours about mysterious shadows
to stave off the mystery in my heart
that collides with the mystery in the world.
There are no ghosts in my house but they talk to me anyway.

In the Pocket

by Suzanne Bouffard

I've never had that nightmare where I'm standing on stage naked, paralyzed in the footlights and the audience's howling laughter. I was born and eventually bred to be a performer, and a big, open stage has always felt like home. But I wasn't brought up to improvise. I was brought up to plan, to weigh everything from my produce to my decisions carefully. Whether it was in dance class or in algebra, I was taught to follow the steps very, very closely. No one ever suggested that I play with them, or God forbid, make them up completely as I went along.

And yet, here I am. Again. Standing naked in front of an audience, but with all my clothes on.

"Can we do something in 7?" I ask Kevin, with an uncertain smile. He throws his head back, slaps the battered but reliable piano cover he's just opened, and pirouettes to face his bandmates. "I love this girl," he laughs. Unusual time signatures, I know, are his trademark, a playful but serious challenge he makes to himself and the musicians in his trio. Almost all arrangements in 7/8, 5/4, sometimes even 3/4 are hard to play, hard to follow, and even harder to improvise in. They're like shooting baskets with one hand behind your back, or attending mass in Latin. This is why so many jazz musicians choose them, and why so many tap dancers avoid them. It's also why I've grown to love them, even if I haven't come to fully understand them yet.

"`Summertime'," I say to the band, half suggestion, half directive. It's one of my tunes, although other tap dancers have started trying to claim it for themselves lately. "I make you no promises," I warn Kevin and the others, equal parts light-hearted and serious. "I might get lost."

I might get lost. I might fall down. I might make a mess.

"I'll bring you in," I call over my shoulder. I set the tempo, and after dancing an 8 bar intro, I signal the band with a nod of my head and a couple of riffs in the direction of the piano, which Kevin has knowingly pivoted to face the dance floor. He's already smiling his kid-at-the-beach grin and his eyes are locked on the rhythmic ideas that are inside me, somewhere beyond my face, beyond my feet, beyond words. Jorge is perched on his cajón, leaning forward like he's waiting for a race to begin, but drumming sparingly so that his rhythms leave enough space to complement mine. The bass player is new to me. His back is nearly touching the wall of this storefront music venue so that I can hardly see him, but I can hear that he's taking it all in and holding it all down.

The first chorus feels like flight. I start grounded, sure of my footing and friendly with the gravity that's keeping me here. And then someone or something removes the blocks under the wheels and pulls back on the yoke, and I'm lifted off the wood floor, first slowly and then all at once. As the four of us go higher, the sounds of the crowd on the ground get farther and farther away, and then they're gone. And it's just us, riding the velocity of this insistent groove that propels us forward because of the missing eighth beat in every measure. Kevin's massaging the keys and inviting me in to the roomy melody; I'm accepting with a metallic trill from my toe taps and then making overtures of my own with a deep heel flam. Jorge follows us, repeating my phrases in the low, wooden register of his cajón. The bass's steady groove ties us all together like a set of sturdy leather straps. It's like we're inside each other's heads. And we keep climbing.

And then I lose it. I lose the 1. I won't be able to shape the piece at all if I can't find it, won't know when to change the tempo, how to trade bars with Jorge, even when to end. I'll be left behind in mid-air, choking in the musicians' exhaust. That is, if I don't send them spiraling down to earth prematurely. I've lost the downbeat. And found the mess.

The old me would have panicked, would have gasped and flailed in a blur of arms and legs and metal and sixteenth notes, waiting for the oxygen mask and the rescue crew. But instead I slow down my steps to listen, and then I grapevine my way over to Kevin, "I'm lost. Can we go into 4?" I whisper. 4/4 time is Western musicians' universal home base. With no hint of disappointment, Kevin holds up four fingers to the other musicians, and at the top of the next phrase, we're back together, seamlessly. We haven't gained any altitude, but we haven't lost any either.

The new time signature turns out to be an opening. Kevin starts to improvise a gorgeous, almost pop melody that feels like it was inside me all along, not in my head, but in that deep part of my chest where the beat lives. We've found our target altitude, and we cruise. The mess, it turns out, was the most necessary part of the piece.

My whole body is hypnotized by the melody and is dancing its bidding. My feet start moving in ways I didn't know were possible. Steps I've drilled unsuccessfully in the studio for hours suddenly trip off my toes with no effort at all. My normally stubborn left foot does a wing it's never been able to do before. Technique has become an indispensible tool for a higher purpose. My brain doesn't feel a part of the equation at all. I'm not thinking about riffs or rhythms, about masterpieces or messes. I'm not thinking at all. In this moment, I am most and least in control, most unaware of the world around me and most connected to it.

When I've finished, I notice some of the other dancers smiling to themselves, remembering their own moments of connection, shaking their heads from side to side in the way that usually means "no" but sometimes means "I know." Some of my students glance sideways at me, searching my face and my feet for clues. I want to reach over and hand them the keys, but I don't know how, don't have anything else to give them beyond what I've just put on the floor.

In the weeks and months that follow, this desire returns to me again and again as I work with students, the ones to whom I teach dance and the ones I mentor as researchers in my not-so-secret double life. And then one night, I'm perusing TED talks online, those inspiring 15-minute presentations by accomplished people from every field imaginable. There I stumble upon the language I've been looking for, in the words of the German psychologist and one-time student of Carl Jung, Mihály Csíkszentmihalyi. I first encountered Csíkszentmihalyi's work on creativity as an undergraduate psychology major and I was fascinated. But in the decade that has followed, my artistic and research pursuits have grown further apart. I've forgotten about Csíkszentmihalyi's major contribution to psychology — the concept of "flow" — but I've been experiencing it.

According to the research Csíkszentmihalyi has conducted with artists, athletes, academics, and others, flow is the phenomenon of feeling singularly focused and completely immersed in an experience, to the point that the self and the rest of the world temporarily cease to exist and all that remains is the work or feat they've accomplished. The people he has interviewed describe remarkably similar feelings and mind states when they're in flow, saying that the performance or the action feels like it's happening without or even in spite of them. Athletes and dancers describe realizing only after leaving the stage or the field that they're bleeding. Many of these people use phrases like "in the zone," "in the groove," or to borrow a phrase from jazz, "in the pocket." But so many of them have used the word flow or the imagery of being carried along by a river that Csíkszentmihalyi has adopted it.

Flow was not a concept any of my teachers ever taught when I was a kid, or as far as I could tell, ever thought about. Like so many others I've seen around the country, my dance teachers focused, very explicitly, on control. "You must CONTROOOLLLLLL that leg," ballet instructors would drone as we students labored at the barre, using the word as if it were the most essential quality of a dancer. Indeed, control is important, insofar as it refers to the mastery of skills and the ability to use them effectively. But it isn't enough. As artists, or as researchers, or as any other people striving to do something meaningful, we have something higher to reach for.

When I signed up for the only tap class my college had to offer, I had a vague sense that I was looking for a more creative, more authentic experience than the ones I'd been having in my suburban dance studio, but I didn't know what it was. I certainly didn't expect it to involve improvisation. But I quickly discovered that I had been in a naïve love affair with an art form I didn't really understand. My sharp-footed and even sharper-witted tap professor not only knew rhythm tap's history, she had lived it. With her hilarious, often off-color stories, she taught me about how the old masters created and then stole one another's steps, practicing on street corners and in the back rooms of dance halls. And with her insistence that we learn a repertoire of standard jazz tunes and improvise to them — one dancer a time, right down the line, in every class — she showed me the form's roots, its lifeblood. I learned that early tap, like the jazz music with which it grew up, borrowed from older traditions from places like Africa and Ireland and then used improvisation to add its own ever-changing spin by ensuring that every night, every performance, every moment was different from the previous, and different from the audience's expectations. I discovered how the dance had influenced the music. I learned, for example, that Baby Laurence (who I had never heard of) had laid claim to the invention of bebop through the rhythms he'd create on the spot with the band, and that some of the great drummers of the era, even those who could have taken sole credit like Max Roach, gladly shared that credit with him.

I tried improvising, at first because my teacher gave me no choice. And then I kept trying, because she had shown me that the art form gave me no choice. I had come to understand that improv is non-negotiable in rhythm tap. Discovering this was like finding the daredevil side of a lover that I hadn't seen at first, a side that thrilled but terrified me, because of its capacity to highlight my own cautiousness and inadequacy. I wasn't a terrible improviser, but I wasn't good, either. Never a risk-taker, my improv was uninteresting and unimpressive. In the years after college, I'd show up to dance with the local tap jam's house band once a month, with a song or two in my head, a few favorite steps in my pocket, and a wave of nausea in my stomach. I'd try to control the encounter by picking the perfect spot during the jam to solo with the musicians, late enough into the evening that I'd be warmed up, early enough that I wouldn't have witnessed the intimidating tricks and flash moves of the guys who had been improvising, at pickup basketball games and on first dates, since they were kids. I'd stride up to the band, pretending to be self-assured, waltz through my tune with total awareness of every part of my body and every note of the music, and then shuffle away with an undefined but certain dissatisfaction. "Pretty," the other dancers would tell me when I sat back down. Pretty is a compliment in most places, but not here, not among tap dancers, not to me.

After the fact, I would have long conversations with my mentors about these experiences. They dropped hints here and there that stuck with me like those parables from children's stories that continue to influence you long after you've forgotten the details of the story. There was the hilarious but hell-bent dancer who taught me the fine art of bullshit and gave me the novel permission to "Make a mess!" while I danced with him in his studio. There was the 74-year old diva whose book told me to "Always take risks." And there was the frequent reminder from an unlikely but simpatico collaborator, written in his email signature and down his left arm in black ink: "The only way to be different is to be yourself." These people never described flow in words, but they did with their bodies, so clearly that even before I felt flow for myself, I could hear it, see it, almost touch it.

And one day, at a tap jam just like the dozens I'd attended before, I did touch it. After years of searching for the route, and walking alongside it, I was on it. I had lost myself in the music, and found everything.

Now when I work with my students, I stress the paradox of control. "Whether you're doing cramp rolls or counterpoint, the only way to create what you really want is to understand what it is, work on it, and then let go of it," I tell them. It's not an easy lesson. And when my students stare at me with that baffled look I used to give my teachers, and they wonder aloud if they'll ever get there, I ask myself: Is the experience of flow necessary? Yes, is my unequivocal answer. The first time I felt flow was like the day I got my first pair of glasses and suddenly realized I hadn't been able to see.

I still get nervous almost every time I improvise in front of an audience, and in the moments before I dance, the nakedness still feels risky at best. Sometimes I even wonder in that moment, "Why do I do this every month?" But I do, and then it ends, far too quickly. Afterwards, I sit in the audience with some of my students, in my car on the way home, in my office with a graduate student the next day, and I wonder just the opposite: "Why don't I do this every day? Why don't we all?" But having experienced flow doesn't guarantee it will happen again; it's only that, when I lose myself, all the rest falls away.

Away from my Dream Desk

by Peter Ramos

The machine powers up bad. Time
to grow summer, hours of green
and forgetting. Learn to fake it,
right, Señor Somebody,
Sir Hurts-a lot & beauty hack,
everyone's et cetera and star-

fucker, leech. Vertigo troubles
the old bones, this side of the galaxy.
Order in moonlight.
Sprout yellow legumes, rack
the portable fruit bombs.
Fly my gone-fishing
flag. I'll carefully
studies my I.

Keepers

by Michael Badger

I know that on good nights they'll drink a decent bottle of wine or two and sit on their kitchen counters and play Catchphrase. They'll yell at each other with purple-teethed smiles and clap when someone has the insight to name the unnamable thing. They've lived right next door to me for years and the walls in the building are thin.

On bad nights there will still be drinking but amidst crying, and instead of games someone throws a toaster or a cast iron. Usually he drives away much too fast. The cops call and say he's been yelling around the cemetery again. She picks him up from the station, but it's all right because he's had to pick her up, too.

The little time they spent together started shading their time apart, where anything could happen fidelity-wise. And it quickly made noticeable rifts. His daydreams lean toward a beat up Westfalia, hers a swing set in a back yard, a 401k. He wants cash stuffed under a mattress, a dog—and she'd rather adopt instead of tearing her vagina open again. She's candid about this.

Tonight he and I are at The Bison Room—the pub down the

street with stuffed and mounted bison, two lynx, a bald eagle, three California condors, a grizzly bear and its cub, two big horn sheep, and an ocelot. Tonight she's driving north, leaving for good this time. She starts a new job tomorrow morning in the city—she used the words *career* and *accumulating savings* when she said she'd be doing simple photo-manipulation for some corporate office. She's rented a place and has encouraged him to visit when he's in town, not quite inviting him to move in. But nearly. She's probably slamming her steering wheel with her palms and blasting sad, loud music because that's what she does. He slams an empty shot glass down and turns to me. He says, "Life is futile, it's *death* we need to understand." I tell him he's being melodramatic.

She takes pictures of dead animals. On the side of the street, in pastures, in the water, underneath rocks, anywhere and any kind. She has a book published. The first picture in it is of a German shepherd's skinless body washed up underneath a dock somewhere out on the coast. She framed a bunch of other ones and hung them up around their old place where he still lives.

Sometimes, during Catchphrase, they would laugh so hard and shout so loud they'd wake Jeri and me. They'd shush each other and at that point I could only lie awake, picturing them getting real close, falling into each other's arms, giving into stained kisses and anxious groping. Even though their bodies matched well and they'd gotten to where they didn't have to futz with how it all worked between them, the attempt inevitably faded out. He's told me this in confidence.

He doesn't like to say, but I know their sex is infrequent. This is why she thinks his constant trips to Oregon are much more than visits to comfort his crippled mother.

Tim, the bartender at The Bison Room, who wears a patch over his left eye, says to him, "Get over it, Adrian." No one calls Tim the bartender Righty, or One-Eyed Tim, or Patch. Just Tim the bartender. He has a good one about a one-legged woman and a man with a wooden eye that ends, "Well screw you too, peg leg!"

Adrian slams down another, and Tim the bartender takes the glass away, says, "You're done."

Adrian says, "Do I look like a turkey? No. I'm *finished.*"

"Go on," Tim the bartender says, and waves like he's brushing us off.

The street's damp from rain during the day. Adrian steps in a puddle and kicks his soaked shoe in the air, cursing. "She's probably hydroplaning into the median right now," he says, deadpan. I disagree. She knows how to drive. Or maybe she has her teeth clenched and her eyes are dry and both hands are wrapped firm around the wheel, knuckles bloodless, her seat belt fastened.

We kick through more puddles down the streetlight-lit road, moving in the direction of our building. "There's a bottle of scotch at my place," Adrian says. I'll end up listening to him rant between long pulls from the bottle. When he gets this way, usually when Lucy's out of town or sometimes when she's sleeping, he carefully takes down every picture she's hung up in the place and hides them somewhere he's sure to forget. Once he put them in a plastic box, sealed it with duct tape, wrapped it in a sheet and hung it just out of sight off the porch. "I can't stand them, but the frames cost so much," is his excuse.

He does exactly that when we get back to his place. He removes the picture of the mallard, split down the middle, stacks it on top of the headless raccoon, the ball of flies trapped and rotting in a jar of red ooze. This time he hides the pictures in the oven.

The difference now, in the morning, is that she hasn't come back before he's awake to put the pictures back in place, like normal. So he wakes up to beige walls with squares of cleaner beige accenting the absence. I hear shouts and cursing and banging and stomping. Soon there's a knock on my door.

"Someone's stolen the pictures," he says. His eyes are bloodshot and his shirt is on backwards. "Do you know how much those are worth?" I don't because he's never told me, because he's never been scared like this before. "A whole fucking lot," he says. "You didn't take them?" I didn't, no. "Jeri did?" Jeri didn't, no. "Lucy must've." Lucy didn't, no. But I'm not going to tell him that. He's desperate. He wants any excuse to see Lucy. So do I, sure. I can tell because he's talking as if he *doesn't* want to see her. He goes on about how he needs my car, how I can just tell my girlfriend that the bus works perfectly fine, that I can't come because I've got to work. And no, I don't have to work, which isn't true, and Jeri, well she doesn't leave the place so it hardly matters, and because Lucy, even if she wouldn't say it, would ask me to do this for him—so he and I are going together.

He smokes all his cigarettes then starts in on mine. The drive is about two and half hours.

On one of their bad nights, Lucy came to my apartment before she went to pick up Adrian at the station. "I'm making him wait," she said. Her smile was weak and her invisible braces looked like plaque. Jeri was asleep so I touched Lucy's shoulder. She sighed and slid away and sat on the recliner and said she was fascinated by the way people personify domesticated animals. She told me Adrian reads the dictionary. When they fight he uses the words he's circled. She thinks he uses them wrong, and then the fight becomes about the definition more than anything else. Inevitably the huge, weighty dictionary is brought out to the counter and opened and forcibly flipped through and it tends to get thrown rather than used. "Discussion over," she said and sliced her hand through the air. I told her yeah, make him wait, but not for too long. I told her Jeri was sleeping, but she took that as a sign to leave.

Adrian is restless and twitchy. He's out of cigarettes, as am I, and he's fidgeting with the window—powering it up and down, down down, up down up. I don't ask him to stop. There are words under his breath, but they're no clearer than the sky over us. I ask him what he's saying. "You and Jeri got it nice, you know." I don't agree, but stay silent. "You guys are quiet and neat and simple. Easy. Never hear *you* fighting, nope," he says. I laugh. It's the first laugh between us since last night and it startles.

When we get into the city it becomes clear that Adrian has no idea where Lucy's new place is. "But she works at a place," he says, a finger to his nose. "GraFix or GraFight or… Graph-bullshit-ting-nothing. I don't know." I tell him it's on 14th and Legion, corner building. Adrian stares. "She told *you*?" I tell him she did and that she told him too, but he'd been drinking. "Well, then," he says.

Breakfast first. Breakfast first because he's nervous.

At some corner diner on the edge of the city proper, we stare out the window at kids walking to school with backpacks weighing them down, curving them backwards. "What is this, Africa?" Adrian says. The comment doesn't make sense. I tell him he can't just march into her office and demand the pictures back. "That's *exactly* what I'm going to do," he says, but the way he spins his fork between his fingers says he's unsure. "Got any more smokes?" he asks.

The waitress is young and throws the menus at us. Coffee spills over the mugs as she puts them down. I smile hopefully and Adrian says, "Whoa, there." She hustles away and slams the door to the kitchen. I tell Adrian he needs a plan, some bigger excuse than just pictures. The coffee's too hot. "You were a waiter for a bit, right?" he asks. I was. "Never treated someone like that, I bet," he points with his thumb. I did. A lot.

Some kid taps on the window and points at something across the street. He's excited. Adrian waves him away.

Lucy used to come into my restaurant and order decaf coffee. She'd just sit at the counter and stare into the fake wood paneling. I'd ask her about the day and she'd say she hated such and such a professor. The local college we went to then was crumbling and most rooms still had chalkboards. "Art classes are nothing but excuses to get all masturbatory," she said often. I refilled her coffee often. Adrian didn't live in town then and I hadn't met Jeri.

A bunch of kids are gathering, forming a circle around something on the pavement across the street. Adrian can't resist, so I follow. The guts and blood look fake, spilling out of the corgi like they are. This wasn't some side-street hit and run. Someone had very obviously massacred the dog and arranged it here. "God. *Dammit*," Adrian says, but doesn't look away.

"That's cool," a kid says, and pokes the body with a stick.

"My dog got hit by a car once," another says.

"Dog. Is. Dead!" Adrian proclaims, fist in the air, but the kids don't get it because they're all really young. He gets a picture of it on his phone. The kids *ew* at him. Adrian slaps one of their backpacks and says to me, "Let's go, that waitress is looking at us."

The coffee is still too hot so I order breakfast and an ice cube. "Okay," Adrian says. I say okay back. We make up some excuse to be in town—Adrian checking it out to maybe potentially take Lucy up on her invite—and decide if that doesn't sound right for the moment, then there's a show or a strip club or some other bogus anything. Even though she wouldn't say it, any excuse would be good for Lucy. "She'll want to see me. She has to," Adrian says. "Plus," he holds up his phone, "present, right?" I nod. She'll like that. The waitress slides the plates over our table and stomps back into the kitchen yelling in Russian or Greek. "She forgot the ice cube," Adrian says.

I know that technically they had a kid. It came out of Lucy blue and silent. Lucy told me when I had to pick her up from the police station because Adrian was in the drunk-tank at the same time. We decided to let Adrian stay. He was asleep anyways. He'd be fine. She though, she was puffy from crying and hoarse from screaming. Her wrists were red and rubbed raw—she's allergic to certain kinds of metal. She laid her head on my shoulder. I stayed very still, trying to take the turns easily and slow. She eked out a few words here and there. I walked her from the car to her sofa, her face pressed against my chest, my arm around her shoulder the whole way. She tried to kiss me and I kissed back. Falling against the armrest, she said, "No, no," her voice cracking in and out of a whisper. "You wouldn't like it in here. Everything's broken and torn." She waved at her crotch. We stayed up talking from opposite ends of the couch until the phone rang and a mildly-sober Adrian asked for a ride. Jeri never asked where I had been.

Outside Lucy's building Adrian breaks into a sweat. He does this profusely when he's nervous. The smell is earthy and everywhere. When he's like this he can't explain himself and his whole body turns into a stutter of gesticulations. He doesn't have much hair to pull at—he says it's the bad genes, Lucy says it's because he's a trichotillomaniac. "Balls," he says. I nod. "Balls shitting Jesus," he says. I ask him what's so hard about talking to someone you've been with for the past four years. "I'm giving *in* is what," he says. "I'm letting her *win*." I think it's absurd, but I don't say it. Jeri is gaining weight and she doesn't leave our place. She has this online job where she types what other people are speaking at about 90 words per minute and that kind of typing is clacking and loud. It's left her hunched. When she starts typing I immediately leave the apartment. We never fight because I can't stand the sound of her voice. I tell Adrian that it's not about winning; it's about being there. "That's a crock," he says, and I think he's right.

Adrian moved to town the year after Lucy graduated. They met at a party where everyone was told to wear a mustache and drink pink lemonade spiked with something almost like ecstasy but with more visuals. I stayed in a corner twirling my mustache and talking to Lucy who wore a Fu Manchu. Adrian walked in at 1:00 am with a forty-ouncer and wearing a small square of hair under his nose, Hitler style, and went around the room asking, "Have you seen Kyle?" Lucy loved it. She thought it was ballsy. I fell asleep in the back of my car and Lucy told me that she and Adrian screwed in the tiny shower and someone walked in on them and joined. Then another and another. And the party basically turned into an orgy. Lucy had keys to my car then, and when I woke up we were going 75 down a back road and she hadn't noticed me. I stayed silent and pretended to sleep and she only realized I was there after she parked and called me and my phone went off right there in my pocket.

In the driver's seat, now, I look over at Adrian. He breathes quick and stares at the dash. "Doin' it," he says, and rushes out of the car like if he'd stayed one second longer he wouldn't have. But he would have.

The building is small, one story, and has pane glass windows as walls so everything on the inside is basically seeable. The cubicle walls disembody everyone's head as they walk around the place. Adrian doesn't bother with the receptionist, who is visibly confused. And once he's through the main door of the office, heads start popping up at whack-a-mole intervals. Adrian walks briskly. No one moves to stop him. He's peering over the walls, throwing his hands in the air, moving on. Doing this is more an act of love or passion than one of spite or revenge. He'd tell you that it was the opposite.

Lucy appears from an unseen hallway off in the corner of the room, all heads turn first to her then to Adrian. Lucy doesn't move. She has a stack of paper in her arms. A tall older gentleman is a pace behind her, he puts a hand on her shoulder. Adrian points at her and the guy slowly removes his hand. I can only guess at what's being said or accused. Adrian, still pointing, is weaving through the cubicles, side stepping things, making a wandering line toward Lucy, who is visibly angry. She thinks she's passive and unemotive, but she's obviously never looked at herself in a mirror, really studied her own expressions.

Adrian is up maybe two feet from Lucy and is still pointing at her. I want to imagine he's saying, *You stole the only thing I had to remember you by, you took part of me when you took those pictures, you took away how you would always be around me, you left me and took your memories with you, I want them back,* but I know he's not. Sounds like something I would say. His mouth moves in clipped and inelegant ways. And of course, when Lucy responds in the slightest, Adrian waves his arms and rolls his head, which can only mean he's lashing out with some maddening retort. The older guy behind Lucy steps between them and Adrian pushes him. The stack of papers in Lucy's arms goes tumbling, the man falters back, but his attention is still on Adrian who yells, I can see, what? what? like he was raised somewhere other than middle class suburbia, and Lucy is fumbling and trying to catch what is clearly futile to try and catch, but she's back there, waving her arms and bending lower and lower as the papers float and sway downward. There are too many pieces and because she's trying to catch all of them so she gets none. No one pays her any attention as there is a scuffle between the guys, and Lucy is focused on picking up each and every piece, her knees bent and instinctively closed together because she's wearing a skirt. Her hair is in her mouth. She's wearing elaborate make-up. She looks perturbed. She looks up and squints out the window, but there's no way she can see me.

The older gent takes a swing at Adrian who ducks and moves to Lucy who pushes him away from her bended position. Adrian is trying, by pulling her elbow, to get her up, to get her to leave this corporate hell hole where her soul will surely be sucked into oblivion and she'll drown in the greed and corruption and sexuality of dubious older men, he's yelling at her to come back home where *everyone actually* loves you, where the sheriff has our neighbor's number on speed dial, where anyone can be counted on to support our mutually self-destructive relationship because it's okay, it's just Adrian and Lucy, they *love* each other. But I don't think he says any of this, really. I see a few people on cell phones, doubtless calling the police. Lucy's up, ignoring the paper, and she's crying. Her crying has always made me smile, hiding any worry.

Adrian's running for the door. A large man stands in his way. Adrian dodges around him and almost topples the receptionist who spins comically. Adrian is nearly hit by a SUV as he sprints across the street. The car's already on and he gets in and says, "Go motherfucker! GO!" And we go.

I don't know if we should leave town or find a place to stay or how, even, to make sense of what Adrian is trying to say. He's a mess of body language, distressed and under-forming sentences. "She doesn't have the pictures," is his only clean statement. I ask him if we should go home, but there's no clear answer. We're driving along side streets and through alleys, past Asians in chef hats and bums smoking on dumpsters. It's an erratic and aimless drive as Adrian's adrenaline is enough for us both. "Where're the fucking pictures?" he gets out. I keep asking him what I should do, where I should go. But Adrian pays no attention, never answers.

Soon we're near the river, the nice and touristy part of town, but at this time of day it's packed with traffic going downtown and we're stuck. "First opportunity, pull into that park." Adrian points at a long green belt between the river and us. People are jogging through it. "They'll never look for us there," he says. And he's probably right, but there's probably no one looking for us. I'm scared. He's paranoid.

In the parking lot, Adrian swears a lot and I recline my seat all the way and close my eyes. Adrian needs a cigarette, as do I, but my need is much less obvious. "She doesn't have the pictures," he says, calmer than before. "Where are they—" he begins, but I cut him off and I tell him it was never about the pictures, it was all about coming here, getting in close proximity to Lucy. Pictures are just pictures, not even of her, just hers that she took. "No," he says. "No, it actually *was* about the pictures." I call bullshit. He needs to recognize what he's doing is for Lucy, not for the pictures. "Bullshit on *you*," he says.

I ask him to please open the glove compartment and hand me what he finds. It's a green, unopened pack of cigarettes. He's very angry about this. I unwrap the plastic and lift the cardboard lid, pacing myself while Adrian twitches. I take two out and light them, handing one to him. I tell him where the pictures are. "How'd they get in there?" he asks. He's accusing me. I tell him that, yes, I put them there. He believes me and releases a long sigh and a cloud of used-up smoke.

He finishes his cigarette quickly and asks for another one. I tell him no.

We're not going back home until he talks to Lucy properly.

"We're not stalking," he says. But we are.

We ditched the car for these bushes. A different side of Lucy's building. Adrian's face is full of fern because he's taking this quite seriously and has hid himself entirely in the bush. I'm just on the other side of it, messing with the dirt. The sun's going down. Lucy still hasn't left. "She probably went out another door," Adrian says through the leaves.

I know that one night, after Lucy left in a rage, Adrian had a woman over. Everyone in the apartment building knew this because he shouted his end of the conversation with her. Everyone had heard the fight, no doubt, and Lucy slamming the door, so Adrian's logic was that he was covering his tracks by yelling stuff like, "HELLO THERE, UTTERLY PLATONIC FRIEND," and "HAVE A SEAT ON THE OTHER SIDE OF THE COUCH, FRIEND." Twenty minutes after whoever it was—her voice was light—had shown up, Adrian stopped yelling. They started to screw. I know this because who moves that much furniture at two in the morning? I never told Lucy.

But she didn't go out another door, because here she is. Adrian almost chokes with surprise and I kick him in the shin. We watch as the old gent escorts her to her car. They're somewhat obscured by the failing sun, but it's obvious—at least to me—that's she's been crying. I can tell by the way she opens her car door—like the faster she can get in the better because she doesn't care if cars can't drive through large bodies of water, she'll drive off the nearest dock just to prove a point.

The man touches her elbow and Lucy turns, holding the door halfway open. He asks her something and she waits. Waits. Nods and shuts the door and they start walking. Her car beeps as she locks it.

Adrian curses and I unclench a fist full of dirt.

We end up across the street from a small bar that's carved into the side of a brick wall. Lucy and the old gent are inside. Adrian is pacing. We're in the shadows of a large billboard that says choice and has a mutilated fetus on it. It's huge and lit up and horrible.

"Do we barge the place?" Adrian asks. We can't do much else. I tell him I want to be privy to this and hand him a lit cigarette. "Privy?" he says. I tell him yeah, privy. I want to be there to help when things get rough, when the bartender asks us to leave and we refuse, when the old guy who's trying to steal Lucy starts to defend himself to an un-listening Adrian who, while loudly insulting the old guy, is really telling Lucy he loves her. His own way.

"That's not happening," Adrian says and I say maybe it will. I say maybe he should try to see that even though the good nights with Catchphrase are few and the kid they almost had creeps its way into their thoughts every time they try to screw, every time they talk to each other, they are each other's and they are inevitable, they happen. I tell him that of course Lucy told me about that and she's told me so many other things, but it's time to make sure no one gets in the way of us three again.

Adrian clicks his tongue and I stand still.

I tell him after everything works out tonight, I'll call Jeri and tell her I'm not coming home because we, not her, are starting this new life and she'll make that sound she makes when she shrugs. She'll tell me she's had enough and I'll know it's because I've never given her enough, and that's all right, I'll say, because I've been giving enough of my everything to someone else for a long time.

He flattens the cigarette with his foot. He looks at me, skeptical if he's ever really seen me before.

Lucy and the old guy are still sitting at the bar across the street. The lights are dim. He's turned toward her and she's resting on her elbows. "All right then. Let's go," Adrian says. And we go.

Adrian pushes the door open. I flick my cigarette into the street, a galaxy of embers. The muffled roar of conversation in the tiny bar rolls out as we follow a quick breeze in. Lucy's to the left, she sees us and her back goes straight, her glass halfway to her lips. She looks first to Adrian who's moving too quickly, too narrowly, too determined. Her eyes find me and they're instantly pleading — it's the look she's had so many times at 4 a.m., crying and worried about herself, worried about Adrian. She mouths my name. She's pleading for me to fix everything that's about to happen. But I can see, so obviously, that as Adrian grabs the old man's shoulder and the barstool wobbles underneath, that it's already impossible — we can't be altered, we're firmly fixed.

David Sedaris is
Sick of Himself

by Carmen Nobel

David Sedaris and I were riding down Commonwealth Avenue in the backseat of his media escort's Chevy Impala. I was trying to take notes without getting carsick, and he was pointing out local businesses, wondering aloud if their owners were important enough to rate a Wikipedia entry. "Would the head of that Dunkin' Donuts rate? Would the guy who owns the Dugout rate?"

He asked me whether I had a Wikipedia entry, and whether I knew anything about the website's notability requirements. I didn't tell him I had avoided creating a Wikipedia page for fear it would be flagged for insignificance.

David Sedaris met Wikipedia's notability requirements, of course, but he never looked at his page because friends had told him it was riddled with errors — that the page claimed he'd gotten his start in stand-up comedy, for instance, when he'd never done stand-up comedy in his life. He said he never looked at best-seller lists online, either. "Every writer I know is obsessed with his book's rank on Amazon.com, but I don't want to know," he said.

I already knew that *When You Are Engulfed in Flames*, the memoir he was in town to promote, ranked #1 on Amazon.com. I didn't tell him that, because he said he didn't want to know. And I didn't tell him I'd never written a book at all, which was one of the reasons I didn't deserve a Wikipedia page. I'd written investigative reports about cell phone companies, mostly, until I had quit the technology trade magazine to start freelancing, which was a hit or miss pursuit. More recently I had crafted an 800-word review of seven floor mops for *Boston Home* magazine, headlined "Grimes and Misdemeanors." Hanging out with David Sedaris was the best gig I'd ever had.

He was hanging out with me because the *Boston Globe* had hired me to feature him in its ongoing "Hanging With…" series, in which the writer went out and did something incongruous with a famous person. (In my favorite of these, my friend Meredith had hung with aging porn star Ron Jeremy at a paint-your-own-pottery studio, where Ron Jeremy had painted a ceramic turtle and named it "Ron Jeremy's daughter.") I had planned to take David Sedaris to the Armenian Museum, maybe, or for a ride on the swan boats, but he asked nicely if we could go to the Jack Spade store on Newbury Street. He needed a new tote bag.

At a stoplight, he inventoried the contents of the old tote bag in his lap: a set of coasters made out of Turkish newspapers, some multicolored tongue depressors from London, two boxes of Greek safety pins, and a t-shirt from *The Daily Show*, where he had been Jon Stewart's guest the previous night. He collected little gifts for children who attended his readings, and he liked to carry them in a new bag. He bought a new bag every time he published a new book.

Sally, the media escort, was mostly quiet in the driver's seat.

"Media escorts are so discreet," David Sedaris said. "I was asking a media escort about one author, and he told me, 'All I can tell you is that she kicked me in the stomach, twice.'"

I asked him who the author was.

"Maya Angelou," he said.

Sally said Maya Angelou had been really nice to her.

We talked about other writers, too. The week before he met me, he had met David Foster Wallace. If I hadn't read Wallace's "Consider the Lobster," he said, then I should.

"I love his writing," David Sedaris said. "And he's a really funny, kind person. Some people can set you at ease."

I admired his shoes as we walked into Jack Spade, and David Sedaris told me that he hated his feet. He wished he could just screw them off and screw on some new, better feet. I told him I loved a line in his new book where he said his feet were shaped like states.

"I worked on that line forever," he said. Up until then he had been in performance mode a little. But now he sounded disarmed and happy. He smiled, and I felt good because I had complimented the right line. I knew how good it felt when someone complimented the right line.

At the time I was dating a guy who was really good at complimenting lines. Mark would pinpoint a couple of good phrases in articles I wrote, parrot them back to me, and add, "That's awesome." I suspected he didn't read the whole article sometimes, but it still felt good, and it's one of the reasons we stayed friends after we broke up.

David Sedaris smiled with his mouth closed. In addition to hating his feet, he also hated his teeth, which he compared to gray fence posts. More than his teeth, he hated the glorification of virginity, which came up when I asked him about his considerable teenage fan base. "When I go to a high school or a college I tell the kids they should be having as much sex as possible," he said. "To have an abstinence club when you're 19, it's ridiculous. When you're old and masturbating alone, you have nothing else to look back on other than the sex you had when you were young."

I asked whether teenagers might be too young to handle oxytocin, the bonding hormone, which was triggered by sexual activity. "That's not an issue if you have sex with someone you don't like," he said. "And that's the best sex of all."

The sound system at Jack Spade was playing "Downtown," the Petula Clark song, in Portuguese. I waited for David Sedaris to comment on that, or for the store clerk to recognize him, but neither happened. He tried a few bags and chose a rust-colored satchel that cost $235. "I could have bought two of these with the money I just gave to fucking public radio," he said. (Earlier in the day he had visited WBUR, the local NPR affiliate, and when he signed the visitor's log he wrote, "In: 1:30pm. Out: $500.")

There was a brasserie next to Jack Spade, and David Sedaris and I stopped in for a bite of Tarte Tatin. He deemed it "just as Tatin-y" as the Tarte Tatin in Paris, where he and his boyfriend were living at the time. When he finished eating I asked David Sedaris if I could take his picture for the article, even though his publicist had told me he'd say no. He said no.

"I just absolutely hate having my picture taken," he said. "There's nothing I hate more. But at book signings, when people ask to take my picture and I say no, they're like — CLICK — and they take my picture anyway. And I say, 'Hey, I said not to take my picture.' And they say, 'But I wanted one.'"

Would he be willing to draw a self-portrait instead? In case he would, I was carrying a small sketchpad and two Prismacolor markers. Sure, he shrugged, and sketched a tiny reasonable likeness, in profile, with tiny squares coming out of his mouth. They looked like confetti.

"I drew myself throwing up," he said. Underneath the portrait he wrote, "David Sedaris is sick of himself."

Over coffee, I asked him about his recent decision to quit smoking, the primary topic in *When You Are Engulfed in Flames*. In a previous book, *Naked*, he had written about his lifelong struggle with obsessive-compulsive disorder. His saving grace had been to start smoking, which itself was an obsessive behavior, but a relatively socially acceptable one, and it more or less had cured the rest of his OCD.

"Has your OCD returned, now that you're not smoking anymore?" I asked.

"Only when someone reminds me of it," he said, not unkindly, but I felt bad anyway.

His new obsessive behavior involved focusing intense pressure into the heel of one foot, which was less obtrusive than, say, licking door knobs. "It's almost like you put pressure on it and think about it until you're hobbling," he said. He was wincing a little. "But I have this book signing tonight, so I won't think about it."

Sally called just then, wondering where we were, because the people at the bookstore were waiting. She picked us up in front of Jack Spade, and on the ride to Harvard Square she asked David Sedaris if he'd do his impression of Billie Holliday. He said he didn't do that anymore — that he wouldn't even do it when Terry Gross requested it.

"I felt like a real skunk saying no to Terry Gross," he said, and laughed at the word skunk. I almost told him I felt like a skunk reminding him of his OCD, but caught myself before I reminded him of it again.

He worried that the bookstore might give him another mug. Bookstores were always giving him mugs, he said. It was as if they thought he might not otherwise have anything to drink from while he was on the road. "You know, when they give you coffee in a hotel, they actually provide the mug," he said. "It's just a loaner, sure, but they have you covered."

A young woman met us at Harvard Bookstore and brought us

to a table in a back room, piled with books to sign.

He asked to use the restroom first, and then he told me about this urine leakage problem he'd been having since turning 50.

"I pee," he said. "And then I pee again, and then I stick my penis back in my pants, and it pees some more. I just told that to someone the other day, and apparently it's called 'breaking the seal.' So, on this book tour I'm asking people about what to do about breaking the seal."

It didn't seem strange, him telling me this, because I was in journalist mode, and because I had heard of this problem from other men. I even knew someone who knew how to solve it: Mark, who was meeting me at the reading.

After David Sedaris read an essay to a packed room, and before he started signing books, I introduced them. David Sedaris asked what Mark did for a living, and Mark gave him the elevator pitch about his small gourmet nut company. (He had given me the same pitch when we met, and I had asked him if he planned to branch out into trail mix. I had been kidding, but the joke fell flat because that's exactly what Mark had been planning to do).

"That's great," said David Sedaris. "You don't meet enough nut salesmen these days."

I cut in, eager to help. "David, I think Mark knows how to solve that urine leakage problem you mentioned."

I said this softly, in part because I always speak too softly, and in part because the room was chockablock with dour Cambridge women, those of a certain type who never seem to find anything funny except, specifically, for David Sedaris, whom they find hilarious. I thought they might be offended by a public, albeit practical conversation about penises. Mark wasn't concerned.

"I HAVE THIS TECHNIQUE I CALL THE PEENLICH MANEUVER," he yelled, although he would insist later that he hadn't been yelling. David Sedaris took a pen and a little notebook out of his jacket pocket and waited for Mark to continue.

"AFTER YOU TAKE A PISS, AND AFTER YOU SHAKE, YOU REACH DOWN AND PRESS HARD, RIGHT BEHIND YOUR TESTICLES, LIKE THIS. SEE?" David Sedaris began to take notes, and a few women within earshot began to frown.

"THE REST OF THE URINE SHOULD SQUIRT RIGHT OUT."

David Sedaris wrote down everything Mark yelled.

He hadn't written down anything I had said all day, and a familiar pang shot through me. My gregarious friends had been cornering the spotlight for as long as I could remember, and here Mark was now, getting all noteworthy with David Sedaris. But whereas Mark was a salesman and David Sedaris was a writer, I was a journalist. Part of my job was to connect experts to those who needed the expertise. And I had done that.

"Thank you so much," David Sedaris said. He was talking to Mark. But a week later I received a postcard in the mail. On the front there was a picture of a painting by Francis Picabia called *Cacodylic Eye*, and on the back was a note from David Sedaris. "Dear Carmen," he wrote. "Thank you for taking the time to talk to me the other day, and for advising me on my new bag. After Boston I went to Philadelphia, where it was 98 degrees and I signed books for seven and a half hours. The last two thirds were air-conditioned but by that time I was a sweaty mess. Sincerely, David Sedaris."

Later that year I interviewed the lead singer of a boy band called the All American Rejects, who disputed an entry on his Wikipedia page, which said that he sported a tattoo of the hip-hop artist Akon on his right butt cheek. To establish fellowship, I shared David Sedaris's Wikipedia page error story, because I still didn't have a Wikipedia page of my own. It was kind of like when my friends talk about their children, and, since I don't have any, I talk about my niece.

Istvan

by Lauren Haldeman

[I woke up in the Mercy Hospital bushes]

[Surrounded by dots, swallowing a chandelier of thinking]
[Vowels filled the aquifer without spelling a word]

[Which way the river?]

[The history book you had told us how to get to my address]
[It was this year's history]

[& You? You were Istvan]

[Higher than the beat of your cap]
[Your glowing head around your head glowed]
[Blue blue jay jay] [Heating the outdoors]

[We traveled home]

[By a chunk of the moon on this wax tip went we]
[Kabashing the discourse of the system of the saplings and]

My thoughts that often mount the sky

Go search the world beneath

Where nature all in ruin lies

And holds and holds her sovereign death

[Istvan, how much can the brain be
A bird on the wall or a bird in the wall?]
[Wherein beating high, its high¬hat lights up,
Knowing its coordinates by the color assigned it]

The Memorialist

by Kelly Matthews

The heart-shaped pink granite headstone he had picked up south of Boston made it hard for Alex to sidle his pickup truck into a parking spot near his wife's apartment. The granite weighed half a ton, and Alex was conscious that it shifted the truck's center of gravity as he swung first the flatbed, then the cab into a metered space on Commonwealth Avenue. After many years of small-town driving, he had lost the habit of parallel parking. He worried that Leslie could be watching as he struggled to align the truck to the curb, but when he finished and looked up at her building, he saw no interested faces looking down. He realized he didn't even know which window was hers.

He had purposely arrived early so that he could catch a few words face to face with Leslie before their son Teddy finished packing his duffle bag for the drive home. Now Alex stood at the parking meter and wondered how many minutes he should hope for. He dropped a quarter into the slot and dug in his pocket for more, but was interrupted by Teddy's familiar "Hey" from behind him. Alex turned to see his tall, skinny son ready to go, his bag slung over his shoulder, earbuds plugged in as always, their tail tucked into his hooded sweatshirt.

"Hey," Alex said, casting his eyes over Teddy's shoulder, looking for Leslie. "You're already packed?"

"Yeah," said Teddy. "Mom told me to wait in the lobby till I saw you drive up."

"She's not coming down?" The parking meter ticked over: fourteen minutes left.

"She said she has to get ready for her African dance class." Teddy opened the door of Alex's pickup and stuffed his bag behind the passenger seat.

"What about the schedule?" Alex asked. It didn't seem right that he had trimmed his beard and washed his truck just to park unnoticed for two minutes outside Leslie's building. "Did she say when I should bring you out here for your next visit?"

"She said she'd email you." Teddy climbed up into the passenger seat and pulled the cab door shut behind him.

Alex turned once again to look up at the blank windows of Leslie's building. It was an unremarkable block of cream brick, like most of the other buildings on the street, with limestone cornices and windowsills and slate steps leading up to the locked front door. For this she had left their little granite house in Hudson, its lintel adorned with lilies and ivy carved by Alex's great-grandfather. She wanted to be anonymous, she said; she was tired of being known to everyone in town just as Alex's wife or, worse yet, Mrs. Bilodeau, though she had never legally given up her name.

Alex considered the memorial stone that was strapped to his flatbed and remembered the stout, well-dressed couple who had driven in from Hopedale to order it. They had been arguing before they walked into Alex's shop; he could tell by the wife's self-effacing smile and the husband's sullen refusal to do anything more than grunt in assent as they paged through Alex's sample book.

Neither was sick, as far as Alex could see. They were just being sensible, preparing for the inevitable, making sure their children wouldn't be burdened with deciding how or where to bury them when the time came. Still, as often happened, when confronted with page after page of headstones and memorial sculptures, the common sense that had led them to their appointment with Alex gave way to the finality of what they were doing. When at last the wife pointed to a picture of a heart-shaped marker with a line from Psalm 23 carved above its base, and the husband shrugged in his surly way and said, "Whatever you think," Alex closed the book and saw that the woman's eyes were brimming with tears. In one well-practiced motion, he reached behind his desk for a box of tissues and slid them onto the table between her and her husband, as if unsure which of them might be in need. "I know you'll be happy with this design," he assured the couple as he filled out their order forms. "The rose granite costs a bit more, but it's worth it when you see the results." The woman took a tissue and smiled weakly at Alex as she dabbed her eyes; the man reached inside his jacket for his checkbook. Despite their differences, Alex would carve their names and their birth years into the stone, side by side, leaving a blank space below, and the marker would stand in the village cemetery in Hopedale—once a utopian outpost, now just another dying mill town—until their remains were ready to return to the earth. Alex hoped that the marker would bring them comfort in the intervening years, that knowing they would be interred together would keep their quarrels in check. He took one last look at Leslie's building and climbed into the cab beside his son.

Alex drove out of Leslie's neighborhood, past block after block of faceless apartment buildings, laundromats, and take-out pizza places, and found the onramp for the Pike, which would take them back to central Massachusetts. When he glanced in his mirror, he saw the city receding behind him, the cold, gray sky reflected in its tallest glass tower. It was lunchtime on a Monday—Teddy's school was closed for faculty training, but other districts were open—and traffic was light.

Teddy kept his earbuds in, rocking his head almost imperceptibly to the beat of his music, shaping the lyrics to himself under his breath. The electric thud of the bass line reached Alex distantly, working its way into his brain like a burrowing worm.

"Hey," Alex said, after waiting unsuccessfully for a break between songs.

Teddy kept on nodding, mumbling the song to himself like a member of some monastic order, one whose members all wore their baseball caps turned backward and who knew each other by the earbud rosaries they displayed around their necks.

"Hey," Alex said again.

No answer. Alex reached over and grabbed Teddy's shoulder, shook him, and shouted "Hey!" a little louder than he had intended.

Teddy sat up, blinked, and looked at Alex as if he had just been woken from meditation. "What?"

"I can't drive with that incessant noise coming out of your ears," Alex said. "Can't you turn your music off when we're in the car?"

Teddy shrugged. "Mom lets me."

"Well, I'm not Mom," Alex said. "And when I'm driving, you need to keep the music off."

Teddy turned off his music and reluctantly took out his earbuds. Then he slouched low against the seat and crossed his arms tight over his chest.

Alex was startled by the sudden silence. "Thanks," he said, relieved that Teddy hadn't defied him.

They drove on without talking for several miles as the barren tree branches on either side of the road flickered by, a monotonous expanse of brown. Alex waited for Teddy to say something about the weekend, about Leslie. No words came.

"We could listen to the radio," Alex suggested, when the silence between them became too much to bear. "I think *Talk of the Nation* is on."

Beside him, Teddy shrugged and made a non-committal grunt. Alex decided to take this as a yes. The self-assured, rational tone of public radio always steadied him, and as the show's host introduced his guest speakers, Alex glanced sideways at Teddy and caught a glimpse of alertness in his eyes, a slight shift in his posture that gave Alex hope he was paying attention. The topic of the day was the presidential primary campaign, and Alex was momentarily lost in the memory of explaining the election cycle to Teddy when he was starting sixth grade. Back then Teddy was always brimming with questions, talking so excitedly that Alex had had to make a new rule for the road: don't ask about the Republicans when Dad is trying to merge into traffic.

They listened together in silence as the two guests reviewed and dissected each candidate's latest gaffes on the campaign trail. He and Teddy laughed at the same jokes made by the host and his commentators, and gradually Alex felt his sense of inner balance returning. Above them, a red-tailed hawk wheeled and glided across the sky, its outspread wings catching each successive current as it rose higher and higher on the wind.

It was coming up to the half-hour, and the talk show host paused for news and station identification. Immediately, the perky voices of the local station's morning show hosts cut in, describing their Valentine's Day fundraiser: a bouquet of long-stemmed roses from a high-end florist, which could be sent to the listener's beloved for a pledge of seventy-five dollars. "You know you need to send these," a woman's voice said cheerfully, "and when you do, not only will you make your special someone happy, you'll be helping to keep public radio on the air."

"That's right," said a man's upbeat voice. "You can send these to your wife, your husband, your girlfriend, boyfriend, mother or grandmother as a way to say 'I love you' and support your favorite station at the same time."

"They really are beautiful flowers," said the woman. "We have a gorgeous bouquet here in the studio, and I know if my husband had these delivered to me on Valentine's Day, I would definitely be swept off my feet."

The man on the radio chuckled. "So call right now and support public radio while you sweep your loved ones off their feet. A seventy-five dollar donation is all it takes."

Leslie had fallen in love with him, Alex liked to think, watching him in the sculpture studio of their college art department. She sat on a high stool in the corner, wearing a HEPA filter mask and safety goggles, observing as he cut and shaped a block of sandstone for a competition sculpture, great clouds of stone dust shooting upward from the spinning blade of his diamond-edged saw. His own face was hidden by his mask and goggles, his hands were covered by thick leather safety gloves, and he never felt more like a man than in those moments, with Leslie watching him from her corner, her body alert and taut as an archer's bow. He believed she could see more than his straining biceps as he handled the screaming saw (though he hoped she saw those, too, of course); he believed she could see his mind at work as he guided the blade over the edges and corners of the stone, that she could see the vision he carried in his very soul —for the sculpture and for the two of them, together, as they carved out their place in the world. After these studio sessions they would shower down in their separate dorms, then meet in his cinderblock bedroom and fuck gloriously for the rest of the afternoon while his roommate Stuart sat downstairs at the security desk, his weekend work-study job. When the sky outside the dorm's plate-glass windows darkened, Alex and Leslie would gather their clothes, shower again, and then meet for dinner in the cafeteria, proudly exuding the aura of sex, at ease in their young bodies, connected from one end of the cashier's line to the other by the spark that had leapt and arced between them in bed. Alex was sure he had never been happier, before or since.

He looked over at Teddy, who was still staring straight ahead out the windshield, immune to the radio's Valentine's Day exhortations. On either side of the car, pre-split granite loomed over the road, blue-knuckled icicles gripping its dark craggy face. The local station's host read out a few headlines, the latest stock exchange numbers, and the weather forecast: misty and cold, with a chance of rain. The pledge drive hosts cut in again. "You only have a few more hours to order roses for your sweetheart in time for Valentine's Day," the woman said. "So do it now. Show your love and affection, and show your support for the terrific programming you've come to expect from public radio."

The man repeated the pledge drive phone number and urged listeners to call before it was too late. *Talk of the Nation* came back on the air, heralded by the somber tones of its theme music.

Alex gripped the steering wheel, trying to stop the woman's voice from running on an endless loop in his mind. *Your sweetheart, that special someone, say I love you, sweep her off her feet, show your love and affection.* He had known it was almost Valentine's Day, of course, but he and Leslie had never celebrated it much in the past—a Hallmark-manufactured holiday, Leslie called it—so he hadn't thought the day would make any difference to him now that they were living apart. He caught himself on that phrase, living apart—one that he had used when explaining their situation to family and friends, even to Teddy himself. *We're going to try living apart.* The thought of those words now was enough to bring tears to his eyes. He blinked ferociously and glanced sideways at Teddy, who still showed no sign of understanding what was happening in his father's heart, just a few inches away from his as they traveled at seventy miles an hour along the Mass Pike. Alex was stilled by the thought that if he sent Leslie flowers this year, she might not even accept them, might tell the delivery man to take them back. He imagined her standing in her apartment doorway, arms crossed, her face expressionless before she closed the door and the roses were taken away, and he felt unspeakably sad. Beside him, Teddy laughed softly at another political comment on the radio, but Alex no longer knew if the topic was the Republican primaries, or if the discussion had moved on entirely. He looked at his own eyes in the rearview mirror and saw that they were hollowed and hopeless.

He had been only half-joking the first time he asked Leslie if he could draw her in the nude. They were alone in Alex's dorm room, lying naked on his single bed under the blue thermal blanket he had taken from his grandmother's basement, and Leslie was stretching her bare arm toward the ceiling, turning her hand slowly, gracefully, examining her own body as if it had been newly bestowed on her. Alex could hear laughter in the hallway and the loud voices of other boys who lived on his floor. A stereo in another room was playing "Close to Me" by The Cure.

"Arms are weird, aren't they?" Leslie said at last. Alex loved it when she came out with simple things like that, when she dropped her Econ-major persona and forgot her inclination to spar with him over his affection for socialism. He turned his head and kissed her cheek, then ran his tongue along the outer ridge of her ear.

"That tickles," Leslie giggled. She kept her arm raised high, twisting and turning it, joining her two middle fingers to her thumb to make a shadow-puppet coyote. She whimpered like a puppy as she brought the coyote's snout down to nuzzle Alex under his chin.

He laughed, and Leslie stretched up both her arms, trying to see which was longer. "Don't you think arms are weird?"

Alex loved the way her smooth skin absorbed the fading sunlight from the window between his bed and Stuart's. He could just see the fine blonde hairs on her wrists, the flexing patterns of carpals and metacarpals under her luminous skin. Before he could stop himself, he blurted out an idea he had saved for his own private daydreams, for times when Leslie was in class or the library, or home with her parents in Swampscott.

"Let me draw you," he said. "Naked."

Instantly he regretted saying it. He waited for Leslie to laugh and call him a pervert, to shame him into disowning the idea as an adolescent fantasy.

Instead she lowered her two arms and turned her head toward him until they were eye to eye across the pillow. Slowly, languidly, she gave him a mischievous smile. "Only if you're naked, too."

His erection was returning, and he knew Leslie could feel it pressing against her bare upper thigh. He blushed at the thought of revealing it in the open air, trapped behind a sketchpad while Leslie posed perfectly still. "Can we fuck again first?" he asked, sheepishly, cringing at the querulous sound of his own voice.

Leslie raised her eyebrows playfully in response. "No." She giggled as she threw back the blanket, exposing the lengths of their bodies to the ripening afternoon light. She nudged him out of bed with her hip, then cocked her shoulder and brought her hand to her hair like a centerfold model. "How do you want me?"

Alex stood motionless for a moment, naked, aching with desire while Leslie teased him with a series of pin-up girl poses. At last he dived for his sketchpad, snatching it off his desk along with a stick of charcoal and a kneaded eraser. He sat himself on Stuart's bed, propped the pad on his knees to hide his waning erection, and flipped open the cover to a blank page.

Alex and Teddy drove on without speaking until *Talk of the Nation* was over. After the show, the local pledge drive started again, with continued banter about Valentine's Day. "Everyone loves roses," the perky woman asserted, "so send some now to that special person in your life. Valentine's Day is just a few short days away."

Alex stared ahead through the windshield and clenched his teeth against the urge to tell the radio host to shut up. Above all he did not want Teddy to know he was perturbed. He had read plenty of Internet articles about separation and divorce, and rule number one was always Don't Drag Your Children Into Your Marital Conflicts. He clung to the hope that his son could emerge from this period in their family life unscathed, and he knew that behind this noble wish lay the delusion that he and Leslie could someday return to being the happy couple he had always wanted them to be.

"I need to go to the bathroom," Teddy said, the first full sentence he had spoken since Alex made him turn off his music.

Alex pulled off at the next exit and kept the truck running while Teddy went into a gas station. The radio pledge drive was still going, and by now the hosts' insistently chirpy voices were grating against the sorrowful tissue at the forefront of Alex's brain. He glanced into the gas station and saw Teddy waiting outside the locked men's room door, his earbuds plugged back into his ears, his eyes staring vacantly ahead as he nodded along to his music. He took no notice of his father, outside in the parking lot, buffeted by the relentless chatter of the Valentine's Day pledge drive.

The male host read out the station's pledge line number again, and Alex pulled out his cell phone. As the man's voice repeated the numbers, Alex punched them in, knowing this was a misguided attack even as his index finger stabbed the last digit on the keypad.

An elderly woman answered, her slow voice wavering but cheerful. "Thank you for calling the pledge line. Would you like to send one or two dozen roses?" Behind her Alex heard the murmur of other voices.

"No." Alex glanced toward the gas station, where Teddy was receiving a key on a long wooden stick from the man coming out of the restroom. Alex watched as his son disappeared behind the door. "I don't want to send roses. I just want the station to think about this pledge drive and how hard—how inappropriate it is for anyone who's alone."

"Oh." The lady on the phone sighed, and the brightness faded out of her voice. When she spoke again, she sounded fatigued, as if Alex's demand had thwarted the momentum that had carried her into the radio station. "I'm so sorry." She paused. "Have you lost someone recently?"

And suddenly Alex could see her clearly, could see her surrounded by others in the station's makeshift phone bank—probably just a conference room with some instant coffee and a box of doughnuts—trying to buoy herself amid a sea of aging women, widowed and alone, taking calls from strangers as a way of bridging the distance between her solitary life and the shoals of healthy, young humanity that streamed by her on the television, the radio, the sidewalk and street outside her apartment complex or her empty ranch home.

"No," said Alex hurriedly. "Not lost—she's not dead, we're just getting divorced. Or separated, anyway. I don't know."

The lady on the phone sighed again. "I really am sorry to hear that. And I'll tell the volunteer coordinator what you said. I hope that you and your wife will be all right."

Alex imagined her face, kind as his grandmother's, and her

white hair, freshly permed. He saw her sitting at the phone bank flanked by other white-haired ladies from her church or bridge club, all of them wearing radio station T-shirts stretched over turtleneck sweaters. Maybe they would all go to lunch afterward; he hoped they would. He wished he could be there to pick up the tab. "It's not your fault," he said, abashed. "I'm sorry I bothered you." He saw Teddy emerge from the gas station's front door with a bottle of electric blue sports drink in his hand.

"Not at all, sir," the woman said, regaining her pledge line politeness. "I hope you have a nice day."

Teddy opened the cab door just as Alex flipped his phone shut. Warily, Teddy removed the buds from his ears and climbed into the passenger seat. "Who was on the phone?"

"No one," said Alex, shifting the truck into gear. "I was just checking my messages."

Teddy looked Alex in the eye for a brief moment, and Alex thought he saw a flash of sympathy and recognition. "If you were talking to Mom, you don't have to lie to me." He cracked open the cap of his sports bottle and took a long drink.

Alex waited until Teddy buckled his seatbelt, then pulled out of the gas station driveway. "I wasn't talking to Mom."

Alex had found that first nude drawing of Leslie in the attic, along with a sheaf of others he had done over the years, sketches made in stolen moments when she was still enough not to mind being drawn: Leslie at their kitchen table, reading a book, her cup of green tea beside her; Leslie in the garden, wearing her wide-brimmed hat, kneeling to re-plant the narcissus bulbs that had outgrown their beds. The last time she had posed nude for him was when she was pregnant with Teddy, and that drawing was bundled along with the others: Leslie standing, draped in an open robe, her face turned shyly toward her magnificent rounded belly, one hand resting on its side, the other cradling her face, as if she were contemplating the child inside her and the new life that was about to begin.

He and Leslie had argued about that drawing. Alex wanted to sculpt it, the pregnant form, the face of a solicitous mother waiting for a new world to open. He would make the features anonymous, he promised, so that it would be a universal portrayal of mother-hood, not a personal portrait of her. Leslie had cried over the idea, had told him that he didn't understand what it felt like to give her body over to another being, to lose control of her balance, her ener-gy levels, even her bladder and her capacity to sleep at night. Alex said that making the sculpture might help him understand, and he told her he thought she was more beautiful than ever. She said that if he sculpted her pregnant, she would never speak to him again. So he put the drawing away, and massaged her feet until she stopped crying. In the back of his mind he hoped her feelings might change after the baby was born.

Alex glanced sideways at Teddy: in profile, his face had the same shape as his mother's, and the open, unclouded look in his eyes made Alex want to weep for the light that had gone out of Leslie's. He knew nothing except the certain weight of the head-stone behind them and the steep turns on the long road ahead. Facing forward alongside his son, Alex shifted the truck into high-er gear and took the onramp toward home.

Allen Ginsberg:
An Encounter

by Harvey Blume

*at 2:50 PM March 10 1955 reached point in time where life was no
longer suffering but to live was a pleasure.*
—Allen Ginsberg, Journals Mid-Fifties (1954-1958)

When I interviewed Allen Ginsberg I said something right off
that startled him, though what I said was simple and not
raunchy in the least, as if raunchy would ever affront a poet who
liked saying, "Why don't we get right down to the cunt of the matter?"

"Allen," I said, "I want to say something I never say to people
I interview."

I was wearing a sort of newsboy hat. As synchronicity would
have it, he had one just like it in his pocket and put it on.

"Yeah?"

"Allen, I love you."

I have harbored deep feelings for a lot of the people I interviewed — Doris Lessing, Norman Mailer, Oliver Sacks. And I de-

veloped similar feelings for others in the course of the conversation itself — E. O. Wilson, to name one. When I met Wilson in his Harvard lab with untold numbers of ants from different species fulfilling their colony destinies in environments expressly designed for them, Wilson was so generous with his time that his secretary stomped in more than once to glare at me and try to get him back on schedule. Wilson would not be interrupted. He was too thoroughly engaged in changing my mind for good about some mistakes I'd made with regard to nature and nurture, genes and environment. He schooled me.

But back to Ginsberg, in April 1995 at an outdoor table at what was then the Cafe Paradiso in Harvard Square. This wasn't my first encounter with him — far from. I'd been running into Ginsberg — known in certain circles as Ginzap — in one context or another ever since as a Brooklyn high school kid wandering the Lower East Side, I happened into a coffeehouse where he was declaiming Howl to a chorus of bearded Beats.

"I saw the best minds of my generation destroyed by madness, starving hysterical naked…"

"Stomp the shrinks! Stomp all shrinks!" came from the crowd, many of whose members, however mad they might have been, did not, therefore, relish their encounters with psychotherapy.

Then there was the time at Columbia College when Ginsberg appeared onstage with his friend/lover Peter Orlovsky, and recited a poem that went into some detail about one or both of them having bent penises. This prompted male faculty members from the English department to rise up in tweedy gentility to escort their female companions, shocked or not, out of the theater.

Here I skip to the movement against the war in Vietnam, where I might be in a throng chanting, "Hell no! We won't go!" while Ginsberg, bare hairy chest exposed, castanets on his fingers, was dancing nearby to:

"Hare Krishna Hare Krishna Krishna Krishna Hare Hare
Hare Rama Hare Rama Rama Rama Hare Hare"

Then, too, there was that winter evening in 1977 when Ginsberg was reading in Cambridge, at Passim's, and Doc Humes, a New York familiar, got himself busted for — believe it — smoking pot. Suddenly, Ginsberg went into the ubiquity mode he kept in reserve. He was outside, dealing with the cops at the same time as he was inside telling us "Genius is no good if you're nuts!"

Craziness v. sanity, nuts v. not nuts was one of his abiding themes.

There were so many brushes of so many kinds, including conversations. Though I am a strictly secular person, there was a time when I went around saying Ginsberg was my one and only rabbi. It changes nothing that, as you'll see, Ginsberg was indifferent, at best, to rabbinic Judaism.

And the poetry. I won't focus on the famous work — "Howl" or "Kaddish" — which, after initial outrage and faculty walk-outs, are now part of the curriculum, even part of the canon (pronounced "canyon" by him in our exchange). I'll stay with the late stuff, much of which took the form of lament, except "lament" is completely the wrong word. We're not talking Milton, Lycidas, Latinate expressions of grief. We're talking old guy stuff, bowel movements. We're talking kvetch.

In a way, all Ginsberg's poetry was kvetch: in "Howl" on behalf of Carl Solomon *et al.*, in "Kaddish" on behalf of Naomi, his mother, crazed not least of all by history — the Holocaust, paranoid imaginings of the KGB. In his last poems his kvetch is mostly personal, lending a new dimension to the conjunction of poetry and kvetch. From his Richard III:

Toenail-thickening age on me
… weak-kneed …
water —
logged liver, gut & lung — up at 4 a.m.
reading Shakespeare.

He doesn't always get to Shakespeare. Sometimes he can't get past bowels, despite which he prefers to stick around. One of my favorite lines in all poetry is his "American Sentence" *Approaching Seoul by Bus in Heavy Rain* (August 1990):

Get used to your body, forget you were born, suddenly you got to get out!

When I told Ginsberg I loved him, he blushed.

○

HB: What struck me most reading the "Journals Mid-Fifties" is the theme of love. You discuss it on a cosmic spiritual level, but also in terms of a masochism and submissiveness you wrestle with constantly.

AG: I hadn't thought of it as masochism but I guess it's so.

HB: You use the word a lot.

AG: It's kind of a buzz word.

HB: You write: "Love is complete…It never lacks because it is All. It comes on the mind in visions. Watch for it coming! It enters the house of the body without your seeking." You say that, on the one hand. On the other, you say, "That kind of love of mine is a sickness…Am I nuts?"

AG: Almost anybody, from Shakespeare on, who talks about love, talks about the pains of love, the thorns of love—the bed of love is a rose with thorns. It's par for the course, in a sense. Very often, I'm presenting worst case scenarios, too, you know, the worst fantasies.

In the situation with Neal Cassady, we were friends, very close friends, until his death, and in and out of bed together for over 20 years. With Peter Orlovsky, though there was a lot of struggle in connecting with him, we were together from 1954 to the present, more or less. So they're the birth pangs.

HB: This passage stays with me: "I have held on to self-pity so long as a primary source of emotion in love, I hardly know what would replace it in my feelings if it went."

AG: The awareness of self-pity is the medicine for self-pity.

HB: The desire for total surrender to someone—or total union with someone—runs through your work.

AG: Or total mastery, one or the other, it's the reverse side of the coin.

HB: It also comes across as tenderness.

AG: I wonder if the masochist aspect cancels out the genuineness of the tenderness. That would be the logical question.

Probably I always felt kind of stupid and inferior and ugly and fell in love with people I felt were beautiful and more true than myself. Probably the quality of devotion and desire, or the intensity of devotion or desire, were the strongest and the most permanent elements in the relationship. So that which was considered, say, inferior or weaker was, because it gave rise to devotion and intense adoration, the cause of a stronger durable passion. Nowadays a lot of that devotion is transferred over to Buddhist dharma and the relation to the teacher, the master, the meditation instructor.

HB: You still practice meditation.

AG: I'm very much involved, and have been for many years, with the Naropa Institute and activity related to the spread of dharma through education. With Gelek Rinpoche, a teacher from Ann Arbor, a Tibetan teacher. Philip Glass and I are students of his. We've done a lot of benefits for the Jewel Heart Meditation Center in Ann Arbor, and I see Rinpoche a lot, visit Ann Arbor and seek advice, go on retreats with him.

It's student learning, setting other people before myself and trying to listen to them and pay attention to them rather than trying to dominate them.

HB: A theme that runs through the dreams you record in the "Journals"—and you pay a lot of attention to your dreams—is that of acceptance. You have recurrent anxiety dreams about being outside the academy, outside a career path. There's a dream in which T.S. Eliot is reading your poetry. You're in tears; T.S. Eliot's reading your poetry!

AG: That was a very funny dream, particularly the idea of Eliot putting me to bed in his digs in Chelsea, getting me an English hot toddy, whatever that is, a hot water bottle you take to bed with you to keep your feet warm.

HB: Do you still dream about Eliot?

AG: No. Bob Dylan.

HB: But Dylan likes you.

AG: In the dream.

HB: Doesn't he like you in reality?

AG: Yeah.

HB: So it's not a problem.

AG: But it's more overt in the dream.

HB: He likes you even better.

AG: It's more demonstrative.

HB: There's a good deal of discussion of canons now, canon-making, canon-breaking. "Howl" set off similar kinds of debates in the 1950s. Someone like Trilling didn't want to discuss your work as poetry at all.

AG: Oddly enough, Trilling changed his mind, and in his monumental anthology of world literature, he included me with Shakespeare and Sophocles. The poem "Aunt Rose" is what he chose. The Jewish family sense in that poem, and the emotion, finally got to him and he realized what I was doing was grounded; it wasn't hippy-dippy and it wasn't crazy.

HB: The same dismissive attitude has been taken up by Harold Bloom.

AG: I don't read him. Specifically? He actually talks about me?

HB: Bloom's always been concerned with constructing canon; who's saved, who isn't. You're not saved.

AG: He may be good on Blake and earlier things but I've looked at the choices of contemporary materials and they're not very inspiring.

HB: He's a canon-maker.

AG: Not really. In ten years it will be obsolete.

HB: A would-be canon-maker.

AG: Everybody's a would-be canon-maker. He just advertises himself as a canon-maker but he doesn't make the canon. Readers make the canon.

And much of that has changed. As of this last year, Kerouac is becoming more recognized as a monumental writer of the late-20th century who knew what he was doing, better than Truman Capote in terms of writing. There have been several reviews that point out Kerouac accomplished a work with vast scope, as distinct from the Updike, Joyce Carol Oates, middlebrow view that he had one interesting book, "On The Road," and the rest was not readable.

But among poets, Kerouac is known to be a seminal influence not only on me but on Bob Dylan as well Gary Snyder and Robert Creely. It's obvious that Kerouac and Ma Rainey and Robert Johnson will be in anthologies sooner or later. To the extent that someone like Bloom doesn't get it—it never occurred to him that American Black blues, early century up to the '30s, might be part of the canon like the Scottish border ballads or the anonymous 14th-century lyrics are in the Oxford Book of English poetry—to that extent he's missing the mark. Burroughs was understood all the way through. Everybody from Mary McCarthy on paid homage to Burroughs as a great writer, even Samuel Beckett. Nobody has disputed that except a lunatic fringe. You could call Bloom part of the lunatic fringe in that sense.

HB: I'd love to call him part of the lunatic fringe.

AG: It's at such a disparity with intelligent opinion. I don't think he puts Burroughs in the canyon.

HB: I think he does put him in the canyon.

AG: Burroughs has an enormous influence on high culture, low culture, an all-pervading influence. Probably get a Nobel Prize if it weren't for the disrepute of his personal life. But that's no different than Francois Villon or Christopher Marlowe or any number of Nobel types.

Gregory Corso is another in my personal canon. I would also point out John Weiners here in Boston, a great tragic poet. Creely is a great poet, a great academic poet, too.

HB: What was it about William Carlos Williams that led him, it seems alone of his generation, to see the virtue in your early work?

AG: He wasn't alone; there were any number of others.

I had known Williams in Paterson. I had written him some letters which were, for him, a welcome response from the streets of Paterson. Then I sent him some poems that were imitations of his. He wrote me a little note saying, do you have more of these?

Years later I sent him "Howl", which he didn't quite get because of the long line. He was interested in measuring the short breath but he read "Howl" to some younger people who were knocked out by it. He saw there was real emotion and wrote me a letter saying so. I asked him for a preface and he did it, understanding that I was dealing with new verse. When I got to "Kaddish" he balked, afraid that the use of the paragraph abandoned the search for an American measure. But he changed his mind and realized I was doing something valuable emotionally or artistically, and he wrote a little poem about it.

It wasn't just Williams. Many of his contemporaries, like Carl Rakosi, Louis Zukofsky, George Oppen, Charles Reznikoff, responded. Even Pound liked it. According to his daughter, he said, this is Ginsberg's hell; I'd be interested in seeing his paradise.

HB: Williams would be open to you because he was listening for an American voice.

AG: There was one time we visited him. Me and Peter Orlovsky and Gregory Corso and Kerouac came to visit him in Rutherford. While Kerouac went in the kitchen with his wife and charmed her—she said he was very handsome and very sweet—we sat around and talked poetry. Gregory read him some new poems, and he liked them. At the end we said, well Dr. Williams, here we are ready to go, do you have any wise words for us? And he pointed out the window, out on Ridge Road Rutherford, and said, "There's a lot of bastards out there."

He was scared of the fame and publicity that came and wasn't sure we could handle it. Because what happened with the Beat writers was pretty astonishing for someone of the older Modernist school whose editions were limited to one or two thousand. And it was actually surprising to me that "Howl" went into more than that. We originally printed 500, thinking of it as an esoteric book to be appreciated by connoisseurs.

I don't think people realized that I grew up in a poetry atmosphere.

HB: Your father was a poet.

AG: It was a family business. I knew rhyme and meter and stanza from my eighth year and memorized endless Yeats, Vachel Lindsay, Edward Arlington Robinson, Edna Millay and knew what was necessary to know as a basic rhythmic specialist. There was the idea of Beat writers splashing their stuff spontaneously which spread like a Frankenstein image among younger poets so everybody thought they could just get away with writing anything they want.

HB: You did say, first pass best pass.

AG: No. First thought best thought. Actually I didn't say it; a venerable Tibetan lama said it: first thought is best in art, second thought in other matters, meaning you have to rely on your ur-thought, your intuition, your organic understanding, your flash, your primordial mind.

"Journals Mid-Fifties" is one out of three of my journal volumes published now. There's potentially another 40 volumes. That's a lot of writing, a lot of fidelity to the idea of art for art's sake, catching your mind, catching yourself thinking.

HB: Do you dream as intensely as you did?

AG: Yeah. I had a great dream the other day of Carl Solomon who died several years ago. I meet him in the afterlife and say, "How is it there?"

He says, "Oh, just like the mental hospital. You get along if you know the rules."

I say, "Well, what are the rules?"

He says, "There are two rules. First, remember you're dead. Second rule, act like you're dead."

I woke up laughing.

HB: I reread "Kaddish" yesterday and was moved again by the story of your mother's madness. Did she know in her blood what was happening in Europe? Was that part of what drove her mad?

AG: I think very much. She had a hyper-sensitivity; she just saw it in a mirror image and didn't realize that exactly what she was complaining about in America was going on with all the Jews in Russia. She thought there were wires and secret police and they were out to get her. Well, it was happening in Russia and in Germany. In an attempt to rationalize an unconscious awareness of that, she projected it on her own scene in America.

That wasn't the only thing. There were family troubles, genetic things. Remember, my mother came over from Russia at the age of twelve or so and had already seen Cossacks coming down.

HB: After the experience of her madness it might seem you were especially foolhardy to spend your time out on a limb seeking visions.

AG: But I also had been inoculated by the notion that once everybody in the world disagreed with me, I should check back on my perceptions and not insist, moderate the violence of my insistence.

HB: You learned something.

AG: How to stay out of the bughouse.

HB: At the same time you were seeking visions by all means possible.

AG: No no no, they came on their own. Then I was checking them out with psychedelics to see what approximation psychedelics would bring to the natural experience. And I was reading William James's "Varieties of Religious Experience" and various other books that dealt with out of the ordinary mind states.

There's always been a visionary aspect to America, from Whitman, Thoreau, Emerson, the Transcendentalists on. That's one of the mainstreams in America's melting pot. There's a lot of mainstreams, unless you want to say the homogenized Time-Life television consciousness is the mainstream.

HB: The effect of jazz on your generation has been much remarked.

AG: We were listening to old blues and new jazz.

HB: How did the music affect your work?

AG: There was the myth Kerouac had about Lester Young blowing 69 successive choruses of "Lady Be Good." The idea was the increasing excitement—building chorus after chorus until you hit an ecstatic orgasmic rhetorical rhapsody. The stream of verses, "Who, Who, Who, Who," in "Howl," was an imitation of that chorus after chorus as was the plateau of rhythmic ecstasy in the Moloch section.

HB: Is it significant to you that today is the last day of Passover?

AG: Well, I had a couple of seders. I went with my brother and his whole family and I will be going tomorrow to another gathering.

HB: Are they meaningful affairs for you?

AG: I've been going to seders for years, not so much as a monotheist recollection but as a historical cultural recollection. Monotheism—the Judeo-Christian-Islamic monotheist tradition—I think, as Blake thought, is one of the curses of mankind, the idea of a single authority in the universe. Blake said, "Six thousand years of sleep since the Garden of Eden." Unconsciousness, sleepwalking, depending on a creator.

The Buddhist theme is, "Daddy, is there a God?"

Daddy says, "No."

The kid says, "Whew."

Taking the roof off the box. Getting out of the claustrophobic box of monotheist dictatorship.

The Pain Scale

by Julia Story

Today is a good day so I can offer
or try to offer connective parts like
connective tissue, invisible: what
extends between us. So it isn't so
much offering as pointing out: we
are connected by invisible tissue.
You ask me over and over every
time I come to give you the definition
of this thing I carry with me which
in so many ways has gone beyond
pain: a burning hand that takes me
to sometimes even a trail of beauty;
dying trees covered in scaffolding,
a map of crushed stuff at their feet;
heron voices. The longer I stay
and look the more the distant box
stays open and I can warble or crawl
toward it instead of just trying to sit
here in this chair. I don't really know
how to be here either but the longer
I make the path, the more lookouts
appear. There is a skull with light

in it, a holy shovel until I'm nailed
again to the sky in my head and we
stand here together like clouds.

The Tonic of Wildness

by Christina Porter

Some of the least transcendental moments of my life have been spent at Walden Pond, chaperoning field trips. I teach high school English right outside of Boston in Revere. It's a city; our students are "city kids." They wear urban style clothing, listen to rap, and rarely venture out of the confines of their neighborhoods. Therefore, when our eleventh graders study American literature, including the transcendentalists, it seems like an English teacher sin to live so close to Walden Pond and not to take our students. A few years ago two colleagues of mine, Kelly and Diana, decided that this is exactly what we should do. We thought that at the cost of a short bus ride, we would be able to better connect them to Thoreau, his writings, and his ideals about the beauty of nature and importance of simple living and simplicity. We had no idea what we were getting ourselves into.

"I am a monarch of all I survey, my right there is none to dispute."

Before the first field trip, we suggest the "proper attire" to our students: very casual. Sneakers and t-shirts are what we have in mind. But apparently, "casual" in city high school context means something different altogether, or so we learn when Kevin shows up in jeans that look like a parachute, hooded sweatshirt with silver airbrushing, black baseball hat, and brand new suede construction boots. As the tour guide begins to lead us along the flat 1.7 mile trail that encircles the pond, I get a funny feeling about Kevin. While the other students lament the lack of cell phone service (and our resultant vulnerability to bear attack), Kevin keeps glancing back to see where the teachers are. This is always a bad sign, so I try to keep a tracking eye on him. As we stop to hear about Thoreau's favorite fishing spot, I see Kevin whisper to a friend, who hands him something that he shoves into his pocket. He then slips through the trees into a little clearing, and I follow, to catch him in the act. Probably smoking, I think. Maybe something more serious.

Instead, I see Kevin sitting on a tree stump with his suede boot in his hand and a packet of tissues in his lap, lovingly trying to clean a spot of mud from his shoes. There is a small pile of discarded tissues on the undisturbed forest ground near him.

"What's going on?" I ask.

"Miz, it's nasty here! I have mud all over my boots!" he informs me. "These are $120 boots!" He believes that this fact should certainly justify his actions.

"What about the pile of tissues you have there?" I ask.

"Miz! They're tissues? Who cares?"

I try to appeal to his sympathy for wildlife. "Maybe the squirrels who call this clearing home will care."

"Are the squirrels gonna pay to have my boots cleaned?"

"How would you feel if someone threw muddy tissues all over your living room?"

"I'd punch them in the face!" he replies.

I see that we are getting nowhere fast, and I hear the group moving off on our tour. "Kevin, just please re-join the group." He glares at me in triumph as he replaces the boot onto his left foot and struts off toward the path. I stoop to collect his pile of trash, utterly frustrated.

"I went into the woods because I wished to live deliberately..."

"Nicola!!" I yell, running down the narrow path. Nicola's friends move reluctantly out of my way as I follow the puffs of cigarette smoke drifting to the back of the line. "Nicola!" I trumpet again as I close in on her. "Nicola, are you smoking!?"

"Miz, you really need to calm down, we're outside!" she informs me, tapping ash onto the hallowed ground.

"Nicola! This is a state park. We are in the woods. Haven't you ever heard of Smokey the Bear?! You can't smoke here, now please put it out!"

Nicola glares at me through heavily lined eyes. Some of her friends laugh nervously at this standoff.

"Whatever, Miz," she says, stamping out her cigarette on the ground, and leaving the butt for the wildlife.

My husband is a "Leave No Trace" master. This is not a made-up title; he has a laminated card from the Appalachian Mountain Club displaying his credentials. People are supposed to erase any trace of their visits to the wilderness. No candy bar wrappers, water bottles, or even orange peels. Thoreau might well have subscribed to it 150 years before it had a name. Nicola, with all the advantages of that century and a half to consider the question, does not. Her discarded cigarette joins the crumpled tissues in my pocket.

Further down the trail, I hear the elevated voice of Diana, another of my colleagues. I hustle past a group of students and see Diana admonishing a small group of kids standing at the pond's edge.

"But Miz! I've seen people do it on TV!" Juan is trying to defend his actions.

"Juan, that's true, people do feed ducks, but they usually feed them pieces of bread." Diana tries to explain.

"But Miz, they like it! Look, they ate all of them!"

"That's because they don't know any better Juan, but I really don't think it is good for ducks to eat jalapeño Doritos." She tries to explain this with caution, trying not to hurt his feelings. It seems like we should have taught these kids more than just Walden before bringing them here.

"Simplicity, simplicity, simplicity!"

All of a sudden, they are quiet. Our teacher instincts kick in as Kelly, Diana and I exchange warning looks, and move off down the path towards the gift shop. We are at the end of the day, our ropes, and our sanity. We brought them to Walden to experience nature, the sublime, solitude, maybe even the universal oversoul. We ended up picking up trash, preventing forest fires, saving the digestive systems of waterfowl and reassuring the students, "Yes, we are still going to Burger King on the way home!" This trip had achieved none of our lofty expectations, and now all we hear coming from the kids is ominous silence.

In the distance, we see them all standing in a group near the horse paddock. The state police have a few horses at the pond stationed near the gift shop. Our kids are standing there, motionless and quiet under the trees. We approach, and see a very large palomino horse standing near the fence.

I know this is a palomino only because my best friend growing up, Adrienne, rode horses. Just like my students, I am a city kid. In fact, I grew up in Revere, and left it as rarely as they do. Never mind Walden: Boston, just a ten-minute train ride away, was a place my friends and I never visited on our own until after we were in college.

I did, however, have some exposure to nature and to the woods. Adrienne's family had a summer home in New Hampshire and they would take me with them on vacations. Unlike many city kids, I had the opportunity to play in the woods and ride horses. I learned an appreciation of the beauty in nature I would not have had otherwise.

Steven, the tallest and possibly the loudest of our students is dwarfed next to this large animal. I hear Steven do something he has never done in my presence before…whisper. "Miz, can we touch him?" he asks me. These kids have never seen a horse up close, and they don't know what to do. They don't try to feed it, tag it, or offer it a cigarette. They are simply in awe of it. I walk Steven up to the horse. "Miz, is he gonna bite me?"

"No Steven, he thinks you might feed him," I reassure him. I reach my hand up to the bony snout and pat the horse. He jerks his head back a bit in horse reaction as he rolls his lips.

"Yo! Miz, watch out!" The students back off at this noise. I tell them to look at his ears. When horses get mad, they pin their ears back. This horse's ears are sticking straight up, so we are fine with him. Now it is Steven's turn. He doesn't want to look like a wimp in front of his peers, especially when I had already approached this huge animal first. His eyes on those ears the entire time, ready to bail if they so much as flicked, he extends a tentative hand, and lightly touches the animal's jaw. One by one, the kids take out their cell phones, and snap pictures for their followers. After Steven breaks the ice, a few other kids pet the horse as well, making sure to document this with their cells.

This interaction does not necessarily fit in with our lofty goals and expectations for how our students would react to Walden Pond, but there is something significant about it.

By the time we return to school, the horse was been transformed by imaginations and tough talk into a beast of epic stature. The kids did not pet it; they tamed it. It was ten feet tall with red eyes and vampire teeth. I hear about it all week from my other students. "Miz, did you hear about how Steven rode that HUGE horse??"

Despite the re-telling liberties taken by our kids, in my memory, the moment exists in simplicity. A group of city kids enter Thoreau's woods. They litter, give ducks indigestion, and still manage to commune with nature, if even for a moment. For some students, the "simple" attention they gave to the horse's ears may have sparked them to respect Thoreau's vision and realize the natural world has much to tell us if we know where to look. Or if not, if they're not more sensitive to the nobility of living simply in the woods, maybe they've at least wised up enough to wear grubby sneakers next time they visit Thoreau's peaceful pond.

Holy Family Holds the Line

by Tom Zygiel

I guess it all starts with school. When I say school, I mean Roman Catholic Parochial School and, specifically, Holy Family Grammar School and Holy Family High School. Mine was taught, administered, and watched over by the Sisters of Mercy. Back then, they, along with the country, were at the height of their power, confidence, and influence. It was a unique experience. Ask anybody the nuns educated at the time. They'll have the scars to prove it.

One of the "gifts" I received from my time with the Sisters of Mercy is a permanent problem with authority. I have gotten into scrapes with dentists about the proper procedure for filling a tooth and then accused the billing clerks out front of deliberately obscuring the charges. On a perfectly beautiful June night, at a Triple A baseball game, I watched my pregnant wife edge away from me, red-faced, while a traffic cop and I "discussed" how best to navigate through a crosswalk. I can break into a cold sweat approaching a baggage claim or airline ticket counter.

You need to know that school was not just school.

It was a generational tapestry of intricate relationships, where schoolmates' mothers and fathers had been schoolmates. My uncles, my Mom, me, we spent dozens of years walking the same hallways, having the same classes, and playing in the same asphalt schoolyard. We heard the same church tower bell and smelled the same smells, learned the same subjects, shared the same rituals, and believed in the same values, superstitions, and biases. We hated and feared the same things. And we all wore the same uniform.

It led to an overwhelming sense of belonging. I belonged to my block, to my family, to Holy Family, and to God's family. Not just Mary and Joseph but all the angels, and saints, and celestial bodies. The connections went deep. I remember when I was eight and first saw the Pieta with my family at the World's Fair in New York. I felt the agony of Christ. The marble captured a moment past the withering of His pain and of the comfort of Mother Mary holding him. It was complete compassion and complete surrender. And it showed the undying love Mother Mary had for Jesus.

I tugged at my mom's blouse sleeve and told her that it seemed so real; the emotion seemed alive.

She asked, "What emotion?"

"Of compassion, of the pain of crucifixion and of Mary's love."

She said, "All of it is the same for you."

"What do you mean?" I asked as we stared at the sculpture with the hot lights on it, and a security guard close by.

"It's there for you," she said. "What is true for the sculpture of Christ is also true for you."

Holy Family immersed you in this type of world. I loved that I lived in a known and conquered universe where all the tough questions had been asked and resolved, all the philosophies thought out and refined, all the mysteries explored and penetrated. And the reason I was on this block and in this schoolyard was so these forces could be distilled in me.

Holy Family was the first parochial elementary school ever

built in New Bedford; built with the pain of Ireland, by the sons of the Irish. Hard-working parishioners with last names like Donovan, Doyle, Donaghy, and Dwyer scrimped, sacrificed, saved and finally built the church and the rectory and then the Grammar School and the High School.

To come into the schoolyard was to feel the force and center of gravity that the church grounds produced. The church itself jutted out onto County Street as if it wanted to impose its order onto the world. And it wasn't an abstract battle. The nuns gave us detention if we didn't bow our heads and make the sign of the cross as we traversed the Tabernacle at the center of the altar even if we were outside on the sidewalk on County Street.

Mornings when my father dropped us off on the way to the mill, my brother John, my sister Mary and I watched as the morning sun rose above the Acushnet River and engulfed the top of the façade of the red brick schools and the grey granite church tower with a soft, golden light. On school grounds, I felt close to God and had no doubt God was active on this block.

But the glow from the schools and church was not enough to keep all trouble at bay. The nuns pointed to a clear and present danger right at the border of our confine: the Clarence P. Cook School, standing diagonally across the street from, and seemingly in direct rebuttal to, Holy Family and our way of life. Clarence P. Cook was named after a ship builder or someone connected to the Underground Railroad during slavery. No one at Holy Family was ever clear on it and no one ever bothered to look it up. But one thing we were sure of: it was not named after a Catholic.

Cook School was in fact the public elementary school in the neighborhood, but I and all my schoolmates for years and years called it, incorrectly, the Protestant School. We had no friends or acquaintances at Cook School and knew we never would. They hated us, which was okay because we hated them.

All the kids over there seemed strange and foreign. They wore no uniforms, carried fewer books, and had no lunch boxes. Still, all of us at Holy Family felt sorry for them because they were not going to receive the illuminations that we were promised and so their reality had certain limits and grayness to it while ours soared and ended in majesty. The nuns told us they had a library, a gymnasium and a cafeteria. We had none of these. Somehow, we offered this sacrifice to God and somehow we felt better than them for it. We were prepared to inherit the earth. As if some ancient rite had to be honored, we thumbed our noses, stuck out our tongues or spat at the Protestant School boys and girls when they came too close to the cast iron fence of our schoolyard down on County Street. Actually the Cook School kids got the message and they mostly veered away from the fence to cross the street. The girls, especially.

The nuns felt the same disdain for Cook School kids that we did except they couldn't show it as openly. The nun on schoolyard duty would turn her whole body away from the Protestant School kids the way you might turn away from a bad car accident that you witnessed and wanted to forget immediately. These "lesser lights" that walked by our schoolyard affronted the entire sensibilities of the nuns and kids.

So all through the long school year we eyed each other warily and suspiciously. Occasionally, a rock fight broke out between schools, but all in all, we remained much like I imagined the tension that surrounded Northern Ireland —- a forced peace always on the brink of war. If in the morning we came back to school and our window panes were broken, then the very next morning Cook School sported broken windows too. The nuns never mentioned the broken windows and in this way OK'd our schoolyard justice. Maybe imagining that if Cook School got control over us they would recreate what all my friends' grandmothers referred to as "The Troubles" right here on our sacred block. Like in Belfast, they'd have us working for them. They'd have us forsake our greatest yearnings, desires and beliefs. They would not acknowledge us as a legitimate force with legitimate wants, needs, and rights. This is what all our grandparents thought we had escaped, and here it was staring at us from right across the street.

Cook School fed our block a constant tension. All our mistrust of foreign people and ideas were directed at them. The nuns probably loved that Cook School stood diagonally across the street. They pointed at it and intimated it was a pagan place full of philistines—and so we had better buckle down in learning the Ten Commandments and all our other lessons.

◌

But the underlying fear that Cook School struck in us was not apparent to me during my first days at Holy Family. What I was aware of was the power of the nuns.

On the first day of school, our very first official act was to attend Mass. Even Mr. Sullivan, the school custodian, had to go. The nuns marched the older students around, barking orders, pronouncing students' last names with a certain bite and madness, with a demeanor that suggested it would be great if some kid did something really stupid and they could make an example out of him.

The nuns held us responsible even for the things they chose not to explain. They could count on the older kids, out of their own traumatized memories, picking up the torch of any fallen protocol.

For example, when the bell rang the very first time everything stopped. After an eerie suspended animation fell over the schoolyard, another bell rang and all the older boys were released to quietly retrieve their belongings. We, as first graders, mimicked what we saw. I found my lunch on the hard asphalt schoolyard next to other lunches. Then we stood in the middle of the schoolyard again not sure what to do. Just frozen, knowing our life was about to change and knowing we were getting on a track that lasted a whole twelve years — a lot longer than we had been alive. All of a sudden, a boy at the back of one of the lines, someone's older brother, took a chance and waved us over.

He cupped his hands and whispered, "You'd best line up over there at the top of the line before you invoke the wrath of the Bulldog." He pointed to the top of the schoolyard.

We found out who "The Bulldog" was when the principal, with her fiery red complexion, pug nose and eyes fiercely set on us came through that oversized door. Her chin jutted out from her face in a way that welcomed a punch, and her stiff upper lip looked like it had never given forth the word "Uncle." The Great Protector of our school, she marched us first graders to our classroom directly from the schoolyard. As we entered Sister Susan's classroom, she said to the first grade nun, "Here's a new batch."

After "The Bulldog" departed, Sister Susan allowed us our alphabetical seating assignments only long enough to repeat the Our Father and the Pledge of Allegiance. Then, taking a deep breath like something momentous was to occur, she invited us to stand, to take up our first responsibility and first act of service to our school and our Lord: to lead the entire student body into church. When the bell rang she told us to put the palms of our hands together, locating them about chest level like my dad taught me when we prayed to God at night. "Walk like this," she said. "Follow me."

We marched silently behind her out of our classroom, into the hallway, down the stairwell, out to the schoolyard once again into the bright sunshine and onto the walkway that led down to County Street. As we walked in the schoolyard, I looked over to where we had stood. Minutes before, we were lost, directionless, uprooted and alone. Now we led the entire Grammar School, High School, altar boys, Auxiliary Bishop, priests, and nuns into church for Mass. How had it happened? I felt the power of the line — its history and responsibility. I felt we trudged a beaten, ancient path that brought us close to God as we fulfilled His mission and were ushered by the nuns from the profane into the sacred. For the first time, I felt like a classmate and a schoolmate. Twenty minutes ago we were not even in school, had no identity and lacked both power and direction. Now, we were responsible for the entire church complex.

Auxiliary Bishop Gerard, who was our pastor, concelebrated the mass with three other priests. Standing with them was every altar boy from school. In full command of the center aisle, the priests carried with them burning incense, candles and of course, the Cross of Christ. The organ lady sang, filling all the empty spaces with her music as the priests turned their backs to us and faced the mystery of the tabernacle.

The nuns started beaming at the priests from the time they eyed them outside church. By the time the priests were in church the nuns were positively beside themselves, gazing in adoration at spiritual giants. By contrast, the nuns scowled at us. It was amazing the depth of their scowl and the contrast of their mood. We had already been tried and convicted and they were having a hard time holding in their contempt. It communicated a clear, unspoken message: At this place you don't complain, or talk about your hurts, or venture to figure things out on your own. The Sisters of Mercy carried the mantle of justice. They were ready for a long year and would take on any comers.

○

Kids at Holy Family, though, were not about to roll over for the nuns even with their huge power differential. Everything in our makeup indicated we couldn't. For starters, New Bedford was too tough a town. Add to that the fact we had Irish blood and knew the Irish saying our dads and uncles knew: Is this a private fight or can anyone join in? So, our instincts, heritage, and skills said fight.

Our response to the nuns' discipline was to be measured, tactical, and muted, but if a lot of boys tested the limit of the nuns' power, challenged them, and stayed unified we could establish a beachhead. And then we might expand those beachheads incrementally.

But challenging the nuns was always hard—they held so many trump cards. Not just the backing that comes directly from the infallibility of Rome, but our families' firm support.

If a nun whacked you at school and word reached home, then you got whacked at home. No questions asked. The message was pretty clear: nuns aren't wrong and parents are on their side even if they are wrong. So, the nuns exploited it and loved calling a kid's bluff and watching him back down.

Wayward kids received lots of punishment. Extra homework or its threat might change a kid's attitude. If things got real bad the nuns called for the dreaded parent's conference. Here they knocked your parents around. These meetings were full of drama. Successful parents had to show just the right blend of contrition and piety, otherwise more trouble brewed. If none of it worked, like Lucifer, you were banished; the school remained cleansed and the nuns' power intact.

Nevertheless, we put up active resistance. There was a belief around the schoolyard that the nuns clamored for a final victory. They wanted us broken. If they turned us into goody-two-shoes, choir boys, altar boys, or momma's boys that was an ultimate victory. The thinking in the schoolyard went like this: If they made us obedient maybe we might hear The Call and if we heard The Call maybe we might enter the seminary. It was said the nuns had informal, secret competitions within the Diocese between the Parishes for bragging rights on who sent the most boys and girls into the seminary and convent.

The farthest reaching example of our rebellion toward the

nuns came from the type of boy the nuns referred to as the Rough-necks. They earned the name from Sister Augustine, who in 4th grade roamed the hallways seizing misbehaving boys' ears and hauling them round to demand, "Just what do you think you are doing? Are you thinking of becoming a Roughneck? Well, you had better think twice about it, Buster."

For the most part these boys were not just rebels they were outlaws—cultural heroes at Holy Family who had all our hearts with them. If the nuns had given way we'd all have joined them in a second. So their rebellion against the nuns, and the nuns' continual reimposition of order, gave our school its imprint, set the tone and attitude for the whole experience.

The nuns and the Roughnecks played a game of brinkmanship for the hearts and minds of the student body. At school the tension was constant. A question hung in the air: Which way were you leaning? Toward the Roughnecks or toward the nuns?

All the kids at Holy Family knew who the Roughnecks were. In my class, they were Mike Rossi, John Conlan, Mike Driscoll, and Paul Koczera. Every kid with a brain at Holy Family appreciated what the Roughnecks accomplished.

I liked the Roughnecks, but some were rougher than others. Teddy Hughes and Paul Sullivan occupied the fraternity's outer edge. They were a few years ahead of me. But they were angry—violent. Hughes and Sullivan indiscriminately soaped cars, flattened tires, pelted eggs at homes, and put sand in gas tanks. They tortured cats probing the theory that they always landed on their feet. They poured gasoline on frogs before striking a match.

Once, while we were walking home from school, we spied Hughes and Sullivan on Mrs. Petersen's porch. Everyone liked the widow Mrs. Petersen. Her house was one of the premiere stops on Halloween Night on account of she gave out this great Norwegian candy that we never saw anywhere else. Hughes saw us and yelled over.

"Hey, you guys. Watch this. We got dog shit in this bag."

We stopped.

Evidently, Hughes had put dog shit in a brown paper bag. We watched him drop the bag on the old widow's wooden porch in front of her door, and light it with a sure strike of wooden match. When the bag was up in flames, he rang her doorbell and they both hid behind some shrubs that offered a great view of the porch and the front door. They laughed like hell when the Old Lady Peterson came out and in her alarm and emotion started stomping on the bag until its contents were all over her! Hughes and Sullivan were delighted. They looked like their whole life was coming together. They felt giddy, young and revitalized. Finally, they must have thought, life gained meaning.

They probably loved most the indignity that overcame Mrs. Petersen. Her sunny disposition tampered out. It was replaced by the confusion, the insecurity and the fear Hughes and Sullivan felt and knew so well. Maybe spreading it around, they didn't feel so alone, so isolated, so alienated.

And yet the nuns ultimately had ways of handling even this sort of pain and violence, even with this sort of kid from broken families that couldn't or wouldn't back them up: they kept them on a shorter leash and had a double standard that they had no problem invoking. They might stroll down the aisle toward the kids with the inside knowledge of his "home situation." They might talk about the danger of drink, getting hit for no good reason, or going to bed hungry. Or they might call on a Roughneck in class when they were introducing a new concept knowing full well the kid didn't have the right answer. And by embarrassing them publicly they knocked them down a bit.

But, in the last analysis, our dissent was limited by practical matters. If we got thrown out, where would we go? Over to Cook

School, to be constantly vilified and harassed by the Protestant School kids, and then mocked by Holy Family every morning we skulked by? We were in what my grandmother called a pickle. Boxed in, we were all basically a lock to go the distance.

◌

And yet. Our parish was not the whole of New Bedford. The nuns' stranglehold diminished a couple of blocks from school grounds. It didn't matter if I walked east to the waterfront or south or north toward the mills, or west toward Buttonwood Park, the influence of Saint Lawrence Church and Holy Family waned. Astonishingly, those ancient, mighty forces of the parish diminished.

Even right outside the church and school complex you felt it happening. You emerged from the church and breathed a different air, scented with candy and dust from the corner variety stores. Halfway across the street and you broke free of the nuns' power; you felt like sprinting away from it. But you were still in the parish, with the church nestled into it like a piece of a puzzle that had long ago been snapped into its place. Rows of tenements stretched entire blocks and made them feel narrower than they actually were, occupied by longstanding communicants who never moved—or moved, in the case of married daughters, only as far as the next floor.

But it was when you took Mill and Hillman Streets down the hill through town and to the waterfront boundary where New Bedford faced the open sea, that you felt the dense webs that connected the church with its surrounding parish give way entirely. The wind blowing from the harbor brought the smells of low tide, of life, of adventure even as far as the church itself. And the closer you got to it, the more it overwhelmed and upended the forces of the parish, swallowed them whole like the whales Herman Melville wrote of, when he was a sailor out of this same harbor, on the bark Acushnet.

In Melville's day, of course, the waterfront was different. New Bedford was one of the richest ports in the world, renowned as a magnet for all sorts of dreamers and drifters, merchants and malcontents. For a long time now, though, with the decline of first whaling and then the mills, a general feeling of collapse had taken hold, spread to houses, rules, economies, yards, and the social order. Warehouses stood abandoned. Discarded shopping carts, broken bottles, and old refrigerators were strewn around. Anything metal rusted. Danger, lawlessness, the sea—instead of adventure, there was a sense of despair, brokenness, and chaos. When fights broke out at The National Club, the Pequot or Haskell's, the police brought backup.

It was forever low tide for the forces of the parish down here. The men and women who earned their living by the sea didn't care what the nuns thought or what line the parish was trying to get the parishioners to walk. That kind of control didn't begin to make sense against the restlessness of the sea, the risks they took. The waterfront was a place not of faith, but superstition. Fishermen braved weather, currents, the price of fish at auction, and migration patterns they could barely ascertain. They faced the chance— higher than in any profession—that their 14 days out, 4 days in would become a permanent watery grave. It haunted them, and they responded by never setting sail on a Friday or December 31st. They didn't bring bananas or a black bag on board. They would not rename a boat, ever, or have a woman come aboard. Lots of fishermen hardly set foot outside this area. No other part of the city understood them, their rhythms were so different from the eight-hour shift workers'.

Their families were New Bedford families, though of an entirely different sort than the parish families I knew. Right before the start of a trip you'd see the weathered crew members milling around the dock smoking cigarettes, drinking coffee from Styrofoam cups, and shuffling back and forth. Nobody talked. They hardly acknowledged each other. They waited for the captain to signal completion of the inspection of the boat and yell "all aboard." Their girlfriends and wives were there, too, saying just as little, standing facing the boat and taking long, hard, frightened looks at their husbands and boyfriends. At the very best, it was two weeks of loneliness, silent prayer, worry and responsibility for broken furnaces, sick mothers, lost dogs and kids.

The sons of such families were different, too. Their demeanors mimicked their dads'. Their body language communicated to outsiders to leave them alone. They, like their dads, underdressed for the weather as if to prove they were impervious to the forces shaping them. They ordered cheeseburgers at BPM's lunch counter the way their dads did— a sense of disdain and a measure of discomfort about the whole transaction. They had a short fuse, easily lit, as if an inner fire was the only answer to what water might eventually do to them.

I remember one kid from down below County Street in particular. Eddie was a fisherman's kid and a Cook School student. Even for a Cook School kid, Eddie was different. He dressed in work pants like the men on the waterfront and wore flannel shirts. He sported a scar plainly visible under his left eye and had strong shoulders that supported a strong, thick neck. His long forehead and deepset eyes gave him a look of resolution. Eddie clearly thought he had figured out a few of life's basic premises.

Yet, he also looked like he yearned for the world to understand him, when he knew it never would. He was without a shepherd. His whole demeanor was different than mine. He walked jauntily, testily with a beezer—a botched homemade crew cut. His face was mean and hardened by life. It contrasted with the faces at Holy Family. Our faces seemed fresh, waiting and wanting to receive instructions from the nuns on how to feel about the world and how best to navigate through it. Eddie did his own navigation.

Each morning we saw groups of Protestant School kids headed to Cook School. They wore no blazers or ties. They had on their play clothes, even for school! Evidence they didn't take school seriously and were not enlightened. Even at this young age I could not help but see them as diminished characters.

Among this group, Eddie was easy to spot. He had an unlit Lucky Strike in his mouth and the collar of his shirt was turned up. He wore no coat, had on his customary work pants and a flannel shirt. And instead of just walking by, Eddie did the most preposterous, defiant and almost sacrilegious act thinkable. He came up to our schoolyard on County Street and walked right past the fence and inside Holy Family.

None of the Roughnecks tried to stop him. Not John Conlan, Brian Hogan, or the MacMullen brothers (there were five of them), not the Farlands or the O'Neils or even the nuns tried to stop him. He kept on cutting diagonally through and it seemed like our schoolyard just opened for him like the Red Sea. I could not believe the invasion of our sacred space and, to use a nun's phrase, his boldness.

As he came farther onto school property, I noticed he carried with him a fishing rod instead of books. Eddie never had a book! And at the end of the pole he had not a fish, but a dead rat. It was a City Pier rat with black, oily, darkened fur. It was a wharf rat that had lost its grey color and turned black from being on the pier so long. It looked like a mutant type of rat. Its dead eyes gave it a wild and bewildered look.

Eddie was not a fisher of men or a fisher of fish. He was a fisher of rats. He measured the reaction alone. It was like he stood outside of us and our world yet was a real part of it. A shaker and mover. Sr. Camilla, the nun unlucky enough to have the schoolyard monitoring assignment, murmured under her breath, "Bold as brass."

All schoolyard activities halted. Everything went still. Hushed. I don't even remember any cars motoring by on County or Mill Street. The only movement came from Eddie. We all watched him and the rat. They both seemed to know how tough life could be. I secretly admired him, but I knew then that I did not envy his fate. I bet Eddie's not alive today.

Still I envied Eddie's complete defiance of and contempt for our city block as he trespassed against us. Sr. Camilla's face was flushed and full of expression. The whole schoolyard read her thoughts, as she stood powerless against this onslaught to the One True Way. It was as if the Devil was let loose in our schoolyard. Sr. Camilla's posture was erect. She stood with military readiness. I never saw her posture like that again. Her eyes never left him. She tried, it seemed, to escort him out of the schoolyard by pure will.

Eddie continued on over to the girls' side. As he approached the imaginary line that separated the boys and girls, breaking taboo upon taboo, all the boys became even more frozen, powerless and diminished. The entire atmosphere changed. Now that we were out of immediate danger we saw the situation in its entirety. We all knew if Eddie hit a girl or kicked her it permanently diminished us and our place. We'd have to have a compensatory act of retribution. It would be like Archduke Ferdinand being assassinated in our schoolyard. An irrecoverable chain of events would be set off that might forever change the entire composition of this city block. Our standing in the eyes of the girls and the nuns was now in jeopardy. Eddie stood to alter the whole sociological and cosmological order of our block: the nuns' authority, the boys' machismo and the girls' sense of chivalry, all of which constructed the world as we knew it. Every kid in the schoolyard that day felt and knew what was up for grabs. We waited as Eddie held our fates in his hands. The boys were willing him to go as fervently as Sister

Camilla had done.

Eddie walked slowly, deliberately, in a diagonal line toward Mill Street. At one point, he brought the pole down in front of him, shook it, and the rat mimicked being alive. The girls cowered at the prospect that what they thought was dead had come back to life. They braced themselves. The boys held their breath. Then Eddie smiled a smile that only he understood, and shrugged his shoulders, as he got to the end of the schoolyard. Out on Mill Street he slung his pole back over his shoulders the way Huck Finn might. As he headed toward Cook School he didn't look back. He just kept walking, his head held high.

Whenever I spotted him in the mornings after this, I watched him spellbound as he passed by. That day school and the schoolyard felt differently right up to the final closing bell.

Goodbye Climate Change, Goodbye Global Poverty?

by Paul Adler

In September 1969, Nixon administration councilor Daniel Patrick Moynihan wrote a prescient memorandum about the rising carbon dioxide levels in the Earth's atmosphere. Although noting the need for more scientific research to understand this trend, Moynihan felt confident declaring that it "very clearly is a problem." He warned of a possible "apocalyptic" future if global warming caused sea levels to rise, declaring it would mean, "Goodbye New York. Goodbye Washington."

A few years later, Moynihan (now U.S. ambassador to the United Nations) again raised the alarm about an international crisis. In this case, Moynihan's concerns focused on the challenge to U.S. hegemony posed by a coalition of Global South countries demanding the creation of a New International Economic Order (NIEO). Moynihan opposed the NIEO agenda, believing its implementation would weaken U.S. power while also proving economically ruinous to rich and poor nations alike. He thus urged the U.S. to oppose the "emergence of a world order dominated...by the countries of the Third World."

More than forty years later, Moynihan's calls to action on climate change and global development are still salient. Yet, where he saw only danger, humanity must find opportunity. For the world to effectively confront the climate crisis *and* end global poverty will require a new world politics — one that treats the climate crisis with the utmost seriousness, while drawing on the spirit of the NIEO to ensure justice for the vast majority of the world's population.

Seeing climate change and development as inseparable is not a new idea. Where once "sustainable development" was the watchword among policymakers and advocates, today "adaptation" is increasingly the rallying cry. In practice, adaptation means implementing policies that deal with climate change as a problem of the present. Already in communities around the world, local groups, international NGOs, and some aid agencies are designing development projects that can survive intensified droughts and storms. Yet, it seems unlikely that local or even national adaptation efforts can be sufficient to meet climate change's challenge without a parallel international politics.

A political agenda for dealing humanely with climate change will have to come from the Global South. Northern countries will, to varying degrees, provide aid and support for adaptation, as they are legally obligated to do under the U.N. Framework Convention on Climate Change. However, as the histories of so many past crises (such as the Great Depression) suggest, absent political pressure from below, it is unlikely even sympathetic policymakers will do what needs to be done.

The need for the world's poor to exert political power is magnified by the frightening trends occurring in the politics of several key Global North countries. Ironically, as the realities of climate change have become more apparent, denial of the problem has also increased. Twenty years ago in the United States, Canada or Australia, the existence of anthropogenic climate change was not controversial. Rather, arguments about climate change focused on disputes over what policies could best ameliorate it. Recently, the terms of the debate have regressed. Now, in several of the most powerful nations, we are reduced to debating elementary science and facing political forces dead set against any action.

Given this context, the idea of a Global South alliance to tackle climate change might seem fantastical. Yet, precedent exists for African, Asian, and Latin American states campaigning to reshape the global political economy. That precedent is the same New International Economic Order that Moynihan warned of. Launched in May 1974 as a resolution in the United Nations General Assembly, the NIEO was a policy and political program intended as a roadmap for reforming the world economy in the interests of the Global South. The NIEO called for the establishment of institutional mechanisms to stabilize global commodity prices, increase foreign aid, and regulate the activities of multinational corporations — proposals that were substantial, but neither new nor revolutionary.

For a brief time, the campaign for the New International Economic Order inspired real concern among elites in the wealthy countries. The strong scrambled to contain the Global South's newfound assertiveness at a time when the rich felt economically vulnerable and the poor seemed able to wield real political power. It was, after all, no coincidence that the NIEO declaration arrived only months after the OPEC-initiated 1973 oil shock.

OPEC backed the NIEO rhetorically, and some of its members (such as Algeria) were key players in the pro-NIEO coalition. Inspired by OPEC, some Southern nations attempted to build similar cartels for other export commodities. Explaining the politics behind such efforts, Tanzanian president Julius Nyerere analogized the global economy to a factory: the rich nations were the management, the poor countries were the workers, and commodity cartels would be the "trade unions of the poor" that guaranteed the South fair treatment.

Southern exertions produced tangible results. The United

Nations created a Centre on Transnational Corporations, which conducted important research on multinational firms and development. In 1976, the European Community signed the Lomé Convention, an agreement that provided a bevy of trade preferences to many former colonies. However, the dream of a reformed global economy was not to be.

The governments of the U.S., U.K., and West Germany rallied against the NIEO, seeking in Henry Kissinger's words to "pull [the] teeth and divide these [Global South] countries up." By 1976, rich nations had succeeded in accentuating divides within OPEC, breaking key nations away from the pro-NIEO coalition. This shift robbed the NIEO coalition of its main political leverage. Meanwhile, the wealthy nations offered only minor concessions in negotiations with the South, while blocking and undermining efforts at deeper change.

Northern resistance and divide-and-conquer tactics were not the only reasons for the NIEO's demise. The pro-NIEO coalition's political incoherence and the economic diversity of its members also contributed to splits forming in their ranks. Most critically, attempts to build commodity cartels failed. The culprit was the free rider problem: it only took one or two members of a cartel deciding to undercut the others to wreck the entire project. The NIEO campaign's death knell struck with the explosion of the debt crisis in the early 1980s. The debt crisis not only forced Southern countries to become supplicants to the North, it also empowered those political forces in the South most favorable to free market reform.

Given this history, the idea of the world's poor crafting a New International Climate Order appears a dubious proposition. Yet, in the era of climate change, expanding the boundaries of the possible is a necessity. Formulating an agenda will be the easy part. Since the early 1990s, a raft of ideas has emerged for addressing poverty and climate change, such as sharing clean energy technologies developed in the North with the South. Many of these ideas fit under an ideological vision of "Climate Debt," which argues that Northern nations owe reparations to the South for the damages that the rich are, after all, predominately responsible for.

As with the NIEO however, such ideas will not go far without Southern political power. Here too there are signs of progress. In 2009, the Climate Vulnerable Forum was created, bringing together many of the nations most affected by climate change to have a collective voice in global negotiations. In 2012, a group of Global South countries (including India and China), formed the Like Minded Developing Countries, a negotiating bloc united by a shared rejection of Northern efforts to shift the burden of climate action onto the poorer countries.

The Like Minded Developing Countries has already solidified itself as an important player in negotiations. This is due to one of the most significant differences between the politics of the Global South today as opposed to the 1970s. Whereas in the 1970s, Global South nations' main contribution to the world economy came through exporting agricultural goods and raw materials, today nations like Brazil or India are economic powerhouses in ways that the rich cannot ignore.

Another feature that augurs hope for today is the richness of Southern civil society. Groups representing indigenous peoples, women, and organized labor are more numerous and powerful than they were in the 1970s. Many Global South movements are engaged with climate change, working with both their governments and Global North NGOs to push for a pro-poor agenda. In November 2013, the tacit alliances between NGOs and governments exerted themselves in dramatic fashion at U.N. negotiations in Warsaw. Frustrated by multinational corporate influence and Northern reticence, a large coalition of Southern governments staged a temporary walkout. This action was reinforced by a walkout by Southern and Northern NGOs, expressing their profound frustration with the proceedings.

Despite the contradictions and hypocrisies easily found in all of these forces, an alliance of imperfect Southern and Northern players is the best hope humanity has. In the Global North, pressure must be brought by civil society and social movements for policy changes that benefit Southern communities made vulnerable by Northern prosperity. Southern governments will need to find ways of exerting economic and diplomatic influence to pressure the North to listen and to change. And Southern social movements will need to work to ensure that their governments serve the interest of the many, not the elite few.

When Moynihan wrote his memorandum in 1969, the dangers of climate change appeared distant enough that his main suggestion involved the U.S. spearheading a "worldwide monitoring system" for carbon dioxide emissions. We are now long past the point where technocratic solutions can suffice. As Indian climate activist Deepa Gupta argues, the way forward lies in "helping people self-organize so that their collective power could also have a large influence." For only strategies that embrace an analysis of political power and which utilize a wide array of tactics have any chance of forging a world where equity and sustainability are synonymous.

In Praise of Nothing

by Eric LeMay

Lately, I enjoy watching nothing. Not nothing in the sense of nothing—not, that is, not watching—but watching nothing happen while I'm watching. In a word, webcams: those video cameras set up around the world that stream images live, in real time, to my laptop.

Through websites like earthcam.com, I watch lights flash and die along the Tokyo skyline or pedestrians stray down Hollywood Boulevard, lingering on the Walk of Fame. On my phone, I have an app that loads random cameras from around the world. I watch the haggard grass in South Africa's Addo Elephant National Park or the evening traffic in Moscow City. My favorite camera frames an altar in what must be a Catholic or Orthodox Church in Borsice, a village in the Czech Republic. The icon at the center of the altar stays lit all night, which for me is most of the day.

I particularly like watching this webcam because nothing ever happens—I've never seen anyone in the church—and it's that nothing I like. I don't, for example, want to watch an elephant in the Addo Elephant National Park. I want to watch the watering hole and the wind-touched grass and the minutes tick by in South African Standard Time with nothing happening but the wind I can't see and light that doesn't change and the slight hitch in the image that happens every thirty seconds that tells me the image is still live, still streaming nothing.

Often, I watch nothing in traffic or waiting for takeout or when other people are checking email or texting. I pretend I'm checking email or texting, but instead I watch nothing. And now, even when I'm watching something, a TV show or movie, I focus on the area of the image that has the most nothing: the out-of-focus parking lot behind the actors, at the far edge of the frame; the knick-knacks in the foreground on the desktop. When video-conferencing, I watch what's behind my interlocutor's head, which is usually nothing.

I'm not sure why I'm drawn to nothing. Perhaps I'm escaping our culture's overload of images through images. Perhaps I'm already so overloaded with images that I no longer need content, just the pure image, distilled to nothing. Perhaps I'm losing it. I do know I get tetchy if the webcam I'm watching shows more than nothing, or the wrong kind of nothing, or aspires in some artistic way to nothing: a nothing that, in showing nothing, attempts to mean more than nothing—a webcam pointed at a webcam, for example, or an intentionally empty room.

My ideal webcam, which I haven't found, would show people only indirectly, by them not being in, but still being signaled by, nothing. I imagine a crumpled beer can, discarded in a brick alley, where weeds have worked up between the bricks and gone raggedy, and every so often the shadow of a car or garbage truck sweeps by, and the can rusts gradually or gets coated with snow, so I can't read the label. I also imagine the corner of a gravel driveway, where the camera sits level with the stones, and the stones catch the hot noon sun.

Two decades ago, I read Joseph Heller's *Catch-22*, and what's stuck with me ever since is Heller's description of the bombardier Yossarian lying in bed, intentionally staring at the ceiling, watching nothing. Yossarian is trying to make himself as bored as possible, because when he's bored, time slows down, and the more time slows down, the more time he has until he has to fight again and so the more time he has to live. "He had decided to live forever," writes Heller, "or die in the attempt." He lives through nothing.

Watching nothing, I don't get bored, but I do, I think, make time. Maybe even see it, and I want to see as much time as I can for as long as I can, even if what I see is nothing.

Living with Pain

*The Desert Fathers and Mothers,
the Hindu Festival of Thaipusam,
and the New York City Marathon*

by Greta Austin

*I*n Singapore my husband and I took our children to Thaipusam, a Tamil religious festival. Hindu penitents carry milk jugs, impale themselves with fishhooks, and walk two miles on nail shoes. Our expatriate friends in Singapore thought we were crazy. "You are taking your children to Thaipusam?" said a friend. He shook his head. He had never gone, but he had heard about it. The traffic was snarled! People drove metal spears through both sides of their cheeks! Expats and Singaporeans alike seemed surprised that Thaipusam went on in Singapore, Singapore with its sleek highrises where the expatriate Westerners swam in blue swimming pools and Filipino nannies handed the children thick expensive towels. Thaipusam and its "primitive" mortification had nothing to do with modern Singapore.

I was not sure about taking our daughters to Thaipusam. They were six and four. We were living in Singapore for six months while my husband taught at the National University of Singapore. Because we both study religion, and because Clark teaches regularly in Asia, our girls have bowed before monks in Chiang

Mai and given them money. They have seen Koreans speaking in tongues in the largest church in the world. They spent six days going through the Hindu temples of Angkor Wat. But watching a spear being driven through someone's cheek? Thaipusam seemed like a ritual too far. Twenty years from now, they might be sitting in leather chairs in psychologists' offices saying, I didn't drive a metal stake through my cheeks but I am scarred!

I told my husband, "We can take the girls to Thaipusam as long as we don't watch spears being driven through people's cheeks."

And then we went to Thaipusam, and watched spears being driven through people's cheeks.

○

Pain and suffering play central roles in many religions. Buddhism, for instance, begins with the premise that suffering is the central human experience. Human attachment—"seeking delight here and there, that is, craving for sensual pleasures, craving for existence, craving for extermination" as a classic text puts it—causes suffering. We want to eat, we are hungry, we eat. Then the meal is done, the dishes are smudged, and we are hungry again in the morning. Buddhism calls attention to the transitory nature of desire and satiation: "the remainderless fading away and cessation of that same craving, the giving up and relinquishing of it, freedom from it, nonreliance on it." When we realize the illusory nature of all attachment, we will move towards a higher level of awareness. I enjoyed that Greek salad, but I have eaten it, and it is gone, and the moment is gone. And beyond that: as my friend Sondra Hausner, a scholar of Asian religions, writes me, "The thing you want is a moving target." Sometimes we want dinner, sometimes love, sometimes money—but they are all shadows cast on the wall, not even shadows of something real, but the shadows of our own hands grasping for something that doesn't exist.

Buddhism formulates the question of suffering differently

than Christianity. Still, suffering and pain play important roles in Christianity, as in many other religions. "The central symbol of Christianity is the figure of a tortured man," Stephen Moore writes in *God's Gym*. The son Jesus calls out to God his Father in the moment of agony, Why have you deserted me? He might as well have asked, Why did you let me die? God permits his own son to be killed. In a way, God kills his own son. Religions do not anesthetize pain. They put pain at the center of their worldviews. But why? Why did people have to drive stakes through their cheeks? Why might they impale themselves with fishhooks and walk two miles?

○

The Christian ascetics known as the Desert Fathers and Mothers, the first Christian renouncers who moved out into the edges of the Egyptian and Syrian deserts in the fourth and fifth centuries, mastered the arts of suffering. One hung a cucumber in front of his nose as he fasted. A handful of famous Syrian ascetics sat on top of pillars for years.

For the early Christian renouncers, the body represented the ties to the world of "passions," and of preoccupations with land, marriage, family, status. The Desert Fathers and Mothers loosened these ties between the body and society. By moving into the edges of the desert, and detaching themselves from the interweaving obligations of late antique society, and rejecting the ties that food and eating reinforced and represented, they made themselves "deliberately not human.... the 'stranger' *par excellence*," as the historian of Late Antiquity Peter Brown puts it in his beautiful study, "The Rise and Function of the Holy Man in Late Antiquity."

Some holy men and women associated the body with sin. "When the body is cherished, the soul is withered," one monk was reported to say. By drawing closer to God, they could distance themselves from the "passions" of the body. A famous Desert Father, Arsenius, admonished a brother to "try hard to make your inner progress as God would have it, and by this overcome the passions of the body." Conversely, people could discipline their own bodies to achieve greater spiritual awareness: "Fasting dries up the channels down which worldly pleasures flow," according to another Desert Father.

The desert ascetics' harsh renunciation made sense to me as a college student. For me, as for some others in my dormitory, the body was a problem, not an answer. One anorexic woman ate only spinach with chickpeas, without dressing. She diminished this to twelve chickpeas. Then she ate only four chickpeas for dinner. I tried and failed to emulate her painful discipline. She reminded me in some ways of the monk fasting and gazing at a cucumber, even though we lived in different worlds from the early Christian ascetics. The Desert Mothers and Fathers fasted in a world preoccupied by hunger and nested with demons. They fasted to find transcendence. We abstained, or tried to abstain, in a world privileged by overabundance and haunted by runway models with angelically thin bodies. In trying to fast, I wanted to get beyond the body, the body which seemed then so heavy, so grossly weighty, veinous, spackled and carnal. Transcendence looked then like getting outside of the body and self-consciousness, rather than encountering the divine through the body.

Fasting exists in many religions. During Ramadan, Muslims fast from sunrise until sundown. Jews fast on Yom Kippur. Medieval Christians observed fast days during which no meat could be eaten, as well as days of completely refraining from food. In preparation for Thaipusam, the Hindu participants eat only once a day for a month before the festival, and they eat only a vegetarian diet. They sleep on mats on the floor instead of beds. The night before Thaipusam, they do not eat at all, bathe themselves in ritual baths, and paint their bodies in sacred ash.

By fasting and sleeping on the floor, the Thaipusam participants become, for a month, like the Hindu ascetics known as sadhus. Like the Desert Fathers and Mothers, sadhus abandon society to pursue transcendence. Sadhus even, unlike the early Christian ascetics, usually move around, rather than living in one place. They loosen every tie, even that of a location. For Hindus attachment itself is the problem. And the body itself expresses samsara, human attachment and suffering. In one Hindu sacred text, the baby enters the universe with clarity and knowledge of truth. But immediately the "power of illusion" of physical objects clouds his knowledge:

> As soon as the living creature has lost his knowledge, he becomes a baby. After that he becomes a young boy, then an adolescent, and then an old man. And then he dies and then he is born again as a human. Thus he wanders on the wheel of rebirth like the bucket on the wheel of a well…

Physicality itself—being a baby, being a human—stands between the human and transformation. And so for sadhus the body itself is a problem. As one sadhu said, "There is no love for a yogi's body. We live in the jungle." The jungle is everywhere, even in the city.

On the subway to Thaipusam, the train filled with Tamils in their best saris and pure white shirts. A Tamil girl adjusted her orange sari, an orchid in her hair. All her sisters and aunts and mother in saris lined with silver and gold threads glittered in a row behind her against the gray wall. Of the three ethnic groups in Singapore, the Chinese, Malay, and Tamil, the Tamils are the smallest group, less than one-tenth of the population. Tamils make up the lowest class in Singapore. They clean the public bathrooms and work in the ports.

We emerged out of the subway to see, in the hot bright afternoon, a nearly naked man encased in a huge birdcage with red and blue feathers. He danced in a circle of supporters. Police stood along the street with low houses and shops, and along the road blocked off by barricades. People were selling garlands of flowers from carts. The birdcage was one form of *"kavadi,"* or burden. Another woman walked past us carrying a silver container of milk on her head. Another man pulled a heavy wheeled structure which attached itself to his skin with fishhooks or with metal spears. He had a spear driven through his cheek.

At the entrance to the temple, volunteers passed out free sandwiches and cups of juice. We shook our heads, nervous about intruding. The cheerful woman said, "It's for everyone! Not just in Thaipusam! Take a sandwich! Come in and see!" The temple was an open courtyard with a roof. Other participants were getting ready in the shade of the temple. Right in front of me, an older man was inserting fishhooks into the back of a serene man, with his friends watching and commenting enthusiastically. Everyone took pictures, like prom night. Another man impaled with hundreds of fishhooks joked with a friend as he waited in line to start the walk. The man with the birdcage attached to his skin with fishhooks looked happier than most Americans in their cars on their Tuesday evening commute.

"I want to see someone get a spear through their cheeks!" said Cecilia, whom nothing bothers.

I looked inquiringly at Chiara, who is more squeamish. She said, "Come on! Thaipusam is great!"

A young, muscled man was sitting in a folding chair. His friend and family circled him. Someone pounded a drum faster. People clapped harder and harder. An older man, spear in one hand, leaned over the young man. The spear was larger than I had imagined. The spear easily passed through his cheek. He winced. The girls watched with a practical interest. "He's not bleeding!" Chiara whispered. "That was great!" Cecilia whispered back.

No one bled at Thaipusam. Some say the holy ash stops the bleeding; others say that participants go into a trance and this prevents them from feeling pain or bleeding. Participants talk about trance as "floating," as "lifted in the air, carried on the wind."

Later someone told me about how his friend had decided to carry a kavadi in Thaipusam but did not believe in it. When the spear was driven through his cheek, he bled effusively, so much that they almost took him to the emergency room.

Why would people inflict this suffering upon themselves? Why would a religion ask this of its adherents? Sometimes, I read, people described Thaipusam as "penitential." But this is not entirely accurate. The kavadi-bearers have made vows to Lord Murugan to avert a catastrophe or to ask for divine intervention. Most participants describe gratitude and thanks as motivating them. One participant made a vow to carry kavadi if his father recovered from cancer. Another carried kavadi as thanks for good results on his university exams. At first glance, Thaipusam looks like a mercenary exchange: physical pain in exchange for earthly rewards dispensed by a divine bank in the sky.

We watched the Thaipusam procession, like float after float going by, and the girls started to step on each other's feet and complain. So we ate dinner. Having small children taught me to see humans very differently. If they were crabby, I asked myself: Are they hungry? Are they thirsty? Are they tired? I started to see my own moods differently, too. A bad mood usually meant I had skipped lunch that day. For us, as for the Hindu sadhus, as for the Christian monks in the desert, the body had its own raw existence of hunger, pain, and pleasure.

A Desert Father named John went into the extreme desert to become an angel. The Desert Fathers and Mothers did not live in the sand dunes of the Egyptian desert near Siwa. Rather, they settled on the arid edges of settled land, as the desert shaded off into brown away from the green Nile delta. John returned after a week. When he knocked on his brother's door, his brother asked who was at the door. "John," he said.

"John," said the brother reproachfully, "is an angel and is no longer among men."

The anorexics became angels. Or they decided to live among us and learned to eat again. It is no longer possible to become an angel. It is no longer possible to eat four chickpeas. We have to eat. The body insists. One aged Desert Father advised another about fasting, "Every day one should deny oneself a little in eating, so as not to be satisfied." (A friend's uncle told him the same thing: "Always get up from the table a little hungry.") The other Desert Father said, "But when you were a young man, didn't you fast two days and more?" And the old man said, "Two days, believe me, and three, and a week… but the old men found that it is good to eat a little every day, and on certain days a little less: and they have shown us this master road, for it is easy and light." Like the Buddha, many Desert Mothers and Fathers taught moderation, not the extremism of angels and cucumbers.

And most Hindu sadhus learn to live with and within their bodies. The body is simultaneously "the most personal symbol of the deluded world of form," but also "a precious vehicle of religious practice and a tool of perception," as Sondra L. Hausner writes in *Wandering with Sadhus*. Even as the body reminds humans of samsara, of suffering, the body simultaneously expresses the divine spirit of Brahman:

In him are woven the sky and the earth and all the regions of the air, and in him rest the mind and all the powers of life. Know him as the ONE and leave aside all other words... Where all the subtle channels of the body meet, like spokes in the center of a wheel, there he moves in the heart and transforms his one form unto many.

For sadhus the body symbolizes and expresses the sacred cosmos: "The individual thinks the individual body is his body; the knower of Brahman knows the whole universe is his body. Others see his body as his body, but from his point of view his body is the whole universe." In Hinduism the body encapsulates an unchanging core essence, one particle of a larger divine force, ātman. As one Hindu renouncer said, "In this body there is ātman. And ātman is holiness." In the very demands of the body, its hunger and thirst, sadhus realize the illusory nature of the world. As one sadhu said, "The wealth of the yogi is his body. There is nothing more precious than this."

So we ate dinner in a crowded restaurant. We ate swirled fried cones with spicy curry and mild curry. Chiara tested the spicy curry. Cecilia— fearless about viewing human internal organs up close in a laboratory, but cautious about tasting spicy food— declined. The girls ate because they were hungry. They stopped when they were full. The parenting books I read claimed that children up until about age five eat when they are hungry and stop when they are full. After about age five, children start to eat for other reasons. The French philosopher Georges Bataille wrote of how early humans lived without understanding themselves as distinct from others. They lived immanently, like "water in water." The girls lived almost like this. They lived immersed in their bodies. They did not see their bodies as either problems or answers. But almost certainly they would lose this sense of themselves.

Night in the tropics drops itself down without warning. We got into a taxi to go home and put the girls to bed. But the girls objected indignantly.

"*What?* We can't go home to bed. We need to go see the end. We need to see them finish at the other temple."

So we went to the other end of the procession. The crowds were crushing and ebullient. More temple volunteers were passing out energy drinks. The kavadi-bearers were struggling along behind the police barricades. The kavadi-bearers looked like marathoners at mile 18 or mile 20, the worst part of the run. Some kavadi-bearers had taken five hours to struggle the two miles from one temple to another. Many looked in pain. As one participant wrote on a blog:

> During Thaipusam while piercing the spikes you will surely feel the pain. No one can deny that, but what one has to do is pray to God to ask for encouragement and strength to overcome all pain. I feel that one has to go through a range of pain and suffering for the sins one has committed knowingly and unknowingly. Taking part in the rituals does physically hurt me, but at the end of these rites I feel as if I had won the battle or accomplished something great.

Just as bravery is doing something when you are afraid, so Thaipusam "works" precisely because it hurts. This pain, for some, transforms them. As one participant concluded: "Thaipusam, in the final analysis, is the alchemy of transformation: becoming a better individual and member of society."

We humans live with pain. Pain is part of the unshakable facts of being human and animal, part of the contract you never sign when you are born. My daughters may not put fishhooks in their backs, but they will go to junior high. Friends will stop talking to them. It will cause them pain. In the dark summer backyard in Connecticut, an animal screams in pain as another eats it. We hear the screams and we cannot help.

But no one at Thaipusam carried their kavadi alone. Everyone we saw had a group of friends and family walking with them. One man pulling a huge cart looked on the verge of collapse. Cecilia pulled on my arm and whispered, "I'm worried about him." His supporters saw it too, and they started clapping and cheering. The man straightened and pulled harder.

Then I realized where I had seen Thaipusam before, or something very like it. People handed out Gatorade and free food. Groups of families and friends cheered on the participants. The participants struggled, in pain, down a paved street that had been roped off on both sides. The police milled about sociably. People cheered. Thaipusam was the New York marathon, with fishhooks and nail shoes.

⬡

People traveled across the desert to ask advice from the most famous renouncers of late antiquity. One aspiring ascetic asked, "'Abba, as far as I can, I say my little office, I fast a little, I pray and I meditate; I live in peace and as far as I can I purify my thoughts. What else can I do?'"

Then—the saying goes—"the old man stood up and stretched his hands towards heaven; his fingers became like ten lamps of fire and he said to him, 'If you will, you can become all flame.'"

For the Desert Mothers and Fathers, the body could be perceived in two ways, as the scholar Patricia Cox Miller argues. As seen against the horizon of immediate objects, the body signified the impermanent, the temporal, which a person might dangerously "cherish" more than the soul. The body fell short of the perfect bodies of humans in the Garden, the divine bodies. "The body was perceived to be problematic, not because it was a body, but because it was not a body of plenitude," writes Cox Miller.

In the second frame, however, the body was located against the flat gold of eternity. And then the body could be "dazzling." The body was not a vehicle or a burden. "A brother went to the cell of Arsenius in Scetis, and looked in through the window, and saw him like fire from head to foot." The body shone "like fire." It was still a body "from head to foot." But it stood against the landscape of eternity, a body which "cast off the perishable to put on the imperishable."

Near the steps to the final temple, the crowd pressed happily against each other. We put the girls on our shoulders. The kavadi-bearers put on giant nail flip-flops to climb the steps to the temple. The nails were pointing outwards. We tried to excuse ourselves from entering the temple but people insisted. "Go in! Go in!" they mouthed over the noise. We had no choice. The crowd forced us into the temple.

The kavadi-bearers danced inside the hot temple. The huge birdcages whirled around their bodies. The body no longer burdened them. *Where all the subtle channels of the body meet, like spokes in the center of a wheel, there he moves in the heart and transforms his one form unto many.* The body was a permeable membrane which divinity washed into and moved out of in waves. Those who worked on the docks and delivered groceries: here at Thaipusam, with flower garlands around their necks, they were the nimbus of the sun. This our bodies can do, radiant against a bright horizon. They dazzled, like the marathoners, after they cross the finish line, stand draped in their silvery heat blankets. Each person took the milk from their kavadis and poured it over the statue of the spear.

An ultra-marathoner fumbled to explain why she runs 100-

mile races to a friend of mine, and then said, "It's great doing something that goes beyond." The going beyond is to a body of plenitude.

○

At Thaipusam, as at the New York marathon, the participants prove to themselves their ability to endure physical suffering. The kavadi-bearers and the marathoners are like my friend Jenni, whose husband's cancer kept recurring. "How do you do it?" I asked her. And she said, "I just keep putting one foot in front of another." The kavadi-bearer keeps walking. The runner keeps putting one foot in front of the other.

By running marathons, and by carrying the kavadi in Thaipusam, the everyday person can make themselves extra-ordinary. As one amateur marathoner wrote on a blog, "We run because if we can make it through 26.2 miles, everything else will seem easy. A moment in time when an average person can... do something extraordinary."

Sadhus and the Desert Fathers and Mothers are the extreme marathoners of religion, the people who run one hundred mile races: atrophied limbs, hair shirts, sleeping outside in the winter without a blanket, sitting on pillars. But most sadhus and most Christian ascetics of late antiquity aimed not to become superheroes, but instead to live more moderate and continuous lives of denial. And modern observers might think that kavadi-bearers, or the monk gazing at a cucumber while fasting, engaged in "primitive mortification," practices which we American moderns have abandoned. But Americans have not abandoned these practices. We run marathons instead—religion poured into new vessels.

The body is a holy problem but also a holy solution. People impose bodily pain upon themselves in order to test the possibilities of their own bodies, and to 'go beyond' in the body itself. The Christian ascetics in the desert, the kavadi-bearers, and the marathoners lived completely as their bodies. The point was to experience the body. *Go in your cell*, taught one Desert Father, *and your cell will teach you everything.*

And the solution of the body is a communal solution, not the anorexic's lonely four chickpeas. The French sociologist Émile Durkheim, who was reportedly a dry and serious man, identified the central place of religious collective experience in religion. He called it "collective effervescence," when collective, group experience bubbles over into ecstasy. You can feel collective effervescence at a Pentecostal service, but you can also feel it in a huge football stadium, with the whole roar of the crowd, or at the finish line of the New York marathon.

Like a marathon, like a football game, religions give humans stories by which they can tell the stories of their lives to themselves, the painful and ecstatic experiences of embodiment. Thaipusam gives people a way to live with the pain and to transform it. They choose to impale their backs with fishhooks. They drive spears into their bodies as an act of gratitude. They walk surrounded by a circle of family and friends, along a street lined with cheering and clapping supporters. For a day, they place their bodies against the shimmering horizon of the permanent. Their bodies exude flame.

As at Thaipusam, as at the New York marathon, as in our very human lives, we carry the kavadi of our humanity and pain. We live in the jungle.

And we want our children to be able to carry their kavadi. Religions teach us how to carry our kavadi. No one carries the kavadi alone. And the bearing of the kavadi can itself be the holy solution—the 'going beyond,' the body in its full plenitude, profiled against the flat gold of eternity.

Chiara said, "Aren't you glad we went to Thaipusam? And aren't you glad we stayed?"

Poem in Film

by Jack Christian

This cocktail you sniffed cost 12 bucks
but did make you clairvoyant on your birthday.

We sure were sure, weren't we,
your new girl would fall for you
if you could cajole her into purchase
of that great in-town apartment
in the heart of Boys Town.

I'm sorry things fell apart
at the Christmas talk with her mother
and her mother's general weepiness
over an old, packaged wedding dress
and the long-dead dad who died beside a football.

I'd like to know at what opportunity
at what crossroads, at what fractal life crisis point,
at what soul-fracking, at what gleaning of soul sands,
at what intra-corpus irrigation, at what headtop removal,
at what hidden arterial explosion,
does one describe himself as a spelunker?

○

If I was wrong when
surprise, surprise
turned out they had my passport behind the counter the whole
time…

If something languished on visits made in gray, Champion sweat-
pants…

If purchasing the black pumpkin stout
on sale for the new holiday
was a sign of a larger internal misfire….

But all that is the plotting of a rust-belt sun-glint weep-eyed dream-
cast
sentimental reform video.

○

The guy at the Petco puppy class where my Patty excelled
said his was a Dixie Dog — Nikita — rescued from a Kentucky
ditch
outside a house-o-fire.

        If I did it in ignominy, if in subtle miscalculation of my own
health…well then.

The Sen. Brown ad was set in Springfield with only white people
in it.

Noons we spent trilling our R's at Amethyst Brook.
Evenings of the tv nudgings.

Evenings after that:

80 minutes college basketball,
one part 2%, 3 parts frozen yogurt,
plus a bowl
and spoon set
earned through our engagement.

I was 19
and all the nurse practitioner wanted
was to tell me about chlamydia.

I beg your pardon
I'm something of a chronicler.

What's good about it
is when it becomes obsessional,

when I can lay it down
in this great non-narrative movie I make

called *Life in In Between Gestures*.

I'm making it even now
with my pirated copy of Final Cut Pro, biorhythmic edition.

X-Ray

by Anne Bernays

It wasn't until Claire Sinkler had hung up her coat, checked in with the receptionist, sat down with only a slight twinge in her knees, and settled herself with a six-month-old copy of People magazine, that she noticed Dr. Steven Fein, her gynecologist, sitting across from her in the Wellbridge Mammography waiting room. He was staring so fixedly at nothing that he might have been mistaken for a wax image of himself. If he saw her, he couldn't — or wasn't willing to — acknowledge that he knew her, let alone that he had been peering between her legs for the last seven or eight years. When, after a couple of minutes he blinked and did see her, he grimaced and shifted uneasily in his chair. And if he was uneasy, then she should be uneasy too.

Claire thought of Dr. Fein not so much as fat but as pudgy, a description for young boys, and one she would have had a tough time defending. His neck, his wrists, and his waistline strained against his clothing. The skin on his face remained youthfully stretched, so that he seemed more like a college kid than a respected member of the Middlesex County medical society. His physical appearance, so unusual for a man in his profession, was one of the things Claire found reassuring about him. Her daughter, April, referred to him as a teddy bear. In Claire's experience with Dr. Steven Fein there was no funny business, no double *entendres*, no narcissistic tricks.

Had she been asked, Claire would have admitted that she would rather be anywhere in the world but here in this overheated room, which seemed to be growing hotter by the second. Its decorator had favored browns and grays and little else. The receptionist, a middle-aged woman wearing a tan cardigan, sat at a desk answering phone calls in an annoyingly nasal voice. "Wellbridge Mammography, this is Loretta speaking, how may I help you?"

Once a year, Claire had been told; but she had let more than two years go by without making this appointment. As if putting it off would decrease the likelihood of anything being the matter instead of the other way around. As a girl, Claire thought all old women smelled of camphor and were shrewd. Rather than accreting wisdom, Claire felt she was growing more superstitious and implausible by the day. At least that was what her son, Evan, had told her, tact not being one of his strongest suits. She had lived almost seventy years without major incident, with two children (Evan, now a man with a so-so job in Providence; and April, who worked in the New York City Mayor's administration), neither of whom had landed in jail or turned into any kind of addict. Both seemed to accept that she, Claire, had done her best with them, though of course they had had their adolescent complaints. Claire and her husband, Amos, shared the same too-large house, even the same bed, but aside from that, acted toward each other more like two people who work in the same office than like a long-married couple. She had adored him, adored him to the point of giving him anything and everything he wanted: her allegiance, her best gourmet cooking, and enough time by himself to accomplish even more than she thought he could. The allegiance remained but not much else.

Dr. Fein was looking at her now; she could feel his eyes on her as if they were fortified with lasers.

"Hello, Steven," she said, "What are you doing here?" It had taken Claire five years to get up the nerve to call him by his first name.

He said, "Oh, I was wondering who I would see here." He was not a happy camper.

What was a man doing in this female place? Dr. Fein failed to answer her question. She figured then that he was probably waiting for his wife. But when the technician stuck her head into the waiting room and called his name, it was clear that the doctor wasn't waiting for anything but to be a patient himself.

Steven Fein was—she couldn't read it any other way—reluctant to put one foot in front of the other. Claire had never seen him any way but briskly cheerful. She knew him as a teller of inoffensive jokes, a schmoozer. He kept his patients waiting but they didn't care because they found him such good company. He had asked her permission some time back to call her Claire.

She watched him leave the room, checked her phone, which she had switched to "off", then felt ice crystals of anxiety sprinkle around her torso, out to her limbs, her fingers and toes. There was no reason to be worried and she wouldn't have been, really, except that her mother had had breast cancer in her sixties—and then had gone on to live another twenty-three years, when she died after a stroke. These breast cancer people had whipped the women of America into a froth of anxiety that, Claire had to admit, did prolong some lives. But was it worth it? In her mother's day, so long ago, mammography resided in the sci-fi category and if and when you found a lump yourself, it was probably too late to do anything about it. There was something elemental, almost refreshing in the notion that the phrase "annual screening" lay far in the future and that you didn't have to go through the worry before and the worry after the event. Early death, then, was a lottery.

"Claire?" Claire didn't like being first-named but let it pass. "How are you today? I'm Chrissie, I'll be doing your exam." She led Claire down a hallway studded with closed doors and into the changing area, a curtained cubicle for disrobing, a locker for her handbag. "Remove your top and bra and put this gown on, open in front." She handed Claire a johnny with strings coming off it.

Inside the dim X-ray room Claire stood facing the sleek works, her nipples decorated with tiny metal tags to distinguish left from right, and, trying to sound cool, mentioned that she had seen a man in the waiting room.

"Oh yes," Chrissie said. "We get men sometimes. You know, like, for lumps on their chest. You have to check it out. Some of the guys who come here act like they're embarrassed. I don't know why."

"Yes," Claire said. Chrissie lifted Claire's left breast, handling it firmly but gently like a baker with a mound of raw dough and placed it on top of a shelf, then pressed a button which brought another, smaller, Lucite shelf down towards the first. When the top shelf was firmly in place — it was uncomfortable but didn't quite hurt — Chrissie turned a knob that continued the squeezing until a dart of pain reached Claire's brain.

"Fresh orange juice for breakfast," she said. She imagined a spurt of orange liquid arcing over the shelf, splashing on the floor.

"Did you say something?" Chrissie said. "I'm sorry, I didn't hear what you said."

"I said my breasts are oranges being squeezed for OJ."

"Oh my goodness," Chrissie said. She retreated behind a glass partition, told Claire to hold her breath, and turned on something that beeped faintly.

"Now the other one," Chrissie said. She was very good at her job. Claire wondered if she got bored by the repetition — or was she secretly excited by the idea that a small clove of malignance might be hiding deep down in that soft tissue?

Both sides done, and Chrissie having checked the pictures, received digitally, on a small screen, Claire was given permission to get dressed. "The radiologist will take a look at these tomorrow," Chrissie said. "You'll get a phone call if we need to get you back here. Otherwise you'll be getting a letter from us in the next few days." This process seemed to Claire to contain a streak of sadism. They would call only if they had bad news for you. So there you were, waiting not for the phone to ring, but for the phone not to ring.

It wasn't as if this were the first time Claire had to endure the suspense of not knowing if they thought she was cancerous. It happened every time she had gone through this peculiar indignity. She told herself she should be used to it by now. Dropping her johnny into a bin already half full of them, Claire got dressed and retraced her steps towards the waiting room. As she unhooked her coat from the coat tree, she saw Dr. Fein again. He was getting into a grey parka with a stand-up collar, his back towards her. That meant that he had been kept there longer than she—because he had gone in first. So they must have been doing something to him, looking for something no one wanted to find. Then he turned around. He looked unhappy. At first he seemed not to want to acknowledge that the two of them were in the same room but then his expression abruptly took on what she could read only as a dart of malice; he was giving her the evil eye. The nasty thing caught her in the throat and she found herself swallowing hard to keep from choking.

She couldn't decide whether or not to respond; finally, seconds later, just as she was about to say something silly and ill-chosen, Dr. Fein, in a harsh, low whisper, looked her straight in the eye and said, "I shouldn't be here." And, after a few seconds, "And neither should you." And with that remark, he opened the office door, stepped through, and was gone. The teddy bear had morphed into another sort of creature, its shape indistinct but with a dark, threatening mouth.

Claire drove home applying a light foot on the gas pedal and an extra dose of concentration, aware that her encounter with Dr. Fein had upset her so badly she was in danger of losing her focus and driving into a tree. It wasn't until she reached her house that she remembered that she had planned to stop and pick up something for her and Amos's dinner.

The house was dark except for a slice of ochre light coming from Amos's study. Claire had long ago discarded the habit of telling her husband most of what she had done and seen and heard during the day. Her little stories didn't seem to interest him the way they once had; these days she rationed herself. When was the last time she had disturbed him at his thinking best during the late afternoon hours, while dusk crept around every corner of the house waiting to turn black? She couldn't remember but it didn't matter, because their marriage was by this time virtually wrinkle-free and promised nothing but more of the same until death should part them.

"Amos," she said, walking into his study, where he sat in a ratty velvet wingchair, something she had been trying to get rid of for years. He was reading one of his philology journals, a pencil hovering drone-like in his hand.

"What's up, Bug?" he said.

"I'm sorry to disturb you but I really want to tell you about the weird thing that happened to me this afternoon."

Amos actually looked up from his book and turned his hazel eyes on his wife. As usual she couldn't be sure what his look said—beyond offering her nothing she could bite into.

"You know I went for a mammogram today," she said.

"I didn't know," Amos said. "And?"

"Well, I don't have the results," she said. "They don't let you know for a while. It's annoying."

"I would think so," he said.

"Dr. Fein was in the mammography office."

"Who's Doctor Fein?"

"He's my gynecologist, Amos."

"I thought mammography was a breast exam. What was your pussy doctor doing there? I don't understand."

That was the issue, Claire told him. Even though the nurse had assured her that men get "lumps" it had unnerved her to see him there.

"And he looked different," she said. "Not his normal jolly self but someone shocked—or frightened. And he said he shouldn't be there—and I shouldn't be there either. He sounded like he was threatening me."

"Are you sure?" Amos asked. "Did he really tell you that or are you just imagining it?"

How could she possibly answer this tooth-grinding question? How could he ask it? Did he expect her to say "You're right. I'm only imagining it?"

"I forgot to stop at the market. We'll have some soup for dinner. I'll make you an omelet if you'd like."

"Anything's fine," he said. "I told Jess I'd finish his article tonight," Amos said, tapping his forefinger on the open journal. "Okay?"

Her phone rang as she walked away from him towards the kitchen. She answered, hoping it was one of the children and not bothering to read the caller's name.

"Is that Claire Sinkler?" The voice was familiar but she couldn't pin it down. "This is Steven Fein. Your OB/GYN. I need to talk to you."

"Okay," she said.

"You saw me this afternoon at Wellbridge? Well, I'd like to ask you not to tell anyone about my being there. This is a favor I'm asking you."

"Of course," she said.

"I want to hear you say you promise. This is very important to my future. You understand, I'm sure."

"I promise," Claire said.

"It mustn't get out."

"Are you okay, Steven?"

"Yes," he said, sounding anything but okay. "It's nothing significant."

Everything he was telling her made it sound worse.

"There was a slight mix-up about my records," he added, deepening the mystery.

"I'm glad you're okay," Claire said. "Thanks for calling. And no, I won't say a word to anyone. I promise."

He thanked her. After hanging up, Claire wasn't sure that Steven Fein believed her. What was the matter with him, anyway?

Claire decided not to tell Amos about the call.

For the next two days, Claire tried hard to follow her usual routine, going to her second-floor office above Main Street, where she edited the Banner, a bi-weekly newspaper. She had been on the Banner's staff for fifteen years before retiring two years earlier. Then her boss, a famous, antiquated editor, was hit by a kid on a bicycle while crossing Broadway, and died a month later. The publisher, who lived in Boca, told Claire he would close the paper unless she came back to run the show, a claim which she knew to be a lie but which pleased her nonetheless; retirement had proved to be a lot less fun than it was cracked up to be. In fact, it was more like a slow and painful death.

Claire sent a reporter to check the status of a semi that had got itself stuck under a railroad bridge and another to investigate reports that a waitress at the town's favorite breakfast place had called a couple of customers faggots. The last newspaper left in her suburban community, the Banner also ran local political and business stories (the emphasis on the latter, which reliably brought the ads that allowed the paper to survive), a bland gossip column, and irregular features about dogs and cats in near-tragic situations. All this time Claire waited for the phone not to ring and the words Mrs. Sinkler, we need to take another look at your right breast. When can you come in for a mammogram? By the end of the day, not having received the dread call, Claire was giddy with relief, the bulky cape of anxiety dropped from her shoulders. She felt so good she went downstairs to Rite-Aid where she bought a Lindt chocolate bar and ate the whole thing while standing on the sidewalk, blinking in the sunlight, finding everyone around her amazing, beautiful.

She finished off the chocolate bar, balled the wrapper and dropped it in a metal trash basket attached to a telephone pole. Then she turned to go back to her office.

"Claire?"

It was Dr. Fein again, who seemed to be trying out various facial expressions, none of which suited him. He was wearing chinos and a jacket under his unzipped parka.

"I work upstairs," she said, pointing to the large letters spelling out the paper's name on the plate glass window above the Rite-Aid store.

He seemed surprised that she had a job. Which was strange, because she wasn't exactly a stranger or a first-time patient, and surely he was aware that she filled the top spot at the Banner. Maybe he concerned himself with and so only remembered facts about the bottom half of women. Like most men?

"Oh, the media," he said.

Claire didn't want to get into a conversation in which the other person's sole aim was to piss on her profession. "Yes, the good old media," she said, wondering why she felt so much like running away.

He told her it was nice seeing her and now he had to get back to work.

"My office is just across the street and around the corner," he said.

"Of course," she said, producing a disarming smile, meant to reassure him that she didn't think there was anything peculiar about his telling her where his office was for crissake.

And as he started walking away he said, as if it was an afterthought, "And don't forget your promise not to tell anyone you saw me the other day."

Once upstairs, sitting at her desk, watching her small but energized staff scurrying to make the twice-weekly deadline, it occurred to her that meeting Doctor Fein had not been an accident. He had planned it, he had been waiting for her. "But that's crazy," she said aloud.

The next two days brought Claire no surprises or moments to brood over. Then her daughter April, phoned to report that she had broken up with Josh, her live-in boyfriend. This caused anguish.

"Just last week we were talking about getting married," April said, close to tears.

Why, at this late date, did girls still assume that marriage would make them whole, as if they were lying around in a thousand little pieces of jigsaw puzzle and needed a male to put them together?

"He got cold feet?" Claire said. "I guess."

"I don't know, Mom. He was such an asshole. He took Chen to his opening."

"Is Chen a boy or a girl?"

"Mom! Chen's a woman. Actually, she's a bitch."

"You didn't tell me Josh was in a show."

"It was a group thing," April said. "No big deal."

"Why don't you come home for a visit? You haven't been here in months. Take the train." April said she would try.

"One more thing," Claire said. "I know you're an adult and I probably ought to let you do your own thing but, well, what happens to you is important to me. No, important isn't the right word, the word is more like central. When you're in pain, so am I."

"For heaven's sake, Mom, what are you talking about? I wish you wouldn't talk to me like this."

"Okay then. When was the last time you had a mammogram?"

"I don't know," April said. "A couple, three years ago I guess. Why?"

"You should have one every year. You know Granny had breast cancer. Didn't your doctor tell you?"

April said she would think about it.

Her daughter's unhappiness, however retrograde its cause, made Claire feel awful. Of course there was nothing she could do to soften the blow of being dumped by a boyfriend, a young man Claire liked in spite of a covert narcissism that poked through every so often. Oh, those pretty boys, how much fun to be with them, how much poison pooled in their veins. She was better off without him, but Claire couldn't bring herself to say this to April.

When she told Amos that night, as he was getting ready for bed, that April and Josh were "a thing of the past," Amos said he wasn't surprised. The boy had plenty of ambition and enough talent to carry it along but there was something missing.

"He would have made a terrible father."

Claire bristled, reminding her husband that he had never, not once, said anything that anyone could interpret as being anti-Josh. In fact, several times Amos had said how much he liked "the boy." Was there no one she could trust? Was everyone a liar?

The next morning, after a breakfast during which Claire and Amos referred not once to their daughter, Claire left earlier than usual for the office, stopping on the way to buy a croissant at Amelia's Bakery. She sat at her desk, eating it as if she were starving, when the desk phone rang.

"This is Steven Fein. You betrayed me."

"What are you talking about?"

"You told someone you saw me at Wellbridge. You made a promise, Claire. A promise is a promise."

"I didn't tell anyone," she said. "No, that's not true. I told my husband, but he wouldn't repeat something like that. Please, you're beginning to make me angry."

"Then your husband told," Steven said.

"That's absolutely crazy," said Claire. "He has no interest in you or in your medical problems. I have to hang up now. I have to get to work. Goodbye, and please don't do this again."

The third Thursday of the month was Claire's day to get her hair trimmed and washed at Dalliance, one of the town's three beauty parlors; she had been going there for ten years. They knew her hair and her temperament and Fran, the woman whose hands fingered Claire's scalp and who bent so close that Claire could smell her sweetish perfume and feel wisps of breath on her neck, was not a non-stop talker like some of them. She didn't seem to mind silence as she snipped. Under her clear plastic cape, her hair sleek like a wet Lab's, Claire saw in the mirror that her face had acquired a couple of new creases. What could you expect? Age creeps along, leaving a snail trail on your face, your neck, your spirit.

"If you don't mind me saying so, you look a little beat today," Fran said. "Been staying up late?"

"Just the years kicking in," Claire said. "Did you know dead is the new eighty?"

"Now that's funny," Fran said. "I think I get it. Did you make that up?"

Claire nodded.

"Well," Fran said. She looked at the clock over the front door. "I'm finished here. Gotta go for my yearly check-up. I just love my primary care physician even though he, like, always keeps me waiting at least an hour. But I've got my new Oprah to keep me busy."

When Claire reached her office just before ten, Dennis, the Banner's intern, rushed at her so violently he nearly knocked her over. An otherwise plausible kid, he was taking a year off from Harvard to learn the newspaper business (which Claire had warned him was a waste of time because by the year 2015, newspapers would be about as relevant as butter churns).

"There was a creepy dude in here a few minutes ago asking for you," he said. Claire noticed that Dennis was cultivating a five-o-clock shadow. So cool. The Banner didn't get many visitors.

"Let me take my coat off, please," Claire said. "What did he look like?"

"Sort of fat, sort of fuzzy if you know what I mean."

The man had refused to tell Dennis why he wanted to see Claire, except that it was a 'private matter.'

Claire sat down at her desk. Hilary, one of her green reporters, a year out of Wellesley, her I-want-your-job ambition as obvious as the money that had gone to buy her designer jeans, fed Claire more details: the man's worn sneakers, his dirty fingernails.

Of course the creepy dude was her ex-OB/GYN (for by this time Claire had decided never to put her heels in his stirrups again). It had now gone way past the joke stage and was entering the next, where you realize you're the focus of someone's obsession and who knew where it might end: in a ditch; in a dozen neatly chopped pieces stored in a freezer; in a shallow grave. And yet, the man had done nothing that would prompt any responsible officer of the law to start sniffing around.

Two days went by without a whiff of her ex-doctor. Instead of reassuring her, Claire found his absence disconcerting as it made her imagine reasons that would explain his silence: he was planning something that took more time and effort than he had been thus far willing to give; he had gone out of state to buy a weapon; he was sick. This last was probably too good to be true. It was time to call the police, though she knew, from any number of reports that had found their way to her desktop, that vagueness never got a supposed victim anywhere; they needed hard evidence. The Chief of Police — she didn't know his first name, everyone called him Petrillo — was one of those people Claire was friendly with because of the work they both did. Otherwise they might never have talked to each other. Claire called the station and asked for Petrillo. Told he was on another phone call, she asked to have him call her back. She had some clout — maybe a three out of a possible ten — with Petrillo, but it was almost five before he finally called back. Just another piece of evidence that newspapers were in a collective coma.

"He's harassing me," she said, after identifying the players in her little drama.

Petrillo said, "I need some specifics, Claire, you know that. Has this guy actually threatened you?"

"Well, he called me on the phone, sent me a text message, and came into the Banner's office looking for me. I wasn't there. He also waited for me outside my office. I'm sure of that."

"That's not a threat in my book. Sorry. I'll ask you again: has this doctor employed any language, any language at all that could be construed as a threat? Has he touched you?"

"Not since I was his patient."

"Oh?"

"You know what I mean, Petrillo. He was my gynecologist. Doctors do have to touch their patients."

"I understand that. But unless and until he uses threatening language either in person, via U.S. Mail, or over the internet, I'm afraid there isn't much I can do to help you at this point in time. I do believe you, Claire, he's a pain in the butt but the law's the law." He paused as if expecting her to come back at him with an argument. She had none.

"Oh yes, he did say he was disappointed with me. Doesn't that indicate that he thinks we have some sort of special relationship?"

Petrillo actually laughed. Fucking no help.

She turned on her computer and began to edit a column by her food writer that was full of misspellings. Then her phone rang. It was April, saying she was coming home for the weekend. Would Claire pick her up in Providence?

"What are you doing in Providence?"

"I'm visiting Evan," April said. "Mom, is something the matter?"

"I'm sorry," Claire said. "A senior moment. I have a few things on my mind. Nothing significant."

"Really."

"Can you take the bus or train? I can pick you up in Boston."

"We can have a conversation in the car," April said.

"Are you pregnant?"

"No, Mom. Maybe. I don't know."

They arranged to meet after Claire left work. Amos would be in Boston at one of his language meetings, long affairs in which a lot of serious men—and occasionally a woman or two—wrangled over the origin of the word "to give," or some slang element that had crept, unbidden, into the lingua franca. It wasn't that Claire had no interest in the subject, but that Amos's focus was like a high-powered microscope, the kind of inquiry that left Claire less than breathless.

"I'll pick you up at Evan's place as near six-thirty as I can. The traffic's hideous at rush hour, so it might be later."

April told her mother it didn't really matter what time she got there. "I have nothing else to do."

Claire called Amos from her kitchen. Noise in the background made it hard for them to hear each other. She told him she was going to Providence to pick up April. "I'm feeling as if I were falling to pieces."

"Really, Bug, I can't do this now. Can't it wait?"

"Of course," she said. "I didn't mean to say that. I'm fine. "

She made herself a tuna sandwich which she stowed in a baggie to eat on the way, heated and poured left over coffee into a thermos, and went out the kitchen door to the driveway. She beeped open the front door of the Saab, folded herself into the driver's seat, pulled the seat belt smartly across her chest and clicked it into place. She keyed on the motor, listening to the gulping sound it made as the pistons went to work, and, checking her rearview mirror, slowly backed out of the driveway into Acacia Street. The street light had yet to go on but she knew the way so well she could have driven its length blindfolded. This was a quiet, unwrinkled neighborhood. Its houses, most of them, had been assembled during the first half of the twentieth century, and were as solid and conservative as William Howard Taft.

She drove down the street, across an intersection, past the Shell station, Aunt Susie's overpriced restaurant, Anchors Away (a nautically-themed gift shop), and the First Congregational Church. She was headed toward the entrance to the Mass Pike when a man spoke directly into her right ear:

"Don't turn around. Keep driving!"

She began to shake as if electrified. Her eyes unfocused and her throat produced a scream of some duration and sound. The tremor jerked her hands off the wheel. Unmanned, the car swerved, heading for the sidewalk. Moments passed before she could yell, "Don't kill me, please don't kill me."

"Be quiet and keep driving," the man said. "Put your hands back on the wheel. Do you want to kill us both?" She recognized the voice: it was Steven Fein. Of course it was Steven Fein.

Instead of doing what she was told, she scrambled to unhook her seatbelt so she could escape. But her thumb proved useless and she couldn't get the seatbelt thing to unlock.

"I mean it!" Steven said. "I tried and tried but you wouldn't listen to me. Now you're going to have to listen. But if you try to get out of the car I guarantee you'll be sorry."

Ablaze with panic and fury, Claire yelled, "Get out of my car!"

"I'm not going anywhere," he said.

Claire stepped on the brake and stopped the car. Again, he told her to keep driving, guessing maybe that she was quite capable of retrieving her head after so noisily losing it.

"I don't want to scare you, but I need you to keep the car in motion. If you're driving you can't run away. You have to listen to me."

"I'm not myself," she said. "You scared me to death. I can't get back...."

"You'll get back," he said. "Just don't try anything."

"How did you get in my car?"

"My secret," he said. "It's easy."

"I don't know," she said. Her trembling subsided a notch. "Look, I'm going to Providence to pick up my daughter. This is terrible. You broke into my car, you scared the shit out of me. I should have you arrested. Carjacking, kidnapping. What do you want with me? Why do you keep hounding me? I didn't do anything to you. I think you're crazy."

"Don't call me that. Don't you ever say that again."

Something told Claire she had better retreat. "You didn't answer me. What the hell do you want?"

"A bargain," Steven said. "If you'll listen to me I'll get out of the car at 128 and take the train back to Boston. That's all I need."

She was scared to ask him if he had a gun or a knife. As a matter of fact, she didn't really want to know. But he read her mind.

"I'm not holding a gun on you," he said. "Or even a knife. I'm not that sort of person."

She was aware that having entered into a dialogue of sorts with Steven Fein, she had already made an accommodation with him. Smack down the middle: half of her was terrified. The other half, sedated by curiosity, and by the fact that she was pretty sure he actually had no intention of killing her, was willing to resist the impulse to throw herself from the car at the next red light.

"I wish you'd move your head," she said. "You're making me very nervous." But in fact, an unexpected coolness, even detachment, had shoved her panic aside. Claire began to realize that she might have some say in what was taking place inside the car. She could sense him hitch over to his right. His image in the rear view mirror presented half a face. His eye was rimmed with pink, his hair haywire. He looked as if he felt not triumphant but miserable. He was thinner than he had been just five days before, the skin on his face sagging like an old man's.

"Why are you doing this? What have you got against me?"

She didn't like the tone of her voice but couldn't figure out how to modulate it.

"Not against you. For you," he said. "I chose you."

"Why?"

"I like the cut of your jib. You have shapely toes. I drew your name out of a hat. You run a piss-pot newspaper. Take your pick. Does it really matter?" He paused and when she didn't answer he told her again that he hadn't meant to scare her.

"Really?" she said. "You break into my car and hide in the back seat until I'm on the road, then you pop up like a homicidal maniac in a movie. How did you think I'd feel? Did you think I'd say, 'Well, hello there Steve, nice to see you again. Why don't we stop for a cup of coffee somewhere and have a nice little chat about the state of the world?'"

He was silent. She could smell him now. He stank of unwashed clothes pasted on an unwashed body.

"Okay," she said, rounding off the silence, "I'll listen to you until we get to the Amtrak station and then you get out like you promised. And if I never see you again, it will be plenty soon enough." She heard herself talking like tough-girl actress Linda Fiorentino in *The Last Seduction*. 'My place, my space.' Claire almost smiled.

"I'll tell you. There's an elephant in the room," Steven said. "And there's a gorilla with the elephant. Okay. There are too many people on earth. This planet's crawling with people who should never have been born. We're ants swarming over a corpse."

"Why are you telling me this?" she said, interrupting him. She figured they were almost halfway there. "Did you hijack me just to tell me people shouldn't have so many babies?"

Steven didn't answer. He was nowhere near through. "Women having baby after baby, never thinking about what another human being will add to the problem. Just my adorable baby, isn't she cute, isn't he the most adorable thing you've ever seen. And you know who're the worst offenders? Hasidim, popping out babies like gum ball machines. The more the merrier, five, six, seven, why not a dozen? Those orthodox men sit on their hairy butts all day reading and rereading the Talmud. To what end I ask you? Where's the wisdom they're supposed to be excavating? When their eyes start to close they go home and *schtup* their wives—and sometimes other men's wives—and make more little Jews to grow up and do the same thing. And you can't accuse me of being an anti-Semite because I'm a Jew myself, like you, right? There isn't enough food for everybody as it is and before long we're going to start acting like those mice they keep so jammed together in a cage they start clawing each other's eyes out. Are you listening to me?"

"Yes," she said. "You paint a pretty grim picture."

"All words," he said. "You're all words."

"If you don't mind my saying so, you don't know the first thing about me."

"I know as much as I need to know," he said. As if he hadn't been challenged, Steven Fein plowed on, turning up the soil and obliging her to listen. They were well on their way to the train station now. The traffic had thinned as abruptly as it had thickened. She stayed in the middle lane, the safest lane. She had to pee but chose to try and ignore the urge.

"And why did I bring up the elephant and the gorilla? Because no one has the balls to talk about the single most urgent problem in the world. In comparison to this, climate change is a little rain on your little parade. No one at the top will tell people they shouldn't have so many babies, no one even has the nerve to bring it up. The Chinese have the right idea, but they overdid it; they should have said two children, not one. But do you think we'd take a leaf from their book? Not on your life. You try to talk reason with women and they'll agree with you—up to when you suggest that after two children it's maybe time to stop. They look at you as if you'd asked them to put their baby on a skewer and grill it. Birth control is racist, right? I swear to you if I could find a way to do it I would sterilize all the ripe women in the world. I would snip their tubes as easily as I entered your car."

And, veering sharply back to his subject, he said, "And at the other end of life? They keep you alive no matter what. All systems down and still they hook you up to stimulants, saline, plasma, blood, drugs, oxygen masks, whatever it takes to give you a few more tortured days on earth. And you know what it takes most of? Your family's money. And if you don't have enough, my money. Other peoples' money. More money is spent on the last six months of a person's life than in all the years that went before. What for?"

Claire's fear had mostly drained, leaving behind a small headache. But the stench was growing; she began to breathe through her mouth. "I want to ask you something," Claire said. "What did you mean when you said that day at Wellbridge that I shouldn't be there?"

"I said that?"

"You did."

"Well, I must have meant that things, bad things, should be allowed to run their course. There are too many people in this fucking world."

"But you don't know why I was there. Why did you assume I had cancer?"

"I didn't assume anything," Steven said. "There's too much testing, too many scans, MRIs, X-rays. We're all glowing with nuclear distress."

Claire decided that for her to drop the subject was not only wise but might also be a life saver. Who knew what he was capable of? Steven had picked up the thread again.

"Medicine runs in my family, you know. My dad was a podiatrist. My brother Bernie decided to be a hand doctor. That's a specialty, did you know that? Hand doctor? And you know why he chose that? Because, he said, he didn't want to have to deal with all that bathroom stuff. It's me that deals with the bathroom stuff. I suppose you think I get off looking at women's pussies all day long? You're wrong again. It's just the opposite. I'm like a dentist—only at the other end: slimy and sometimes rotting."

"Please don't elaborate," Claire said. She felt queasy. The headlights coming at her from the left were too bright. She blinked a couple of times while telling herself to concentrate on her driving and stop listening to her passenger. But how could she stop listening?

"Did I bruise your precious sensibilities? My god, I'm hungry."

Should she pass him her sandwich? Would that shut him up for a few minutes? But then she realized that the large structure to her right was the Amtrak station.

"This is where you get out," she said.

"But I have something for you," he said. He rustled around in his parka. "I want you to print this as an editorial," he said. He reached over the seat and dropped a manila envelope that had been folded and folded again onto Claire's lap.

"It's my analysis of overpopulation and some suggestions for fixing it ASAP. What I've just been telling you."

"You're just like the Unabomber," Claire said. "That Ted-something who wrote wild manifestoes." She didn't mention that he had killed someone.

"You think I'm nuts like him. You don't even have to say so. I can feel what you're thinking."

"By the way, in case you were wondering why you saw me at the mammography place. They did a needle biopsy and found a little something that they're going to keep an eye on. Keep an eye on—one of the more ominous phrases in the English language. Steven Fein comes down with a disease reserved—or so he thought—for females. Who could have predicted? It's a one-in-a-million thing. I admit it threw me off my game, I lost it for a while, went clear off the rails. They might as well have told me that I had ovarian cancer. My wife Susie was no help. At the time she was too busy banging our across the street neighbor, son-of-a-bitch owns a bar near Fenway. Only one in the neighborhood has a hot tub."

"No, I don't suppose Susie was much help. Why don't you send this to a paper or a website or start a blog? Why would you want to run it in a piss-pot paper?"

"Thought I'd try you first. I know you."

"I'm getting out with you," she said. "I have to use the restroom."

"I'm going, I'm going," he said, and still she couldn't sense any movement behind her. She opened the car door and unfolded herself. They were inside a cavernous garage, half empty. Her knees tingled unpleasantly. A car alarm went off. "Get out. You promised."

"That I did," Steven said. He seemed deflated, the fight gone out of him, his purpose lost somewhere in the vast gloom of the garage. She told herself not to let him get to her.

"You'll run my editorial?" he said.

Claire narrowed her eyes at the envelope, then at him. "I can't promise without reading it," she said.

"How will I know?"

"I'll be in touch with you."

"You won't," he said. "I know your type. You already betrayed me."

"I didn't," she said. She looked at his feet.

"Your left shoelace is untied," she said. "Better tie it up before you trip and fall."

Benign Indignities

by Kim Stafford

I have walked a thousand times
this mile at the river to witness
how waves churn, thrash, and ebb.
I have lifted stones once shattered
from bedrock jagged in the river, now
friendly to hand, made shapely by water's
way with time and change. And I have
learned from that tug and surrender how
to fondle what is broken until it is smooth.

So in the book of my humiliations
I am taught to cherish my myriad failures
now rounded by recollection, thorns caressed
until they glisten, secret stupidities pearled
by affection. I have kept no dignity—only
saved this wild museum of errors where I walk
along the water, marveling at what I have
survived—stone by stone, loss by loss,
wave by wave, and step by step.

The Living Dead

by Carol Band

Over Memorial Day, we visited one of those touristy shops at Hampton Beach and I broke down and bought my son a hermit crab. For Lewis, part of the appeal was that the crab's shell was decorated with the logo of the Boston Red Sox. For me, the hermit crab seemed like a good alternative to more complex life forms like geckos, guinea pigs, and iguanas.

"His name is Bruce," my son said lovingly as the crab clamped onto his finger and drew blood. "I think he likes me!" On the ride home, Lewis sat in the backseat with a cardboard crab container on his lap and cooed to Bruce through the air holes.

"Why are you talking to that crab, you moron?" Lewis' fourteen-year-old sister said. "Crabs can't hear you, and even if they could they don't even have brains. They're like lobsters. I think we should cook him."

"Don't listen to her, Brucey," my son hissed into the box. "She's just jealous." At home we found an old ten-gallon aquarium, one that is haunted by the ghosts of deceased goldfish and long-dead gerbils and transferred Bruce to his permanent digs.

"Bruce needs a more interesting habitat," my son said as be proceeded to arrange Lego guys and plastic dinosaurs in the tank. The crab seemed unimpressed. At the store, he had been more lively, but here, amid a T-Rex and sword-wielding pirates, he was a little lethargic.

"Maybe he's just tired from the long drive," I suggested.

We went to our local pet shop to stock up on hermit crab food —even though I suspected that Bruce wouldn't live to consume much of the fishy-smelling powder that Lewis piled into his tiny seashell dish. We also bought a sea sponge, so Bruce wouldn't become dehydrated, a bag of neon-orange pebbles, to mimic his natural habitat and we blew seventeen dollars on a plaster castle that might have added a little more quality to the short life of the now-dead goldfish that once inhabited the tank. This was one lucky crab.

"Bruce is going to be soooo happy," my son beamed as he festooned the tank with our new purchases. He also added a Spider-Man action figure, a handful of marbles and several Hot Wheels cars. The environment in the tank was so rich, so stimulating, that it was hard to even locate the crab. When I did, he looked suspiciously...dead.

"I think you might want to take a look at Bruce," I said in a gentle tone.

"Whadayya mean?" Lewis asked.

"Well, he's not really moving," I said.

"That's because he's sleeping," my son declared.

Who was I to question his expertise? Maybe crabs did sleep. So I took a pair of tongs from the kitchen and moved Bruce into a realistic pose near the sponge. Maybe some water would perk him up.

"See, Mom? I told you he was just asleep," Lew said as he gently dumped more food into the seashell dish. "Bruce is drinking water now."

"Did you see him walk there?" I asked.

"No, but he's drinking; he's fine," Lewis assured me.

The next morning, the crab's thirst was apparently still not quenched. While Lewis brushed his teeth, I used the tongs to reposition Bruce at the door of the castle. He looked good there. In fact, he stayed in that position for several days — until Lewis needed to retrieve his Spider-Man action figure.

"Hey! Bruce is guarding the castle!" Lewis exclaimed when he noticed the crab's new post. I pondered Bruce's next move and wondered how long I should carry on the charade.

I've thought about replacing Bruce with a live crab, but our pet store only sells fish. Even if I could locate a suitable double, I'm not sure that I could successfully lure a new crustacean into Bruce's Red Sox shell or that I could successfully evict the current (albeit deceased) occupant.

Turns out, a dead hermit crab is a pretty good pet. He doesn't eat anything, so his cage never needs cleaning and the faint stench of rotting shellfish emitting from Lewis's room not only adds a waterfront ambience to the whole house, it has given our geriatric cat a renewed sense of purpose. The only maintenance required, is periodically moving the shell to simulate lifelike activity. The dead crab's antics have kept my son amused now for over a month. Sometimes Bruce is atop the sponge "drinking." Other days, he's positioned near his food dish and sometimes, he's wedged inside the Hot Wheels convertible ready to race around the tank.

"I like Bruce," my son said yesterday, "but when he dies, I'm going to make a necklace out of his shell."

I can't think of a more fitting memorial.

Self-Portrait Before

by Anna Ross

In the split between two boulders
behind the blue and orange playground,

the children are building nests
for when the hurricane comes.

Assembly line, they pass small piles of twigs
and—Faster!—last year's leaves,

then climb inside with larger sticks for rowing.
April now, and the last storm has redrawn

all the Atlantic flood maps.
One more year until the Cartaret Islands

go down in the Pacific—
whole forests of nests past all rowing.

One morning last December,
my friend went in to wake her 2-year-old son,

and found him. Causes unknown,
the doctors said—some stuttered synapse

blanking inhale. What tide could bear this?

She wrote his obituary for the local news.

Is it tomorrow? my son asks at bedtime each night,
and in the morning asks again.

Demolition Trio

by Zach Savich

○

Demolition

Or days bounty exaggerated the labor's strain
Grapes thread on a thigh

Has not thirst made the nectar run

And savory the acorn

My elegy is just ongoing consciousness
Trail maintained by flood

I wake early enough to see those whose work begins before heat
Heat precedes me

The Hopelessly Open Gate

Wind where the chimes will be

Beautiful, in a passing way
Thus, more beautiful the more it passes me

Much as those birds that never touch the ground

Is this tree the ground
Is fruit the ground

○

The Final Step of Transplanting

There's little evidence of the bee's contact with the blossom
Outside the blossom

By alternating crops, you make toil easy

Cardinal in some stacked panes, or in each of them

In my time travel dream, we agree to visit the present

Blue

by Leslie Anne Mcilroy

For M. R.

Eyes not exactly blue,
but light and blue metal,
a blue blue that is not,
but rather a hue of intense,
not as blue as the sky
on a cool summer night,
but blue like stone glint
in the sun. Blue after rain,
blue before dawn, the blue
of paintings as they settle into blue.
There is a grey, spelled with an "e"
and a wisp of silver villain.
There is the blue of longing
and the blue of knowing,
the blue of promise and bruises,
oceans and longing. Did I
say "blue," did I say "longing"?
What I meant was
the color of a storm
and its lazy rise to torment,
its thunder yearn and blue,
what might happen next,
what might happen if never

is the shade of blue I am
wearing, what my white
heart does with desire,
how when we get to the end,
we are nothing except
want and vein, except
ink and eyes, except
something in between
longing & knowing,
and dear god,
blue.

By the Pool

by Julie Monrad

Autumn was near over — not that it mattered.

In the dull heat Lady let her feet swirl in the pool, sucking her red popsicle, waiting for something to happen. Her popped-out belly button slowly browned in the sunlight. The white tank top, with brown and green marks of wear, yellowed as sweat dripped into the creased fabric, jammed between stomach and bones. Her belly had grown large and round but no one paid it much mind or care. These things happened in their town. After all, she was very beautiful — so judged the old ladies — and a girl can only turn down so many offers. The older women floated like flies from one dung-heap of story to another, digesting them into rumors. As they told it, Lady had chosen the right offer: a boy off to play the best college football in the country. And not too bad to look at either.

He wandered over to sit beside her, just his normal saunter, hips rhythmic and steady, never a falter from his large feet. His broad hand spread across her belly, absorbing some of the heat. His legs drifted beside her splashing feet, the water perfectly outlining the circle of his upper calf. His hand slid to her inner thigh. It gave a squeeze. He flopped backwards onto the grass.

"The old man ain't here, is he?" His voice reached from behind her back.

"Nah. Florida." She stared across the pool. Sweat slid out from under her hair, trickled down her back.

"How do you always know where people are?"

"Ain't so hard to figure out."

"Want to swim?"

His palm landed on her solid back and rested there. She tilted her head up towards the sky. The sun glinted off the oversized, round frames of her sunglasses. She held the moment—worthy of fashion advertisements—in her mind. Weren't they glamorous?

"Nah. It's too hot."

"Don't make sense."

He lay still another moment then stood and stripped and dove smoothly into the water. He floated on his back a while, his penis adrift as if separate from his body. Slowly, soundlessly, his shadow traveled each inch of pool bottom. She watched his eyes scrunch together against the sun, as if he could never squeeze them tight enough. Then suddenly, he just relaxed everything, eyelids and all, embracing the caress of damaging beams.

Time passed. She sat with her head tilted toward the sun, still as a praying mantis. He hoisted himself from the pool, splashing water. She felt his wet chest against hers and lay down beneath him. Her index finger wiped away droplets fallen from his brow upon her cheek. His palm dragged across her hair, friction tugging slightly.

"You know," he said, face placid, "you're still so beautiful."

He looked a moment more, then rolled onto his back into the grass. The ants hummed sweetly.

Lady closed her eyes against the sun. She rubbed her fingers across her shirt, then extended those fingers between his. So they lay beneath the cancerous caress of the sun, holding hands.

"Hey."

They hadn't heard Skelt approach. Lady didn't care for many of his friends, but Skelt she tolerated, almost liked.

"Old man ain't here?" Skelt asked.

"No," he responded, unabashed by his nakedness.

"You go swimming?"

"Just me."

"Why not you?" Skelt asked her.

"It's too hot."

"Don't make much sense." Skelt sat down beside his naked friend. "Heard you got that football scholarship."

The flies were always buzzing.

"Yep."

"Pretty exciting."

"Guess so."

"Guess so? My mama ain't stopped talking about it."

"People always talking."

"You get to get out of here! Like really get out of here."

"Maybe I like it here."

"Aw shit man, no one likes it here. I mean, what the fuck is here? What the fuck are we supposed to do in this cow-town?"

"Raise cows I guess."

"You want to raise cows for the rest of your life?"

"There are worse things."

"You ungrateful son of a bitch. You can say that because you've got options. Fucking options."

"Quit fussing, Skelt," said Lady. "You know you're smart. We all know what you got on your SATs. You'll have options."

"But a scholarship? How the fuck am I gonna get that?"

"Quit fussing."

Skelt did as he was told. He stared across the pool at the rotting wooden fence, arms wrapped around his knees.

"Old man doesn't take care of his fence."

"He ain't too rich," said Lady.

"Nah. If he was you'd be carrying his kid."

"Not funny."

"You do sure spend a lot of time with him," said the father.

"He's nice."

"Why are you always baking him cookies?"

"I get to eat them too, don't I?"

"Yeah. Still kind of funny," he said. He turned to Skelt. "Tank coming?"

"Yeah. Just getting a thirty."

Lady felt her body stiffen. Her nostrils flared. Ants trickled across her right foot.

"Fuck this heat," Skelt sputtered. She heard the rustle of grass and untrapped insects as Skelt stood up, stripped and splashed into the pool. Small drops of water sprinkled the two lovers.

Lady smelled Tank before she saw him. He dropped his thirty of Pabst Blue Ribbon at her feet, crushing the grass along with who knew how many innocent bugs.

"Jesus fucking Christ it's hot. Store never felt farther," Tank said.

"Put the cans in the pool," Skelt called.

"Catch!"

"Shit!" said Skelt, dodging the flying cans. "The fuck are you doing Tank? You're gonna hit me in the head."

"Don't be such a pussy."

"Asshole."

The father squeezed her hand.

"Gonna take a leak in the old man's bathroom."

She watched him closely as he strode off, wishing him back.

"Come swimming with me and Skelt," Tank called to her.

"No."

"You're gonna fry."

"Bake."

Tank took off his shirt. Lady closed her eyes.

Something damp and heavy landed on her face. She was suffocating. The air was foul and hot. She whipped Tank's shirt from her face and threw it away.

"So uptight today, babe." His toes nudged her shoulder.

He dove into the pool. The crack and gasp of a beer, finally allowed to breathe, echoed across the yard.

The father returned.

"Tank, toss me two," he called out.

He snapped them open, sipped from one, and placed the other beside her.

"Beer ain't good for the baby. Doctor said."

"Good for you though."

Thirty packs went quickly in their group. Crinkled aluminum littered the lawn around their limp, outstretched bodies. They were courteous enough to keep the last drops of beer out of the old man's water. But piss ran freely.

"When you two get married," Skelt said, shaking off his dick, "I want to be the ring bearer."

"We're not getting married," she said, eyes on the yellow-brown sky.

"Why not?"

"It's not about that."

"She's coming to school with me though," the father said.

"If she gets in," said Skelt.

"Either way."

"Parents want him to be a good Daddy," said Lady.

"Fat chance," said Tank.

"What's that supposed to mean?" said the father.

"Nothing," said Lady.

A bee hummed around the sweet aroma of her hair, gently playing in the soft breeze.

"I want another thirty," Skelt said.

"I'll come with you," he said, propping up, away from her.

"I got it."

"No you don't."

They rose and trudged off, leaving her with Tank.

Tank shifted so they were hip and hip. He rubbed his hand across her upper thigh, sliding it inwards. She pictured millipedes scuttling.

"Come with me to Virginia," he murmured.

"No."

"You're actually following him?"

"If I want."

"What about what I want?"

"Means shit to me."

"Don't be a bitch."

"Get your hand off me."

"Why do you toy with me?" Tank rolled on top of her.

"Fuck off Tank."

"I should have told him you were mine."

"Fucking once or twice doesn't make me yours."

"It was more than that."

"Regardless."

"I made a mistake," said Tank.

"No such thing," said Lady.

A bee buzzed in her ear.

"Don't give me that."

"Everything happens for a reason."

"So if I took you right now, it'd be for a reason?"

The buzzing stopped. Tank recoiled with a yelp and curse. Flopping onto his back he grasped his right forearm and moaned.

"For fuck's sake this hurts. Aren't you going to do anything? Jesus Christ."

"Go inside. First aid kit beneath the kitchen sink."

"Don't you have to suck out the stinger?" He moaned.

"It'll come out when it's ready."

Tank had been inside for twenty minutes when Skelt came back with the father. They laughed when she explained where he'd gone.

"What a pussy."

"We ran into Stems. She's coming later. Getting her brother's stock."

She smiled gently, reached her hand up for the father's. He pressed his fingertips around hers.

Skelt freed himself of his sweat-soaked shirt and reentered the pool.

"Throw me some!" he called.

Skelt splashed around trying to catch beers out of the air. A cricket began its song.

Stems came into the yard, pulling herself over the rotted fence. She lay down behind Lady, who used her flat stomach as a pillow.

"Where's my boy?" Stems asked.

"Tank's inside," said Lady. "Got stung by a bee."

"You're heavy these days."

"My head's gotten heavier?"

"Swollen," said Skelt. "It's all the praise you get about your 'glow.'"

"I hate those comments. I've always been tan."

"It's not the same," the father murmured.

"When're you due again?" said Stems.

"Dunno."

"Thursday," said the father. Stems laughed.

"The days are getting shorter. I don't want the baby to be born in the dark," said Lady.

"Don't worry," he said.

Stems brushed Lady's hair with her fingertips.

"What'll you name him? Her? I can't remember."

"Something smart," said Lady.

"Yeah, something smart," said the father. "Don't want him making our mistakes."

"He's not a mistake. Nothing is."

"He wasn't part of the game plan."

"So it's a he?" Stems asked.

"Dunno. Can't remember," she said.

"Of course he is. Already causin' trouble, and he ain't even born yet." The father smirked.

"Trouble yes, but not a mistake," she said. "Some things are just done. And some aren't."

The baby was the result of a moment stolen for just each other. She'd wanted to feel him. He wanted to know her. The countless moments of which they felt robbed by that barrier between had weakened their resolve until it broke.

They became another dung heap for the old women to buzz around.

"Shit, my skin is fucked up," Skelt said, splashing out of the pool.

"Stop getting me wet," said Stems.

"Stems, you got the green?"

"Yeah, Skelt. Nice to see you too by the way."

"Whatever. You didn't say hi either."

"Go get Tank and we can light up."

"Wait, Skelt, I'll come. I gotta piss," the father said.

"Think the old man's got anything hard to drink?"

"Couldn't tell ya."

"Don't take his alcohol, you piece of shit," said Lady.

"You're such a mom," said Skelt.

Crickets began to chirp as the sky turned purple. Lady's eyes drifted across the clouds. One right above her looked like a butterfly. Its right side got pulled by the wind, slowly stretching it apart, until poof! It was something totally different, a deformed, sideways heart perhaps. She wondered: if caterpillars turned to butterflies, what did butterflies turn into? The dust on other butterflies' wings?

"You're still so beautiful," Stems cooed.

She let the comment sit for a moment.

"You know what my mom used to tell me when I was little?"

"What's that?"

"She said that I'm a caterpillar who just needed to build her cocoon."

"That's awful pretty," Stems said.

"Yeah." She ran a hand atop the soft skin of her stomach. He was so still inside.

"You might have a baby in a couple days. Crazy."

"Yeah. That one can't stop talking about it," she said, tilting her head towards the house.

"I mean, he holds your belly, his baby, every day. It's weird for him, too."

"Yeah. I guess."

"Can't believe you kept this one."

"Yeah. I know."

"I always wondered, why didn't you keep the other one?"

The boys exited the house. Tank walked in front, brandishing a bottle of whisky. He winked in their direction. She rolled over onto her side, away from the line of men, head still coddled by Stems' stomach.

"It wasn't the right baby," she muttered.

The sun slid down past the edge of the horizon. To the sound of crickets crying, five pairs of eyes fell shut.

Temptation's Crush

by Allen M. Price

*I*t's nearly 6:00 p.m., six hours before my thirtieth birthday. I've been running on the treadmill for about thirty-five minutes, having arrived here from school, grad school that is. Running is the thing I enjoy most when working out. Weightlifting is good when I'm looking to have the boys ogle me, biking is good when I need to get my legs more defined, but running helps me burn off the energy I've built up throughout my day. There's nothing better than sweat dripping off my brow, headphones blaring techno music, and wet shorts riding up my ass. Okay, that one's annoying.

He usually strolls through the door around 6:10—five minutes to change out of his work clothes, another five to get to the gym. You're wondering who *he* is, huh? *He* is Lee, the man I've had a crush on for over three months now. And yes, he's married. Who am I, you ask? I'll give you a hint. I was born during the summer, and I'm hot like the month. Get it? August. So I've got a bit of arrogance.

Don't fault me for that. I'm only human.

The word HOT doesn't begin to describe how Lee's presence

grabs me, though. Composure is at a halt, focus is nilch, my surroundings are a blur. My blood warms and my skin radiates. I feel alive, energetic—yet when he steps to me, I'm like a kid running downstairs on Christmas morning only to find the tree is bare. Ever had a fantasy become reality?

Be careful what you wish for.

When he smiles, damn, when he smiles, when his lips slightly move to dance, I feel sweat driblets cascade down my legs and create puddles of lust-induced hope all around me. False hope. I know he's unavailable, for a relationship anyway. Let me break it down for you: Lee and his wife are both strippers. She strips in a local gentleman's club that is rather popular among men in neighboring states. Her Latin American look is hotter than J. Lo standing on the red carpet in that green Versace dress that made headlines all over the world.

Lee strips in nightclubs where gay men go, in and around Rhode Island. Why, you ask? Never heard of straight men dancing in gay clubs? Welcome to my world, the real world: married men sexing it up with guys. There are a lot of duplicitous people out there.

It's called on the "Down Low." Doing the ultimate no-no, according to Leviticus 18: 22. This is the same book that says you're not to eat shrimp or pig, three pages back. Leviticus 11: the pig...is unclean for you. You must not eat their meat or touch their carcasses...all creatures in the seas or streams that do not have fins and scales...you are to detest...you must not eat their meat and you must detest their carcasses. Then again, why follow a book riddled with hypocrisy, or a God whose followings are based upon it? I stopped right after that night, that night I heard a faint whisper pierce the night sky, telling me Jesus saves those who save themselves.

God is conditional love.

We've got roughly eight minutes before he walks through the doors, and I'm sure you're burning to know how we met, right? Oh, come on, you know you want to. It was three months ago, when the sun blazed across the sky, gays celebrated pride, and I started on summer vacation. Toxic, a straight club turned gay Thursday during Boston's pride week, is where I saw him.

This particular night I went alone; my straight buddies don't know what I engage in. Secrets. I like secrets. Life would be boring without secrets, don't you think? I am entitled to a private life. It's bad enough God meddles in my business. So get off my back.

I got there, and a patch of shirtless boys stood in front of the velvet rope, hands in the air, hoping their looks were enough to get them through the gates of heaven. The clear night sky with stars hid behind a thick wall of clouds, a dark gray wall of clouds roaring thunderously. I felt it—a chilling wind, tenderly, gnawingly nipping my skin. I took my tank top off, maneuvered my way through the boys, confident that my Indian bone structure, my Latino skin complexion, my Italian jet-black hair and muscular physique would get me waved through.

Gay clubs are a peculiar place, quite different than straight bars. Whoever heard of having to take your shirt off to get in a nightclub? This is something that gays do and straights don't. Usually, you can't wear jeans or sneakers or any type of clothing that's not considered presentable. Here, you can pretty much walk naked and that'll get you in. Strange. Long are the days of Studio 54. Okay, so they did a ton of drugs and had wild sex and STDs ran rampant, but at least they did it with class. Hmm, I just had a thought, a picture image. I'm going to tell you, so relax. You know those rooms that were in the basement of Studio 54? Picture it: the door crept open, the empty cement floor, Lee up against the wall, and me between his legs, looking up at those piercing brown eyes blinking in ecstasy. Just a thought. Nice one, though.

I got in, of course. I'm August. Hot.

The music escalated with each footfall I made to the dance floor. Soapsuds were falling on people's heads like snowflakes falling on a rooftop. Can someone please explain this to me? Why soapsuds in a nightclub? After you spend hours getting dressed and doing your hair, you come out to a club to have it all ruined? I don't get it.

There's something arousing, though, about nightclubbing in gay establishments. It's more than watching hot flesh pressed against hot flesh. It's journeying to a forbidden habitat, a place where rules are nonexistent, a place where I can go without politically correct friends telling me I'm stupid because I like being surrounded by beautiful people. Since when has appreciating beauty become so terrible? We've gotten off track; lost focus on the important things. Embrace it. Acknowledge it. Pretty people are like Michelangelo's *Creation of Adam*: rare, exceptional, priceless.

By the way, right now? It's seven past six; he should be arriving soon.

My eyes aimlessly ran around the warehouse-sized room: laser lights shooting red and green fluorescent; half-naked guys grinding and groping, packed the dance floor; go-go boys in lifeguard attire paraded around on platforms, four of them sat in lifeguard chairs each in a corner of the dance floor—the theme was Sex on the Beach.

I saw Scott walking through the back room entranceway. Scott. Let me tell you a little secret about Scott: he's gay—if that's not the understatement of the year. Came out to his mother at fourteen, told his friends at fifteen, and claims we had sex when I was sixteen. The fact that it's possible still worries me. Don't let your mind wander, he's just a friend. He'd like to be more, though. He's on the hunt for a relationship, any relationship. I hate that word. Think it has something to do with his lack of self. See, that's the difference between him and me. For me it's about having fun: no ties, no façade, no bullshit conversation.

Scott's eyes were locked on some twink's behind; his hands tucked deep inside. Following him was not an option. I don't much enjoy having to clean my sneakers from sticky stuff or having some guy unzip my pants without asking. Not my kind of fun. A text message will suffice.

When you're done hooking, come find me.

Lee's faint-colored skin caught my attention. His legs, his calves, those well-defined, hairy calves are indescribable. My eyes could clock those calves in the middle of Grand Central Terminal during rush hour. His butt gyrated to the beat; his calves sat like two cliffs resting on the ocean shore. His brown eyes bored into mine. It was the moment of truth. He grinned. I smirked. Same thing. Tweeted-out twinkies were awed by the lightning show flashing through the windows that rain banged on, overpowering and distracting us with music of its own. He climbed down the lifeguard chair and trundled to the back room, peeking at me through the crowd.

Lee is not for you.

It appeared across my phone. It wasn't Scott messaging back. It was an unknown sender text messaging me. I scanned the room again. Lee was gone; Scott was busy. I took heed of a fellow gym buddy I'd seen a few times, a man I'd not paid much attention to—his muscles didn't bulge. His laugh lines were dancing; his arms were swinging; his stiff legs were robotic. Not exactly an Alvin Ailey graduate. I left. Why stay? I'd get to meet Lee at the gym, a far better place to exchange interest and find out the real deal. Right? Okay then.

And here he is. 6:10 just like I told you. Ever see calves like that? Jolting like waves breaking on the ocean floor. And that ass.

I almost dropped the bar the first time he spotted me benching. You'd have done the same thing. My eyes peeking up his shorts, noticing he had no underwear on. Lightning struck the dumpster in the gym parking lot. The air tightened, stiffened around me, thickly pumped my lungs, my skull's vessels with harrowing images.

A fantasy I view as nothing more.

"He's not for you," Scott whispered in my ear, sneaking up from behind me.

"Asshole," I said, jumping. Scott plays on my teenage crush, yet he's a kid himself. Freckles still on his pale cheeks; pimples on his forehead. Hair doesn't even grow underneath his armpits. At twenty-nine, you'd think he'd have developed out of adolescence. Scott is my one gay friend. Oh, and he knows about that text message.

"The least you could do is show a little sympathy."

"When you pick a side."

"Not submitting to society's need for labels," I said.

"I'll leave you to your wet dreams," Scott said sardonically, patting my forehead with his towel.

Lee consumed my sleep since that evening, along with those five words: the same two dreams every other night, waking with creamed shorts every other morning. The mornings without wet shorts, I awake to thin scratch marks on my neck and chest. Pain fills my mind far more than my body. Three months of torture and pleasure were wearing me thin. Three months of needing to get laid, despite my frequent hookups with Karen Stoahoyic. This is for all the women of the world: sometimes guys don't care about hitting the 'G-spot'. We just want to get ours. If I were concerned with a chick's orgasm, I'd get married. Not going to happen.

Look at him: Lee, not Scott. Always in the mirror, always peeking out to see who's watching. He takes voyeurism to a higher level. Lee loves to show off his chest, his butt, but mostly he loves to show off his stomach. No matter who's around, whether or not there's a mirror, the shirt comes up and the abs get flexed. What a sight it is, too. He told me one reason he agreed to marry his wife was because he knew it would make him more attractive to guys. How sick is that? I thought I was vain. Maybe we're both just insecure. Anything's possible.

"Working tonight?" I asked Lee, peering over at him racking the leg press machine, on my way to do squats.

"Yup," he muttered, "at Toxic. The wife'll be here."

"Cool," I said flatly, gesturing him to come spot me.

Those calves rubbing mine, our arms intertwined, hands gripping the bar, my butt locked in his crotch like a piece in a puzzle. We squat gingerly. Rain pellets fall from the purplish sky. Darkness leaks through the windows, wind through the cracks. Water drips from the ceiling. Buckets were already in place. Our gym is set in an old warehouse. It needs much repair work. Only $200.00 a year, how can you go wrong?

My phone vibrates on the floor rhythmically to the drumming pellets. How do you answer the phone when you're in a situation like the one I'm in at this very moment? You don't. No way. This feels too good. Not…going…anywhere. Just like when I toss and turn in bed, and my erection rubs the sheets.

Yeah…that's it. Do it. Go ahead. God yes…
…GOD, YES…OH…GOD…GOD…
…NOT…YET…LEE…IS…NOT…GOD…YES!

She's on the treadmill watching. Her name's as mysterious as her voice. But her eyes say so much. She likes to watch, to watch us chase the impossible, the inevitable. It fascinates me how married people's sex lives change once they're no longer single. Does it dwindle or does it just vanish? The disconnect is visible: flirting takes place less than when single, words of lust are trapped under years of marriage, rapid boiling passion simmers to a calm. It's evident what year she and Lee are in, in their marriage. Remind me to thank Scott. You're really asking me why? He's the one who made me realize the purpose of marriage, and that purpose doesn't fill my life, a life with drama. I can turn on *Days of our Lives* for that.

He is not for you.

Those five words linger on my phone again, like blood stained on a shirt. It leaves a chilling effect in my skull, pounding the walls of my mind. What, or rather who was it? The locker room's empty. Lee's by my side changing; his wife's still walking on the treadmill. Scott? Can't be. Not his style. Scott loves to play, but he's not one for playing sadistically. It was ignorable the first time, but now it's infuriating. A stalker? Naw.

Ever wonder what it's like to be stalked? Like when you watch those Lifetime movies and a woman runs through the dark park with a broken shoe heel or ankle being chased? Someone write Hollywood a letter: Let's see the villain be a woman chasing Charles Bronson or Steven Segal through the park. The time has come.

It's in the air again, and close, closer than the scratched-up yellow lockers, closer than Lee's glutes that just bumped me. Untouchable. Invisible. Like Lee's scent permeating the air, yet forceful. Digging into my sweaty skin, climbing into my heart, my soul. Wrapped around Lee like a vine twisting and coiling, slithering up a tree. Achingly suffocating my thoughts, my heart, my soul. So close. So inviting. Touch it. Feel it. Push it.

Love?

It is love. Has to be love. Love's manipulating my mind, our hope, our togetherness. Don't it have a nerve? Its moral authority will not prevail. It's not ruining my birthday. Who needs it? All it does is take the heat, the rawness out of sex. Create havoc in people's lives. Does it really matter, anyway? Love. It doesn't, it really doesn't matter at all, not anymore. It's suicide.

"Look at the little muscle," Lee joked, squeezing my bicep. "See ya later?" he asked, heading toward the entranceway.

Smiling uncontrollably, I asked, "You get me anything?"

"You'll see tonight." Lee said, tittering, walking out.

"Tonight?" Scott said, half question, half answer, entering the locker room. "Oh, brother." Ain't he nosy?

"See ya there," I said, following Lee.

My eyelids blink to pitch-black, sweat beads roll down my cheek. I hear a voice this time around, a voice not that of Lee, a hollowing roar in between his moans and groans. Who needs God telling you what you can and cannot do? In my mind, always in my thoughts, persistently trying to chisel them away. The dream produces an erection, a few long scratches, one under my eyelid. Why does the voice make me cringe? And why is it in the room? So close. So inviting. Touch it. Feel it. Push it.

He's not for you.

Getting dressed is a project. Looking good doesn't come easy. No one just wakes up and looks like a GQ model. It takes time and preparation. And with this heat wave, I get nasty. Get your mind out of the gutter. Nasty means bitchy. I'll never visit a tropical island. I'd rather vacay in Alaska. Still get the same stuff: tranquility, relaxation, beautiful scenery.

No thirtieth birthday party, decided against it. All it signifies is growing older—the start of crow's-feet in my eye's corners, and gray hairs in my goatee are reminder enough. Watching Lee, his presence, his naked torso, is what I consider to be a celebratory evening, a far better reason to throw a party. Besides, Scott is forfeiting the money for our trip to New York City to see *Rent* (my second time) this weekend. That's plenty.

All I want is Lee. How sappy is that? I sound like Mariah Carey's Christmas song 'All I Want For Christmas Is You.' Let's make it Rod Stewart's 'Tonight's The Night.' Janet Jackson's version is a bit more likeable, though. She sings about a guy and a girl, right up my alley. I'm going off on a tangent. Sorry.

It's the bottom of the hour and it's back, again. I feel it. It's in line with me. It's in the cold, misty air, digging into my shivering skin. Poking at my desire, my urge to touch, to free Lee. Caressing my ears softly, gently whispering icy no-nos.

Talk about harassment.

My wish, my one wish I made an hour ago is disappearing with each footfall—the air is nibbling at it feverishly, gnawing at my images of Lee, producing depictions of disparity. I smash the thoughts like a broken heart. Not corrupting my mind.

I am so ready, so sure Lee is ready.

Clusters of naked torsos form a ring around the dance floor. Music hits my mind's walls, trapped in the corners, trying to disrupt my hunt for Lee standing on a platform surrounded with gay boys: sucking face, snorting out of vials, unzipping and sliding hands deep inside pants. Damn he looks good. Those white trunks I could peel off with my teeth. Those calves are getting me going. That butt I could play with like a dog and a tennis ball. I trundle to the bar, keeping Lee in sight, keeping his eyes on me.

HE'S NOT FOR YOU!

Who keeps doing that? I scan the place—full of pretty boys unable to grab my attention, unable to provoke what Lee is able to: to get beneath the trenches of it all—for the first time frightened. Wondering what will happen in fifteen minutes. Something in the Blue Moon is upsetting my stomach, causing it to revolt, to ascend in my throat. Not fear. Not sanctity. Not the hairy, rugged man parading his fingertips over my nipple. His touch feels good, actually. Might just let him touch me there. Maybe not. Maybe the E Lee gave me in the parking lot of the gym isn't agreeing with my stomach.

Here he comes, down off the box, trundling through a circle of boys inside the ring, towards me. My stomach trudging up my throat, I swallow hard, tasting a dark, gory matter slither down the outer lining, soothing the eruption deep below my stomach. I can hear the sounds, the paranoid rhythm my stomach belts out over the music.

It's waiting for me, waiting for me to fail, to fall. It hung above my head outside, now it swirls in my toxic blood. Tainted with an unknown substance. Tickling my bones, my organs, seeping through to my skin. I need to bypass this monumental grotesque joke being played on me. Let's celebrate. I deserve him. Ached for him long enough. Begged God for him. Wanted him all for myself, for keeps, to walk secretly, accompanied only by birds chirping and trees swaying.

Never let your dreams muscle out.

Lee pulls my head close, tight to his face. His fiery lips base upon mine. Ouch. I'm ready. Almost. It shoots back up my throat, and Lee looks…Divine. This is one of those times in life when an image is sketched in your mind's eye. You know, like your first kiss, the first time you make love, the first time you ask God to rid your mind of demons, despite his unfulfilled presence.

Lee's eyes boring into me, his body warm, moist, sensually firm against mine, rocking to the music. In his eyes, I see it—buried far beneath those erotic brown pupils, staring at me intently, searchingly, pulling me in hypnotically. Destiny. Destiny lights up the corners with a fatal mirage. It's funny how life plays tricks on the mind. Educates the mind. In a microscopic way I know it's over.

The floor vibrates erratically, hiding my quivering skin; my blood gassed with the strange and sickeningly sweet toxin, pumping through my vessels at my lungs, pricking my skin. My mouth cracks up into a smile. I'm ready. And he knows it.

He clasps his hand in mine, and whispers, "Happy Birthday." The rain trickling down the windowpanes, the invisible nobodies all around, the pain drowning in it, feels wonderful, an electronic drowsiness flooding through me like a fine vintage red wine.

We trundle to the back room. Scott is here, his hands on the back of some boy's head, crouched down in between his legs, pleasuring him. He smiles, looking at me quizzically, sympathetically, flicking his gaze away. No Happy Birthday? No over the hill cracks? What's his problem? I step over and slip him my last hit of E.

Lee leads me to the back, our footfalls in line. Music fades and thunder escalates, ending at the end, hidden behind a column. Falling into the cement wall, pulling me in, Lee pushes me down. I undo his pants, rubbing my hands over his crotch, peering up at him: red eyes surrounded by a black cast, his teeth long and sharp, his lips dripping saliva, and I wonder how long before Scott follows. He turns thirty tomorrow.

Licensed Outlaws

by Sebastian Stockman

"[Y]ou know, Bluegrass is always held to be like this sacred purity of country music and roots — and it is, for sure — but Bill fielded the question of whether he thought Elvis had ruined his bluegrass. This was from a journalist who was holding Bill in very high esteem, and he said, 'Mr. Monroe, do you think Elvis ruined your song, Blue Moon of Kentucky?'
"And Bill said, 'No sir, them were powerful checks.'"
— Peter Rowan, on NPR's Fresh Air, Nov 24, 2010

*I*n *Outlaw: Waylon, Willie, Kris, and The Renegades of Nashville*, Michael Streissguth is on the authenticity trail. He wants to find it in the guise of the country-music "Outlaw." Specifically, he wants to track "the outlaw paths of Waylon [Jennings], Willie [Nelson], and Kris [Kristofferson] from their arrival in Nashville in the 1960s up through the 1970s, the decade of the outlaw movement."

Setting aside for a moment that the outlaw "movement" these singers and others were purportedly part of was largely a mid-70s marketing niche, Streissguth strains to position this movement as the outgrowth of a coherent artistic stance. And he doesn't stop there. He stretches this argument even further in arguing that the "Outlaw Movement" was of a piece with other significant cultural movements of those decades. Specifically, he wants to examine the way his title characters and a handful of others "have in common their coming of age against the canvas of Nashville's wildly clashing notions about race, education, lifestyle, urban renewal, war, gender, corporate influence, and government interference, [phew!] which sorted the outlaws — musical and otherwise — from the accommodationists." That "otherwise" lands Streissguth deep in the weeds.

Let's take a look. Watch how Streissguth stretches a baggy-but-workable definition of Texas music into the type of hopeless argumentative overreach that characterizes much of his book:

"Indeed, the Texas brand of country music traditionally blended honky-tonk, western swing, and the blues, and was now adding rock elements and ethos," he writes. That's accurate, if anodyne, but the sentence is not over. These elements were added, Streissguth claims, "in a way that recalled favorite son Lyndon B. Johnson's pragmatic negotiations with black America's inevitable push for civil rights."

We might let this pass as clumsy period-setting, a ham-handed attempt to evoke the musicians' milieu, but it's worse than that. The passage purports to describe Texas music at the time Willie Nelson *left* Nashville to return to his home state, in 1970. As an evocation of the period, the sentence fails: In 1970, the out-to-pasture LBJ was no one's favorite, and the Voting Rights and Civil Rights Acts were five and six years old, respectively. The musical analysis is broad. So the honky-tonk, western swing blues blend was "now adding rock elements and ethos?" Whose elements? Buddy Holly's? Led Zeppelin's? What did this new amalgam sound like? Even if we grant, as sociocultural criticism, for argument's sake, that there was something both "pragmatic" and "inevitable" about Texas music's absorption of rock's "elements and ethos," it is not at all clear in what "way" this was like the Voting Rights Act. (Also, who in this scenario is Texas music's LBJ? Willie Nelson? Actually, I'd watch that movie.)

The notion that white musicians' appropriation of rhythm and blues tropes is a kind of civil rights activism is one to which Streissguth seems curiously attached. The notion isn't inarguable, but it does need to be argued. One can't just assert it the way Streissguth does in an attempt to evoke the musical landscape Waylon Jennings faced as he started out in west Texas: "Rising stars Elvis Presley and Carl Perkins had integrated a world that Jim Crow laws couldn't touch, incorporating elements of black rhythm and blues into their beloved hillbilly music." That's one reading. Cooption, thievery, artistic appropriation: the incorporation of rhythm and blues elements by Elvis and others into their own songs has been called many things. Seldom, if ever, has it been hailed as a form of activism.

A self-congratulatory capsule history of Nashville's "outlaws" would sketch out a Texas invasion of the Nashville music establishment, wherein bearded, shabbily-dressed long-hairs showed up with guitars, scandalized clean-shaven Music Row executives, and liberated country music from its "Nashville Sound" prison of pop-radio-friendly orchestral arrangements. This return to authenticity by way of a back-to-the-roots insurgency against the current era's chart-toppers is a perennial cycle in pop culture, but it's especially persistent in country music. One of the genre's great topics is nostalgia: Things Ain't What They Used to Be. Nicely representative are these two lines (and the title) from Waylon Jennings' "Bob Wills is Still the King": "I can still remember the way things were back then/ In spite of all the hard times, I'd do it all again." Things were hard, but also somehow better then. And, anyway, didn't we have fun?

This self-mythologizing is integral to the genre. But the truth is of course more complicated, and it's problematic for a historian to try to build his argument with these creative myths as his foundation. The main problem in this book is that Streissguth has appropriated his subjects' tendency toward mythmaking. He makes claims for the music and the musicians that the facts cannot support. In the process he passes over a more interesting story.

Streissguth's title characters are compelling. Waylon Jennings loved pinball, parties, and cocaine — not necessarily in that order. Willie Nelson, the clean-cut songwriter of Patsy Cline's "Crazy", reinvented himself as America's hirsute, road-loving, pot-smoking uncle. And Kris Kristofferson was a football-playing Rhodes Scholar and Air Force captain who turned down a faculty appointment at West Point for a series of odd jobs in Nashville and the chance to make it as a songwriter.

One of those jobs had Kristofferson flying a helicopter to shuttle workers onto and off of oil derricks in the Gulf of Mexico. According to a story in *Outlaw*, Kristofferson wrote "Me and Bobby McGee" on one of these sojourns. But Streissguth renders the most famous Kristofferson helicopter story thusly: "And according to a story that [Johnny] Cash told, and would have to be dismissed as apocryphal if only Kristofferson himself hadn't confirmed it in later years, the maverick songwriter rented a helicopter, landed it outside Cash's home in Hendersonville, and delivered more demo tapes."

That "more" is telling, as is the way Streissguth introduces the story. We have just been told that, while working as a janitor at Columbia, Kristofferson "had slipped demo tapes and lyrics sheets to Cash..." which is why the helicopter stunt had to involve the delivery of "more" tapes. This story hardly passes the smell test. Cash's assertion would "have to be dismissed as apocryphal" if not

for Kristofferson's confirmation? According to the end notes, Streissguth interviewed Kristofferson at least twice for this book, but
the "confirmation" is not sourced to one of these interviews — or
to anything in particular.

Let me pose an alternate theory: Kristofferson, known around
town as a talented songwriter desperate to be noticed (he'd given
up a tenure-track job, for goodness' sake), very well might have
pressed a demo tape on Cash with one hand while holding a mop
in the other. Let's also stipulate that folks around town knew the
Air Force vet sometimes took on piloting gigs for extra money —
certainly an unusual odd job for an aspiring songwriter. Isn't it just
as likely that Cash — in mid-career, after the apogee of his fame in
the late-60s/early-70s, before his Rick Rubin-produced resurgence
in the 1990s — might have, with a storyteller's exaggeration, braid-
ed together several of these strands and arrived at a pleasing tall
tale that reflected well on both parties? Not only does this fable
confirm Kristofferson as the plucky and imaginative iconoclast
his fans want him to be, it cements Cash as the benevolent elder
statesman of the Nashville establishment who both recognized talent when he heard it (he recorded dozens of Kristofferson's songs)
and was also pretty laid back about helicopter landing-skid marks
in his yard. For Kristofferson, what is the margin in contradicting
Cash's story? A man who once quoted William Blake to Jay Leno
on "The Tonight Show" is surely not above a little self-mythologizing. Not to mention that, in the song he wrote "about" Johnny Cash (I put "about in quotes here because Kristofferson has at
various times also claimed to have written the song about Dennis
Hopper and the session musician Donnie Fritts, among a slew of
others), "The Pilgrim/Chapter 33," the title character is "a walking
contradiction/partly truth and partly fiction."

Cash looms over *Outlaw*. Streissguth's previous book was
Johnny Cash: The Biography (this reader would have preferred the

indefinite article), so he knows what a complicated and compelling figure Cash is. But even in Streissguth's amorphous formulation, Cash can't be an "outlaw". Well-established in Nashville by the time Kristofferson and the other title characters hit town, Cash — prison concerts notwithstanding — was at least as much an establishment figure as a countercultural one. After all, here we have a man who writes in his autobiography of how he was hanging out with Billy Graham in the wake of Watergate and they got the idea to place a consolatory call to Richard Nixon, who they figured would be feeling pretty low after his resignation.

Cash's stance as an avatar of empathy — whether for beleaguered inmates or disgraced ex-Presidents — may be the most remarkable thing about him. Cash at his height was a sort of establishmentarian iconoclast. His ability to be all things to all people while seeming to remain his own man is almost perfectly distilled in this stage patter from a Madison Square Garden concert in December, 1969 (The album, *Live at Madison Square Garden*, wasn't released until 2002):

"Everywhere we go these days it seems like, that, all of a sudden, reporters and people that ask us questions, ask us questions about things that they didn't used to ask. ... [T]hey say things like, 'how do you feel about the Vietnam situation, the war in Vietnam?'"

Translation: Your simple singer of songs has been forced to deal with the issues of this world.

"I'll tell you exactly how I feel about it. This past January ... we went to Long Binh Air Force Base near Saigon. And a reporter friend of mine asked, 'That makes you a hawk, doesn't it?' And I said, 'No that don't make me a hawk, no. No that don't make me a hawk.' But I said, 'If you watch the helicopters bring in the wounded boys, and then you go into the wards and sing for 'em and try do your best to cheer 'em up, so that they can get back home, it might make you a dove with claws.'"

A dove with claws! What a way to split the baby! Who can argue with a man of peace who's not afraid to defend himself?

Another Clintonian rhetorical flourish from Cash can be found late in *Outlaw*, when Streissguth quotes the Man in Black on the 1976 election:

"Now, Jimmy Carter — some of those who say they're voting for him are doing it because they believe what he believes. ... and some of them are voting for him because he believes in something. Whether they do or not they're voting for him because he believes in something."

This is non-endorsement dressed up as conviction, but Streissguth deploys the quote as evidence that "Nashville had found its alternative to Richard Nixon." Once again, Streissguth's straining for a clear narrative line leads him to simplify — and render less interesting — a complicated story.

"Johnny Cash forced change on country music," Streissguth writes. This is true, but it's not quite the kind of change Streissguth has set out to explore in this book. Cash was more of an influence on the subjects of Outlaws than he was one of them. Yet Streissguth wants to draw on Cash's cultural influence in order to make his brief for this book, which is why he spends a good bit of effort telling readers about "*The Johnny Cash Show.*"

On this primetime variety hour that premiered on ABC in 1969, Cash hosted not just country-music luminaries but Bob Dylan and Joni Mitchell (both on the show's debut episode), Neil Young and Louis Armstrong. This eclecticism helped reinforce Cash's reputation as his own man, musically. Here's what Streissguth says it did: "In effect, Cash and his TV show had joined the civil rights heroes of earlier in the decade in communicating to America that the 1960s lived in Nashville." Streissguth foreshadows this breathtaking equivalence earlier in the book when he calls Diane Nash and John Lewis — organizers of Nashville's lunch-counter sit-ins, founders of SNCC, icons of the civil rights movement — "the city's first outlaws." Streissguth doesn't qualify this claim, he doubles down on it: "...Nashville had exported to America the integration of public accommodations ... and *The Johnny Cash Show*. And that had to be worth something."

I suppose it depends on who's doing the accounting.

Speaking of accounting, one thing that's so often missing in music writing is the notion of musicians not only as artists but as businessmen, casting about for a hit, trying to make money. Mammon and The Muses are ever at odds. This notion of artistic authenticity as necessarily separate from commercial concerns leads us too often to a Scooby-Doo version of cultural production. In that story we have Chet Atkins, scandalized by the long hair of Willie, Waylon and Kris, standing in the wings at the Grand Ole Opry, shaking his first at "those darn outlaws."

Atkins is the legendary country guitarist who eventually rose to the head of RCA-Nashville and whom Streissguth strains to cast as the villain in this story. Willie Nelson was unhappy with the way RCA promoted his records (are artists ever happy with their label's support?), so he left. Meanwhile Atkins and Waylon Jennings had fights over various aspects of creative control — would Waylon get to use his band, or did he have to use the RCA session players?

It's OK to stifle a yawn at this point. This sort of recording minutiae is not that interesting even to many of us rabid Waylon fans. But this also seriously undercuts the book's argument. If this is what the "renegades of Nashville" were fighting against, it trivializes the civil rights comparisons Streissguth has been making.

It wasn't that Atkins and his cronies just hated those long-hairs with their irreverent lyrics, it's that they had a good idea of what had been working — the big pop-string arrangements of the Nashville Sound — and wanted to deliver more of the same. That was the job.

The singer-songwriter Rodney Crowell told Streissguth as much. When he first came to town Crowell was signed to a publishing company that Atkins co-owned, "[a]nd I think it probably was just that Kristofferson had made it," Crowell said "so that Harry Warner and Jerry Reed *and* [emphasis his] Chet Atkins recognized that 'this kid, he's got some of that.' ... They scratched their chins and were like, 'Oh, okay, I don't get it, but keep the songs coming. Show up every once in a while.'"

This is exactly right. Atkins and co. were not fusty old stuffed shirts, bristling at the new stuff, unwilling to have their minds blown. They just didn't think they could sell the new stuff. But, like A&R men everywhere, once something got through, they started looking for copycats. Once the suits were convinced the stuff would sell they were on board, and not subtly. Witness "Wanted! The Outlaws," a 1976 RCA concoction that threw together recordings by Waylon, Tompall Glaser and Jessi Colter, along with some old Willie Nelson tunes the studio still owned. Damn! This "movement" instigated by the "renegades of Nashville" co-opted by the man? Streissguth is nonplussed. He tells us that Waylon "had always known that even the outlaw bit was nothing more than another way to sell country music and soon it would be replaced by another hook." This assertion, coming late in the narrative, prompts a number of existential questions in the reader, not least of which is "Why am I here at the end of this book?"

The thing is, there's an interesting story in the material Streissguth has amassed, including his interviews with the clear-eyed Crowell and some acute and prescient observations from the art critic Dave Hickey, whose 1974 *Country Music* article "In Defense of the Telecaster Cowboy Outlaws" was influential in naming the genre.

Streissguth sometimes acknowledges that the history he's telling is mined with myth and legend and just-so stories, but he doesn't do anything with that knowledge. Instead we get empty assertions such as "[y]outh culture was afoot in the western world and Kris symbolized Nashville's contribution to it."

A more interesting book would have interrogated these myths, placing into direct conversation the sentiments Streissguth uses as epigraphs to successive chapters. The first is from singer-songwriter Mickey Newbury: "Nashville's a great place to be right now — like Paris in the twenties — a place where you can get together with people and rap." The second is from the Jewish country singer-cum-mystery-novelist-cum-Texas-gubernatorial-candidate Kinky Friedman — who, with his songs "They Ain't Makin' Jews Like Jesus Anymore" and "Rapid City, South Dakota" (which he described as the only pro-choice country song), actually was a Nashville outsider, one whose songs were never played on country radio.

Anyway, Kinky said: "Paris of the thirties my ass, it was one big con."

A Borrowed Copy
of Ben Fountain's
Brief Encounters

by Eric Anderson

A flutter in the governing hand, and an eleventh finger
extending from the other, uncovering

an upper register, automatic and after, apex plus, *A flat, A flat, E.*
Fountain's *Fantasy.* Uncanny temperament a la

minor arcana. Criticized offhandedly as merely voyeuristic
embellishment. *Polydactyly doesn't happen every. . .* et cetera.

The pianist in transit, pianist in a train, practicing the 19th century
on a crude keypad, Schumann, etude, alien *organa.*

Perfectly wooing, yes, but it's the chicken scratch that taps
into fantastic mess, marginalia moving me to refuse to return

this collection to whoever:
~~Lucy~~ writing ~~Timothy~~, circa 2008,

*Keep the commuter pass, the envelope of notes, receipts, leave me
out of any emails, posts, keep Fantasy, keep Faith, and my flaky
tartlets on your tongue, I've taped the extra apartment key behind
Ben's bio.*

Five-Finger Discount

by Dwight Livingstone Curtis

It was a hot day and they drove out along the Ottauquechee, the two of them sitting up on the pollen-yellow roof of the Volvo with their legs through the sunroof, kicking the headrests and reaching out for tree branches. When they hit pavement the car swayed on its soft springs and Peter's dad pressed the gas. They clamped their feet around the headrests and tipped back, and as Peter's dad hugged the shoulder coming around the bend in the river they reached out and tore off fistfuls of maple leaves.

The ropeswing was off the side of a dirt stretch of the road, down a steep mud bank, and to get down to it they'd have to scramble on their backs, sliding on their heels from root to root, and then Daniel would wade in. Just before the water got to his balls, he'd freeze for a second, tense, and then whoop and dive forward into the river. He'd swim to the sun line and tread water and then all at once kick up and reach for the stringy little tail end of the rope, a frayed scrap line tied like a kitetail to the bulging grapefruit knot at the bottom. When he got it he'd hang there for a second, feeling the whole rope wobble and sway sixty feet up, letting his joints fill up with air, and then swing it back and forth, arcing his whole body and kicking himself up so it was just his hips and legs in the water, and then jerk down and whip the whole bucking rope up to shore for Peter, who'd hang tight off a root, reaching out with one hand.

Today when they drove up there were two teenagers on the bank, shirtless and shiny wet. One of them held the rope, leaning back with his feet planted wide, braced against the weight. He had on black basketball shorts and white boxers, which puffed out over the side of his shorts. The other one was wearing sunset colored board shorts, so low that his pubes fuzzed out through the drawstrings. He had his hand on the trunk of the big tree. Daniel had on a dark blue bathing suit with itchy mesh that now he saw made his legs and stomach look white.

Daniel and Peter crept down from the roof of the Volvo, their backs stained yellow, stepping softly on the rearview mirror and swinging down from the roof rack. Daniel hadn't ever realized you could climb the ropeswing tree, but now he saw that there were little footholds nailed all up its trunk. The guy in board shorts began climbing them two at a time. He had on fat white high tops with the laces untied and water dripped off the ends of the laces as he climbed. His friend with the rope whipped it up and down, sending waves rippling along the rope and up into the leaves.

Daniel backed up against a smaller tree and gently bumped his funny bone. "Fuck," he whispered. Peter had left his flip-flops at the top of the bank and was lowering himself down the muddy rocks, glancing over his shoulder to make sure he was right in everyone's way. The guy in the boxers stared out at nothing and pumped the rope up and down, with his other hand down the front of his shorts. The guy in the board shorts had disappeared up the trunk into the leaves. Daniel cradled his elbow.

From up in the tree a voice said, "I think I'm good."

Daniel stretched out his fingers and a tingle washed over him. He shuddered and leaned against the tree and curled his toes in the dirt. He had to shit, or drink some water, or something. Peter was twenty feet down, hunched in the low rocks down the bank, staring up at the tree. They must be seventeen? Eighteen? The two guys hadn't glanced their way since they got out of the car. Were they pissed? Daniel shuddered again and felt a tremor building in his wrists, which he washed out by swiveling them in their sockets. It moved to his neck and he rolled his head in a circle. Daniel would be, pissed. Four was too many for this little spot. Five, with Peter's dad reading the newspaper in the car. And Peter crouching like an asshole right where they probably wanted to swing. Daniel glared at him, but Peter's eyes were locked on the tree. Daniel held out his thumb and closed one eye.

The guy in boxers stood wide-legged in the dirt above the jumping rocks, nearly in the street, and leaned against the weight of the rope. He went up on his tiptoes, took a quick step forward, and then a couple of steps closer to the tree, moving at a lean. Daniel pressed, tingling, against the rough trunk of a tree. His bathing suit looked frumpy. Up in the tree a branch shifted and a shower of drips glinted down.

He pictured a sharp branch sticking up exactly level with the water. He'd swing out and grab his ankles in the air and break the surface of the water, skewering himself along the branch right between the knobs of his jackknifed knee. Right between the muscle and bone, all the way up to his hip. He wouldn't even sink, just ragdoll off the branch as the whole submerged tree groaned and finally rolled him underwater. Daniel shivered and clenched his tingling kneecaps and sunk half an inch against the bark of the tree, scratching himself in sharp little stripes that heated into an itch. He pressed into the little points, rolling his shoulder blades to even out the prickling sensation, to make it symmetrical across the skin of his back.

The guy in boxers stood at the base of the tree, hanging onto a nailed-in foothold with his arms outstretched, and he had ahold of the rope by the butt of the knot. He started swinging the rope side to side like a jump rope and then swung it hard around and it flopped lengthwise over the trunk of the tree. Up in the leaves it tightened, and when the guy below let go of the free end it swung out on a shortened arc.

Daniel had never seen anyone holding that part of the rope before. For thirty feet it hung slack and vulnerable, where it would have been outmuscling Daniel, bucking and yanking as he scrambled root to root up the bank. At the tightest moments, outstretched like a cross as he climbed, he'd feel half-gravity, the rope like a living thing trying to pluck him off the bank and fling him out into the river. This was a different rope: tame, purring from a soft belly up in the leaves, shuddering down in jerks and ripples that dead-ended into the knot, whipping the kitetail in tight circles.

What if, as he swung, the wind whipped the little kitetail around his ankle, got a wrap in it, and just as he let go the wrap caught on itself and clung? He'd jerk back, and for a moment everything would go slack as he freefell. Then he'd hit the edge of the arc and start swinging, head down, arms forced overhead by his momentum. Would he be able to crunch up and grab hold of the rope, and just barely keep his head above the low rocks? And punch flat against the sloped dirt with the crack of a whole row of ribs? Could he hang low and cup his hands, open his mouth, and try to create enough drag in the water to slow his swing before the rocks? Or maybe everything would happen too fast, and the force would be too great, and he'd swing back in a half curl, reaching for his white ankle, only to collide ear-first with the highest of the low rocks, and spill out like a cracked egg into the yellow-green eddies of pollen.

Whenever he got up to swing, he'd let the rope spin out first, holding it up as high as he could reach and letting it hang out over the bank until it stopped twirling. He'd take the thin tail and hold it in his bottom hand against the fat rope, making a fishhook loop, which he'd rest against his thighs, the grapefruit knot knocking against his crotch. Then he'd swing out, lifting his knees on either side of the loop, and when he released he'd throw the whole loop hard around to his left with his bottom hand where it would unfurl out into nothing. Pissing Peter off to no end, as it came jerking back across the bank ten feet from shore.

The dripping from the tree had stopped and the rope danced, hooking and jerking in the open air above the rocks and the riverbank.

Daniel's head was where the investment was, according to his mother. His undiversified asset. It was protected by an eggshell.

If the person who woke up from the coma was wired differently than the person who fell into it, then that slightly different version would be an enemy of the real Daniel, who had worked so hard for his life up to this point and wasn't ready to give it up to some ungrateful post-accident version of himself.

Daniel scrambled down to where Peter was standing at the water's edge and from there he could see the guy in the tree. He was standing on a thick limb, his board shorts hanging in perfect cylinders, holding the rope with one hand and steadying himself against a higher branch. He'd tied his sneakers. He shifted his feet, spreading his legs wider, pivoting his top foot across the branch and then along it. Daniel watched him lean back against the rope with one hand, then tug it, and high up in the tree a thicket of sunny leaves shuddered.

The kitetail kicked gently toward the far bank. The guy at the base of the tree had his hand down the front of his boxers. The fragmented sunlight made Daniel feel sick to his stomach. He pinched and pulled the mesh of his bathing suit and it prickled free from his ass.

Daniel's balls always tightened into shooter marbles as he stood vibrating on the high rock, braced against the egging of the rope, feet planted and ready to swing, an instant away from freefall. Every muscle hair-triggered, savoring that last shudder of anticipation one split second at a time. And then he'd lift off, and swing down, hurling the rope clear of his ankles, and reach back with one hand to grab his toes before ripping into the chilly river.

He squeezed out tingles from his toe joints, his ankles, his ass cheeks, his hips. He sponged them in as he inhaled, filling his lungs and feeling them uncrumple, and flexed the tingles out one joint and muscle at a time, chasing them around the limbs of his body. He exhaled as far as he could, and then even farther, hunched forward, wringing the air out of his body.

The high-up patch of leaves jumped in the sunlight and the big body came swinging out, fast. He was on a tight arc, swinging ahead of the knot, incredibly high up, his back arched and his knees cocked back. He swung high over the water and then just as he started to rise up out of the bottom of his swing he flung his hips forward and pulled up his knees and let go. The rope shuddered and slackened and pulled back and he grabbed his knees as he flipped, arced, peaked, and began to drop and then unfurled, his white sneakers emerging to smack soles-first against the flat water, way out in the middle where the sun lit up the current.

"Holy shit," Peter said. Neither of them reached for the rope, which came pulsing back at them a moment after the splash. They stood in the shade in their dry shorts, arms crossed tight. Then the swinger broke the surface of the water and shook out his hair like a dog, and lay back and floated on his back and whooped. He flopped over and swam, his sneakers plunking, and when he got to the rope he launched out of the water and grabbed it above the knot, arched and backswung it, his hips rising above the water, and slung it toward shore where his friend caught it easily halfway up the rocks.

Peter had his dad leave them at the edge of the parking lot with fifteen dollars for sandwiches. They padded across the hot dust barefoot until it turned into asphalt and Daniel kept his flip-flops in his hand, letting dirt coat his wet feet.

The door jangled. It was air-conditioned inside the store and Daniel's suit dripped onto his toes, liquefying some of the dirt. They were alone except for a woman sitting on a stool behind the register. Peter went into the aisles while Daniel looked at the menu board. She came over eventually and Daniel ordered. Then Peter came up to the front and Daniel went back into the aisles.

Soldiers got PTSD from war and it rewired their brains and messed up their chemistry and changed their personalities. It could happen to anyone after a traumatic experience. Could the same thing happen in a dream? What if Daniel had a dream so awful, so terrible and visceral and immediate, that it ravaged his brain like a car accident, and spent his neural pathways, and stung some folded, hidden part of his memory so deeply that he woke up wracked with phobia, unable to think or feel normally ever again?

In the small hardware section, hanging on a hook with no label, he found a clear plastic tube with three metal rods in it. They looked like what the dentist used to pick at the plaque on his teeth. Each point had a different shape: one curved, one elbowed, and one straight, and thin enough to fit through a buttonhole.

What if he couldn't even remember the dream? If he went to sleep tonight and woke up with a smoldering hole in his brain? A ghost operation by a ghost scalpel, and no clues to the operation except for some faint pattern to his mental shredding, some sickening network of phobias that might light up at any moment, like a flicked spiderweb?

At the front Peter had the sandwiches and a Cookies-N-Cream bar and a bag of apples on the counter. Daniel put down a Skor bar. She punched it into the register and it came out to $19.25.

"Do you have any cash?" Peter turned to Daniel and asked, eyes wide.

Daniel patted his butt where his wallet would go.

They looked down at the counter and then Peter took the two candy bars and put them aside. Daniel took the candy bars and bent at the waist and put them back on the candy rack.

She punched it in again and said, "Seventeen."

Peter put the cash on the counter and said, "We only have fifteen."

After a few seconds of silence, Peter took the apples and put them back. The woman rang up the sandwiches and put them in a bag and gave Peter the change. They walked out and the front door jangled and Peter stopped in the doorway and cupped his hands against the screen door and shouted "Yeah, thanks!" The parking lot was empty. Daniel took a deep breath and walked toward the road.

He imagined that there was a pebble in his mouth, lolling around between his teeth, resting in the depression of his fattest molar. If he flinched he'd bite the pebble and shatter his teeth. If he stayed calm, and relaxed his jaw, and ignored whatever Peter was doing, he could slowly exhale, and wring out the tingles, and settle down. Some mornings he woke up tight as a drum, breathing like a piston. He conjured the pebble and horseshoed it, clicking, along his gums, clenching and releasing until whatever it was started to boil off and he could hear and blink again. When he finally untwisted, he'd roll the pebble onto his tongue, make a tunnel around it, and fire it out.

Once they got out onto the main road, barely off the parking lot, Peter fished out his drawstrings. He'd tied a buck knife to the ends. The handle was textured plastic, meant to look like wood, with an eagle printed on it, and the blade was about three inches long with a little knob on it for your thumb. He handed it to Daniel. It locked when he opened it and Daniel freed it by pressing in on a little piece of metal on the back of the handle. He opened and closed it a couple of times. He tried the blade on his thumbnail.

"That was on my balls," Peter said.

Daniel dropped the knife in the dirt, and reached out, grabbing the corner of Peter's towel, and jerked it free from his waist. He wiped his hands with it and tossed it back at Peter's chest. "Check this out," he said, and handed Peter a brushed silver Zippo. Peter flicked and it lit.

"That was in my ass," Daniel said. Peter slapped it hard against Daniel's chest and it dropped in the dirt.

"Ouch. Fuck you," Daniel said. "What was up with the apples?"

Peter reached into his shorts and pulled out a Cookies-N-Cream bar. "I hid a bunch of stuff under the apples."

Daniel reached over and broke off a chunk of chocolate.

"I put another knife in there and some candy and stuff."

"And some chapstick?" Daniel asked. Peter looked up at him. "Yeah, some chapstick."

"I saw you picking it out," Daniel said, chewing. "Faggot." Peter stuffed the whole bar in his mouth and grabbed his towel off the ground. He started twisting an end into a rattail and Daniel leapt away.

"You sure you don't want to go back and get it?" Daniel asked from two parking spots pover. "Do you remember which one it was?"

"On the far left," Peter said. "Someone's going to buy it and be really confused."

They crossed the road and moved onto the shoulder so a car could pass. They climbed down to the low rocks and took out their sandwiches. Daniel opened the plastic tube and took out one of the tools. "Think we could pick a lock with this?" he asked.

"Jesus, man," Peter said.

When they got back to the ropeswing the older boys were gone.

Daniel stared at his big toe. There was a black band where the nail met the skin. It was bleeding under the nail, slowly, forming a bubble. It would grow out with the nail, and by that time the blood would have dried into a paste. Last night after dinner they'd gone out to the hot tub and Peter had leaned up against the side, with his dick against the jet, and they'd talked about girls. Falling asleep, Daniel had experienced a kind of zooming-in, as though he were flying forward microscopically into the backs of his own eyelids, faster and faster, and the feeling had gotten so intense that he'd had to open his eyes and sit up and crane his neck out over the matte black backyard, finally finding the low contrast of the treeline, to stop himself from puking.

Peter surfaced and flipped his hair and flopped onto his back, floating for a long time before reaching up and grabbing the rope. Daniel stood on the jumping rock, waiting, clenching his knees and hips, working out a tingle. It shuddered from one thigh across his ass and down his other thigh. He craned his head back, closed his eyes, and opened his mouth. Peter slung the rope up from the water and Daniel caught it.

He looped the kitetail and squared the heavy loop against his thighs, his dick tenting through his damp suit. Peter stood up in the shallows looking the other way, across the river, waiting. Daniel held up his thumb and closed one eye. He set his feet on the rock.

When he was little and first realized he'd been having nightmares that he didn't remember, he'd lie in the dark on the top bunk, eyes wide, ashamed to go to sleep. In class he'd yawn so hard that his hearing would black out and his eyes would clench shut and leak tears.

He wasn't sure what he was going to do with the rope. Throw it to the side, somehow. Peter was out of the water now and looking up at the road. There was gravel grinding and then a door slammed and a shadow, and Peter's dad jutted out over the rocks. Daniel fixed his grip and squinted at the water. He spotted where he thought he might land, out past the sun line, and then almost went, felt his feet get a little lighter on the rock, and exhaled and imagined it again, watching himself swing. He saw himself holding the rope, forced himself to let go, and then he tensed, and felt the floodgates open, all the chemicals sluice and prickle, and he shuddered. His fingers pulsed on the rope. Click click click. He horseshoed one way and then the other.

If they did this forever, eventually they'd wash the mud right out of the riverbank. The rocks would roll one by one into the shallows, leached out by the water they carried up in their dripping suits, and they'd tie on longer and longer ropes until the tree itself tipped sidelong into the river.

He mooshed his lips and sucked air through his teeth and made a tunnel out of his tongue. He let his head fall back so that his head bone rested on his neck bone and his Adam's apple crested in the breeze. He closed his eyes and took a full breath, held it for a second, and then opened his throat and fired the feeling of the pebble hard out into the air, over the rocks, past the shallows and into the slow bright water at the center of the river. He opened his eyes and saw where it had landed, squeezed the rope, leaned back, and lifted off.

Interlude: Yemen

by Effie-Michelle Metallidis

*I*t's Thursday in Old Sana'a, and the call to prayer has yet to rush anyone home.

Our motley tourist troupe — Egyptian, Brazilian, Canadian, American — sits in the corner of a silversmith's shop in Yemen's capital watching the afternoon street exchange. It's a spur-of-the-moment trip from Dubai, born of cheap tickets on Air Arabia between weekends of heavy tribal fighting.

Then as now, stability is tenuous. The Houthi rebellion in the north threatens an already fractured state; Al Qa'eda roosts once again in the Hadramaut Valley; there is scant water; oil, even less; the president has, once again, resigned. Yemen: climbing the Failed States Index since 2005.

But like so many states in the region, fragility depends on the day. On this afternoon in June, the city's rhythm beats as slow and sonorous as the call of the *azan* from Jami' Kabeer mosque. The acacia trees are in bloom; the mountains bring a dry wind; people get on with the business of living.

There are beggars — darkened by the sun, gaunt — who roam

past us ahead of afternoon prayer. Yemen is not a rich country by any stretch, but there's a dance to which everyone is accustomed: a few words murmured by the beseeching in return for the sturdy clink of rials into outstretched palms. The small hands that gather around us — accompanied by bare feet and curious eyes — poke and prod the strange people with their cameras, their sunglasses, their uncovered arms, the women with no hijab who dress in colors.

Aaliya is 12 and wears a somber black abaya; her younger cousins are in soiled party dresses and T-shirts. I ask Yehya, our guide, how soon the pink dresses and curls will disappear under black cloth and gloves. "When they become women," he declares. (Later on, a girl in *niqab*, slightly cross-eyed, will sidle up to me, restrained but assiduous in her begging. She will trail us for blocks before I give her money, and when I look at the cloth around her eyes, I see that it's worn, and her dress is scuffed white with sand at the bottom. Will she be here in 10 years — on the same street, peddling for change, or married, loosed from this routine, these confines?)

Two boys, large, curved *jambiya* knives jutting from their belts to display manhood, straddle an abandoned motorcycle behind a brick building. (The curved daggers passed down from fathers to sons are legacies wrought out of metal: wealth, status, and region woven into silver inlays, carved into hilts, and bound by intricately patterned belts. The ones I buy have Islamic and Jewish metalwork woven into the design; testament to the craftsmanship of Yemenite Jews whose wares haunt the *souqs* decades after their emigration).

"Houm majaneen!" one of them says derisively of the large African family that begs in front of the shop — they're crazy. He is reproached and told to drink his tea. (Later, another beggar boy wanders up, maybe 7, 8, dressed in a large blazer and trousers, dragged reluctantly by his grandfather through the square. The

lucid hazel of his eyes strikes me, as if I can see right through them to the resignation of another week, another hustle.)

If Egypt is *um dunya* — the mother of the world — Yemen is its forgotten grandfather. Its rich legacy as a crossroads of trade and a progenitor of culture in the Arabia Peninsula is eclipsed by its modern woes. Oil-deprived, water-scarce and enervated by *qat*, it moves at the same viscous pace as the honey it is famed for, a timestamp of a bygone era before the rest of the region discovered oil. Before the black gold rush hit Dubai, before Muscat got the Shangri-La, before Riyadh got its first Starbucks, there was Yemen: impoverished, fragmented, volatile Yemen — a modern testament of what could have been had the rest of the Gulf lost God's resource lottery.

In spite of — maybe because of — what it lacks, Yemen remains culturally stable in ways modern parts of the Gulf haven't. Open stalls line the narrow streets of the Souq al Milh and the shops around Bab al Yemen. (In the UAE, malls have become the modern-day agoras; places of ultra-cool congress that erase the backwardness of haggling in the outdoors.) There is gossip and tea and gregarious laughter as the Egyptian barters for me in the crisp outdoor air, chastising me for giving in too early. (When I go back to the U.A.E., where I work as a journalist, the air will be hot and thick and impenetrably dense with sand. Industrial air-conditioners will spew cold into the malls where society congregates, and a slalom run down Ski Dubai will seem normal — an average day in the desert.)

We eat kebabs roasted over a cleft oil drum in the souq. Our place mats are copies of *The National*, the Abu Dhabi-based newspaper that employs me. When it was first launched in 2008, it was touted as "The New York Times of the Middle East." Behind me, a shoe seller opens a copy, sprays it down, and wipes his shop windows.

As we eat, the boys and men around us — there are mostly only boys and men around now — crowd the stalls, grabbing for hot sauce, eggs and ketchup to shove into freshly baked rolls. They peer at us for a while; one man offers me a fresh roll with blackened fingers. Soon, our novelty wears off. We're abandoned. (Later, as a friend and I sit in a female *hamam*, the water tepid and doled out in empty vegetable cans, an Egyptian wife will tell us that men now go to her country for brides, because Yemeni women are circumcised and "not hot-blooded". The henna patterns on her thighs are intricate and vast, spanning the large swaths of her body.)

When we tour the old summer residence of Imam Yehya in Wadi Dhahr later that day, another woman — covered in black, glasses tucked into her face covering — raises her gloved hand and makes a clicking gesture. *"Mumkin asoor?"*

Sure, I'll take a picture. We pose: black robe, black robe, black robe, me (pink shirt and white scarf), giggling children. Not a face in sight, but I'm the unknown quantity in the equation. It's amusing, and strange. Have I seen you at the hamam? I want to ask. Were you the Egyptian wife with the frisky husband? More families now. More cell phones, more clicks, more smiles. Babies are suddenly in my arms, bright green eyes questioning. The other American — ginger-haired, wad of qat in his mouth large as a baseball — is stunningly pale next to their coffee skin. We are the subjects become objects; the animated souvenirs come to entertain the local folk on a Friday afternoon.

When I first came to the Gulf as a recent American college grad, I was drawn by a narrative of progress and modernity. The deft cut of the Burj al Arab and the gild of Emirates Palace painted a seductive vision: oil was the new gold rush, raising future cities from the sand, rife with potential and opportunity to create something new, something better, something different. But as I took in Yemen — poor, broken, no-ski-slopes-for-miles Yemen — I couldn't help but wonder about what development throws away, what jewels of the past get lost in the race to re-make a nation.

I sleep with an open window, six megaphones lashed to the minaret that looms over my room. At dawn, the over-zealous muezzin bellows "*Allahu Akbar!*" so loudly that my bedframe shakes and I flail, falling out of bed.

Below, the devout file into the mosque. Religion, if nothing else, offers certainty in an unstable clime, ritual and routine creating a fixed environment where outcomes are knowable, the playing field safe. I wonder if that is why Old Sana'a clings to these traditions; that in the face of unemployment and scarcity, religion makes the uncertainties easier to bear. In *Arabia Felix*, where things constantly seem on the brink, hope seems the most precious of resources to cultivate.

The day we leave, the Houthi rebellion starts anew; refugees stream in from the northwestern province of Hajjah; and a German family of six is kidnapped and executed. More travel warnings spew from the American embassy: avoid Yemen at all costs; avoid the poverty, the instability, the devalued cost of life.

So we leave, and I return to my tactless and air-conditioned petro-kingdom; to a throng of Indian migrant workers crowding the arrivals terminal; to a skyscraper apartment that does not sit on a lake but a sandpit filled with water; to late-night conversations in sleek lounges around cloying *shisha* smoke. I feel the pulse of the city's potential thrum through my car as I barrel down its 7-lane highway, jambiyas and honey and silver tucked into the back.

Young Man Afraid
of His Horses

by Caryl Pagel

What will keep you from telling it to everyone.

What will prevent you from perpetual disclosure: shame or
privacy—words or the
sense that once said you cannot snatch the story back.

What you say will disseminate and break.

It will split out into the ether outlasting matter—ignoring
teller—resisting
order—beyond reason—escaping even your own hold on
the subject.

It will not fit into history.

You cannot keep yourself from speaking.

Losing Translation to the Marketplace of Ideas

by Alex Green

Last fall, Patrick Modiano was awarded the Nobel Prize in Literature. A French writer, he was hailed by the committee "for the art of memory with which he has evoked the most ungraspable human destinies." Yet nobody in America knew who he was. The few Modiano books ever published in English disappeared from bookstores within a day and none were available again for weeks.

That an author at the forefront of world literature was not only unknown but nearly unavailable in America created a storm of commentary. The Modiano affair was rightly identified as emblematic of how little translated literature of any kind gets published in the United States each year. But focusing on publishing as the issue misses the larger, persistent, worsening problem: we are a society that appears to have little interest in what the rest of the world is saying. Having little access is only the symptom.

It is important to note that the Nobel Prize committee is not made up of Norwegian hipsters trying to one-up us on contemporary esoteric French writers. Modiano has enjoyed a successful career for over four decades. In spite of this, his few translated works were scarce, published by David R. Godine, a small Boston press. Nor is Modiano the only one. When French-Mauritian novelist J. M. G. Le Clézio, author of over three-dozen books, was awarded the Nobel in 2008, the same publisher was again one of the few to have published his works in America.

In telling this story, nearly every Modiano article embraced some version of the following argument: Translation is expensive work. Authors have to be paid for the rights to their books and translators must be paid as well. Talented editors are needed to oversee the process, and it can be difficult working in two languages. On the other end of the production line, books have to have audiences and if audiences are not there, losses can be significant. The risk of publishing unknown foreign authors, especially given the costs, is therefore simply too high to be commercially viable.

With hastily translated Modiano books now widely available, one could conclude that this is a sufficient view. Risk, supply, and demand are the problems. The problem, however, is far larger than scarcity alone, and far larger than just Patrick Modiano. The problem is that scarcity begets scarcity, with significant cultural consequences.

It is important to keep an eye on the real problem because the commercial argument gets less convincing the more you look at the risks and complexities involved in nearly any kind of publishing. Think, for example, of children's picture books. Royalties have to go to the authors, but also have to be shared with illustrators, who translate stories into images. Talented editors are equally necessary and like all books, children's books must find an audience or the publisher loses money. Yet there's money to be made. Behemoth publisher Scholastic, which keeps a healthy number of picture books in its mix of titles, earned well over $100 million in gross profits in the third quarter of last year.

Publishing is always a business of finding the right mix of titles, and there is plenty of evidence that books in translation can sell well. The Swedish-language blockbuster *The Girl with the Dragon Tattoo* sold over 15 million copies in the United States after being published by Knopf, a venerable publisher willing to take an occasional chance on something unknown from overseas.

Something, though, is keeping books from abroad scarce, even as the margins and flexibility afforded by e-books make publishing risks lower than they've ever been. Only 3 percent of books published in America each year were first written in another language. Of those, less than 1 percent are fiction, and most are classics like *Crime and Punishment*.

Part of the problem is self-fulfilling prophecy, surely. Seeing small audiences, large publishers leave much of the heavy lifting of contemporary literary translation to small presses. Without marketing budgets or the Nobel Prize, small presses rarely reach large audiences. A belief that translation is unviable begets the belief that it cannot and should not be done.

But at the heart of this is the question of why the audiences are small to begin with? And here we see another belief: that we, the English-speaking peoples, are actually leaders in advancing the stories of individuals across the globe. The paradoxical effect of this faith in our own preeminence is to undermine it: we assure ourselves of our leadership while having little interaction with the world's great contemporary literature, little understanding of who is creating it, and few ways to figure it out. After years of devaluing the importance of translation, we are not just missing avant-garde things, but works we might all embrace and works we very much need. This perfect storm of self-reinforcing isolationism means that despite our easy access to technology, we are alone. We have lost touch with the world's storytelling *lingua franca*.

The cultural expense of our inaccurate financial focus on translation is immense. When we lose the stories that draw us together, we lose shared cultural fabric and connections with one another. Calmed by our confidence in the democracy of our markets, devices, and platforms, our own creativity suffers and we hardly notice how little real contact we're making. A reflexive disrespect for other cultures grows while our own narrative becomes an incoherent supremacist monoculture that steadily approximates propaganda instead of conversation.

We tell our stories. We read our stories. Nothing more. Screaming over the wall at high decibels, we are not listening.

An End to Impunity?

Protests and Hope for Mexico

by Alfredo Corchado

I have covered many massacres, witnessed too much bloodshed, so many that the latest killings should not have come as a surprise. But it doesn't make it any less painful.

Mexico has a history of horrors. It is a country ravaged by rampant corruption, weak judicial institutions, deep economic disparities and indifference by authorities at all levels, so much that at times I question whether Mexicans have become numb. The impunity rate is right up there with Honduras, 95 percent.

And yet here I was, at the latest protest over the latest massacre, with masses of people pacing the same boulevard. The majestic Reforma Avenue now turned into a river of agony and outrage epitomized by tens of thousands of protesters raging against the latest massacre of 43 students in the state of Guerrero.

Is this Mexico's turning point? I asked myself as I walked away. What, if anything, has changed in this country?

I was born in Mexico, left my umbilical cord buried there and have spent a lifetime searching for answers to those questions, questions that have haunted me since I left my homeland kicking and screaming to the United States. The very questions that pushed me to write *Midnight In Mexico: A Reporter's Journey Through a Country's Descent Into Darkness.*

Since 2006, more than 100,000 people have been killed or disappeared. Tragedies abound, reflected in part by clandestine graves regularly unearthed throughout the country, from northeastern states of Coahuila, Nuevo Leon, Chihuahua to my birthplace of Durango. Guerrero is by no means a stranger to this morbid list.

And yet, this march felt different, the weight of the world falling on this magnificent, yet transfixed valley of more than 20 million people. The grim revelations of deep complicity between government authorities and criminal groups hit a new low, drawing condemnations from such world leaders as President Obama and Pope Francis and widespread anger in cities from Mexico City, Oslo, New Delhi, Buenos Aires and even Boston.

To begin with, the grisly details: Investigators had recovered garbage bags with dozens of burned human bones, ashes and other remains. One bone fragment has been confirmed by independent forensics experts from Austria and others may also belong to the missing students, all teacher trainees at a Guerrero town called Ayotzinapa. Some of the remains may never be identified, officials said Monday. The students were allegedly killed by a drug gang at the behest of the local mayor.

On Reforma Avenue I walked alongside colleagues and protesters that included some of the relatives of the victims. The protesters had seized the 104th anniversary of the Mexican Revolution to show their discontent, still searching for the equality and justice the revolutionaries died for.

Under gray skies and gathering raindrops, some carried pictures of the victims, others signs that mocked the narrative that President Enrique Peña Nieto tried to promote abroad. One sign read: "Visit Mexico" and showed gravesites in the background.

Others carried Mexico's tricolor flag, transformed into another symbol of mourning by coloring its green and red stripes to black.

Indeed, the biggest blow, analysts say, may be Peña Nieto's carefully crafted domestic and international public relations campaign. Since his presidency began in December 2012, Peña Nieto has focused on pushing for major reforms, from energy to telecommunications, and promised to rebuild his party's tattered image as corrupt and decrepit.

The Institutional Revolutionary Party, or PRI, which governed Mexico for 71 years, was kicked out of office in 2000 for 12 years before returning to power with Peña Nieto. The ouster and return of the PRI was hailed as a sign that democracy, albeit messy and violent, had been ushered into Mexico.

The protests unleashed another fury; reports from leading Mexican journalist Carmen Aristegui of a mansion estimated at $7 million belonging to soap opera star Angelica Rivera, the wife of the president. Rivera was buying the home, under construction in a pricey section known as *Las Lomas*, on credit from a company whose owner won large government construction contracts from Mexico State when Mr. Peña Nieto was its governor. Peña Nieto acknowledged the home, but said it belonged to his wife, Rivera, who would answer questions. She did and said she would put the house up for sale.

The allegations of government corruption, complicity with drug traffickers and conflicts of interest underscored a belief: If the PRI, or other political parties didn't change, the people certainly have. Marches, protests, vigils have continued here and across the world with the theme of "Mexico, the world is watching."

Democracy isn't tidy and neat, certainly not in Mexico, or even in my adopted homeland, the United States. Days later I returned to America and saw protests sparked by a grand jury decision not to indict a white police officer who shot and killed an unarmed black man in Ferguson, Missouri. And most recently in New York City. I couldn't help but think of Mexico.

The U.S. protests may lead to changes in how law enforcement authorities operate. President Obama weighed in and supports the idea of police collecting evidence through body cameras worn by officers. I thought of the possibility of such a move in Mexico: Mexican cops wearing cameras? Never.

Never may be too strong of a statement. Change in Mexico, fellow journalist Angela Kocherga reminded me, is usually a series of turning points that may lead to a tipping point. Whether Mexicans can seize the latest moment is perhaps a question best answered by time and those around me: Young and old, poor, middle and upper class, jamming streets leading to the biggest public square in the Americas known as the *Zócalo*.

Social media is proving an effective tool. Mexicans are learning not just to blame authorities, but to shame them before the world with their postings. Hold the powerful accountable.

Indeed, just the fact that people still turn out to protest in the darkest moments is further proof that the best of Mexico lies in the Mexicans themselves.

I strolled the streets of Mexico, looking for cover from a pouring rain, still caught between fear and hope.

— MEXICO CITY

DEAR GRACE

by Collier Nogues

The QR code directs to an online interactive version of this poem. As you move your finger (on a touchscreen device) or a mouse (on a computer) from line to line of the poem, the original document's erased text will reappear.

Dear Grace:

     Please tell
  Ja ne
n Cal   I lo

    ve
them
    — and no one worry
     .
     if it happens, it
will be   a
story.

James , Jr.

Dear Grace:

keep   an

    e   y   e

          out   for

                                        us
        . I

feel   we   have another
              fight on our hands.

            ever y on
                      e will be
hearing a great deal about it in the
next
few weeks.

        James   , Jr.

Dear Grace:

        It looks to me like it
will explode any day now. There is
tremendous   pressure to move

       —and no one seems to worry
about how or to where.
                      it
will be   m
     y
                  corp s
— my estimate
  is

             .

      James   , Jr.

Dear Grace:

        I
will explode any day now. The
               pressure

  i s

     the

suspension of
        tim e the
feeling that
                  our hands

                  will b
ear   a great deal
     .

    James   , Jr.

Dear Grace:

          I look   like

an alien —
       or

                  a corp
          se

James   , Jr.

Dear Grace:

    on   on
        o n
  an d no .
 n o
      out   or i n
  and no one
      or

      one of   us
      or t wo   o r
  n o t   us
and

              not
     our

             no

  James , Jr.

Dear Grace:

                                                 like
                                        Th is

                                        —

                                                 r a t
                                    a
                            r at
                             a

                t at
        t at   a t

                    at   a t

            James   , Jr.

Dear Grace:

                    bab y
                        writ e
                        m e

        p

                            l

                ea

                            s e, Jr.

Contributors

Paul Adler teaches in the History and Literature concentration at Harvard University. He received his PhD in history in 2014 from Georgetown University. His dissertation, *Planetary Citizens: U.S. NGOs and the Politics of International Development in the Late Twentieth Century* examines campaigns by U.S. NGOs in the 1970s and 1980s to reform the practices of institutions such as the World Bank.

Eric Anderson was born in Alexandria, Virginia. A recent graduate of the Iowa Writers' Workshop, his poems have appeared on Granta.com, in *Columbia Poetry Review*, *The Journal*, and elsewhere.

Greta Austin is Professor of Religious Studies and Director of the Gender & Queer Studies Program at the University of Puget Sound. Her academic research focuses on the law of the medieval Catholic Church. She lives with her two daughters and her husband Clark Lombardi, a professor of Islamic studies and comparative constitutional law, in Seattle.

Michael Badger's work has appeared in *Two Thirds North, Black Heart Literary Magazine* online, and is forthcoming in Scotland's *Valve*. Graduating from Lesley University with an MFA in creative writing did his soul well. He does the art thing and slings drinks to the masses in Seattle, WA

Carol Band's humor column, "A Household Word," won numerous awards—including the Gold Award from Parenting Publications of America for two consecutive years—and was collected into a book of the same name. Her writing has appeared in *The Boston Globe, The Boston Parents Paper* (where this column first appeared), *L.A. Parent*, and *AARP Magazine*, as well as Humorpress.com, parenthood.com, and others.

Jennifer Barber is the author of *Given Away, Rigging the Wind*, and *Vendaval*. Her poems have appeared in *The New Yorker, Upstreet, Harvard Divinity Bulletin, Orion, Gettysburg Review*, and elsewhere. She teaches at Suffolk University and is founding and current editor of the literary journal *Salamander*.

Anne Bernays is the author of ten novels, including *Professor Romeo* and *Growing Up Rich*, and co-author of *What If?*, one of the most widely used guides to creative writing. A teacher of fiction writing at the Nieman Foundation for Journalism at Harvard University, she has published essays in *The New York Times* and other major publications.

Harvey Blume is an author (*Ota Benga: The Pygmy At The Zoo*, 1992), freelance writer, and critic, who hails from the other Brooklyn, the part they haven't branded yet.

Suzanne Bouffard's writing has appeared in *The New York Times*, *Parents*, the *Harvard Education Letter*, and other outlets. She is co-author of *Ready, Willing, and Able* and winner of a 2013 Solutions Journalism Network grant.

Jack Christian is the author of the poetry collection *Family System*, winner of the 2012 Colorado Prize.

Alfredo Corchado is Mexico Bureau Chief for *The Dallas Morning News* and author of *Midnight in Mexico*. He was also a 2009 Nieman Fellow at Harvard University. This story is based on his reporting for *The News*.

Dwight Livingstone Curtis is a writer and teacher living in East Hampton, NY. His fiction has appeared in various journals and magazines, including *Explosion-Proof Magazine*, *Yolk NY*, and *The Harvard Advocate*. He is a recipient of Harvard's Louis Begley Prize for Fiction.

Mitchell Grabois has been nominated for the Pushcart Prize for work published in 2012, 2013, and 2014. His novel, *Two-Headed Dog*, is based on his work as a clinical psychologist in a state hospital. He lives in Denver.

Alex Green is the founding owner of Back Pages Books, an independent bookstore and publishing house in Waltham, Massachusetts. Since 2010 he has been a writer and researcher for the Harvard Program on Negotiation and the Harvard Business School. He has been a guest columnist for Boston.com and a contributor to *The Huffington Post*.

Lauren Haldeman is the author of the poetry collection *Calenday* (Rescue Press, 2014). She received her MFA from the Iowa Writers' Workshop, and has been a finalist for the Walt Whitman award and the Colorado Prize for Poetry.

Kalpana Jain is a senior journalist whose reporting played a significant role in elevating public health as an important topic of news coverage in

India. She has been been a health editor with the largest circulating English Daily, *The Times of India*. She is currently pursuing a Master in Theological Studies at the Harvard Divinity School.

Eric LeMay teaches in the writing program at Ohio University and serves as an associate editor for the *New Ohio Review* and the web editor for *Alimentum: The Literature of Food*. His collection *In Praise of Nothing: Essays, Memoir, and Experiments* won the Emergency Press International Book Contest. You can find more of it at http://www.inpraiseofnothing.org.

Matthew Lippman is the author of three poetry collections: *American Chew*, winner of The Burnside Review Book Prize (Burnside Review Book Press, 2013), *Monkey Bars* (Typecast Publishing, 2010), and *The New Year of Yellow*, winner of the Kathryn A. Morton Poetry Prize (Sarabande Books, 2007).

Kelly Matthews' fiction has appeared in *Salamander* and *Jewish Currents*, and her book about *The Bell*, an Irish literary magazine, was published in 2012. She has won writing awards from the Massachusetts Cultural Council and the University of Ulster.

Timothy McCarthy teaches at Harvard University, where he is the founding director of the Sexuality, Gender & Human Rights Program at the Carr Center for Human Rights Policy. Educated at Harvard and Columbia, he is the author or editor of five books, including *Stonewall's Children: Living Queer History in the Age of Liberation, Loss, and Love*, forthcoming from the New Press.

Leslie Anne Mcilroy won the 1997 Slipstream Poetry Chapbook Prize for *Gravel*, the 2001 Word Press Poetry Prize for *Rare Space*, and the 1997 Chicago Literary Awards. *Liquid Like This* was published by Word Press in 2008 and *Slag* is forthcoming from Main Street Rag in 2015. Leslie's poems appear in *jubilat, The Mississippi Review, PANK, Pearl, Poetry Magazine, the New Ohio Review* and more. She is a 2014 Pushcart Prize nominee and managing editor of HEArt—Human Equity through Art. Books and more at lamcilroy.org.

Effie-Michelle Metallidis is a graduate of the Harvard Kennedy School and a former journalist who was based in the Middle East.

Julie Monrad is a graduating senior from Harvard College. When avoiding schoolwork, she reads, writes, cooks at home and in restaurants, travels, hikes, plays squash, and volunteers for an eating disorder hotline.

Elizabeth Moore is the author of *The Truth and the Life*, a novel recently published by Alternative Book Press. Her work—both poetry and prose—explores the sometimes beautiful, sometimes tenuous relationships between nature and the human heart, between the wonders of youth and the uncertainties of experience, between past and present-day lives. She currently lives in Massachusetts with her husband, Nathan, where she works at The MIT Press.

Carmen Nobel is a senior editor at Harvard Business School and a frequent contributor to publications including *the Boston Globe*, NPR Science Friday, and *Inc. Magazine*. She lives in Watertown, Massachusetts.

Collier Nogues is the author of *The Ground I Stand On Is Not My Ground* (Drunken Boat, 2015) and *On the Other Side, Blue* (Four Way, 2011). She teaches creative writing at the Chinese University of Hong Kong, and co-edits poetry for *Juked.*

Pamela Painter is the author of three story collections, *Getting to Know the Weather, The Long and Short of It* and *Wouldn't You Like to Know*. Her stories have appeared in *The Atlantic, Five Points, Kenyon Review, Missouri Review, SmokeLong Quarterly*, and *Ploughshares*, and in numerous anthologies such as *Sudden Fiction* and *Flash Fiction*. She received a grant from The NEA and has won three Pushcart Prizes. She lives in Boston and teaches in the Emerson College MFA Program.

Caryl Pagel is the author of *Experiments I Should Like Tried at My Own Death* (Factory Hollow Press, 2012) and *Twice Told* (H_NGM_N Books). She teaches in the NEOMFA program in eastern Ohio and is the Director of the Cleveland State University Poetry Center. She is the co-founder and editor of Rescue Press and a poetry editor at *jubilat*.

Kiki Petrosino is the author of two books of poetry: *Hymn for the Black Terrific* (2013) and *Fort Red Border* (2009), both from Sarabande. Her poems have appeared in *The Best American Poetry, Tin House, Gulf Coast*, and elsewhere. She is an Associate Professor of English at the University of Louisville, where she directs the creative writing program.

Christina Porter is the Director of Humanities for Revere Public Schools in

Revere, MA. When she is not working, she can be found exploring the outdoors with her two great loves, Andrew and their daughter Norah Kate.

Allen M. Price earned his MA in journalism from Emerson College, and served as a proofreader for *Redivider*. His journalistic work has appeared in such magazines as *Muscle & Fitness* and *Natural Health*, while his short stories have appeared in such publications as *The Saturday Evening Post*.

Peter Ramos is the author of one book of poetry, *Please Do Not Feed the Ghost* (BlazeVox Books, 2008) and three shorter collections: *Television Snow* (Back Pages Books, 2014), *Watching Late-Night Hitchcock & Other Poems* (handwritten press, 2004), and *Short Waves* (White Eagle Coffee Store Press, 2003). An associate professor of English at Buffalo State College, Peter teaches courses in nineteenth- and twentieth-century American literature.

David Rivard's new book, *Standoff*, will appear from Graywolf in early 2016. His five other books include *Otherwise Elsewhere, Sugartown,* and *Wise Poison*, winner of the James Laughlin Prize from the Academy of American Poets and a finalist for the Los Angeles Times Book Award. Among his awards are fellowships from the Guggenheim Foundation, Civitella Ranieri, and the NEA, as well as the 2006 O. B. Hardison Jr. Poetry Prize from the Folger Shakespeare Library, in recognition of both his writing and teaching. He directs the MFA in Writing program at the University of New Hampshire.

Anna Ross is the author of *If a Storm*, selected by Julianna Baggott for the Robert Dana-Anhinga Prize for Poetry. Her recent work has appeared in *Tupelo Quarterly, Salamander,* and *The Brooklyn Quarterly*, and has been recognized by the Massachusetts Cultural Council Artist Fellowships program. She lives in Dorchester, MA, with her husband, daughter, and son.

Zach Savich is the author of the poetry collections *Full Catastrophe Living* (U. Iowa, 2009), *Annulments* (Center for Literary Publishing, 2010), *The Firestorm* (CSU Poetry Center, 2011), and *Century Swept Brutal* (Black Ocean, 2014). His work has received the Iowa Poetry Prize, the Colorado Prize for Poetry, and the Cleveland State University Poetry Center's Open Award, among other honors. He teaches in the BFA Program for Creative Writing at the University of the Arts, in Philadelphia, and co-edits Rescue Press's Open Prose Series.

J.D. Scrimgeour's book *Themes For English B: A Professor's Education In & Out of Class* won the AWP Award for Nonfiction. He has also published two books of poetry, and a CD of poetry and music, *Ogunquit & Other Works*. This past summer *Only Human*, a musical that he wrote with his two sons, was performed at Ames Hall Theatre in Salem, Massachusetts.

Kim Stafford is the founding director of the Northwest Writing Institute at Lewis & Clark College, and author of a dozen books of poetry and prose, including *Having Everything Right: Essays of Place, 100 Tricks Every Boy Can Do: How My Brother Disappeared,* and *The Muses Among Us: Eloquent Listening and Other Pleasures of the Writer's Craft*. More about his music, writing, and films can be found at www.kim-stafford.com.

Sebastian Stockman is a lecturer in English at Northeastern University. His work has appeared in *The New York Times Book Review, The Wall Street Journal, The Boston Globe,* and *The Los Angeles Review of Books,* among other publications.

Julia Story is from Indiana and now lives in Somerville, Massachusetts. She is the author of *Post Moxie*, which was the recipient of Sarabande Books' 2009 Kathryn A. Morton Prize and *Ploughshares'* 2010 John C. Zacharis First Book Award. Her recent work has appeared in *Sixth Finch, Salamander,* and *Denver Quarterly*. Her chapbook *The Trapdoor* will be published by Dancing Girl Press in November 2014.

Tom Zygiel is a lifelong resident of Massachusetts and a graduate of Boston College. He has traveled extensively in Concord.

In Praise of Nothing is reproduced here courtesy of Emergency Press

Portions of *Allen Ginsberg: An Encounter* first appeared in the Boston Review, August 1995, vol.2 #7. "Allen Ginsberg" by Ryan Origami, All Rights Reserved, Used With Permission.

About Pangyrus

Pangyrus is a Boston-based group of writers, editors, and creative professionals with a new vision for how high-quality writing can thrive on the internet. Now also a print publication, we aim to foster a community of creative individuals and organizations dedicated to art, ideas, and making culture thrive.

Combining Pangaea and gyrus, the terms for the world continent and whorls of the cerebral cortex crucial to verbal association, Pangyrus is about connection.

INDEX by AUTHOR and GENRE

POETRY

Eric Anderson	A Borrowed Copy of Ben Fountain	226
Jennifer Barber	Motion Harmony #3	7
Jack Christian	Poem in Film	157
Lauren Haldeman	Istvan	81
Matthew Lippman	Crime Shows	50
Leslie Anne Mcilroy	Blue	192
Elizabeth Moore	New England February	46
Collier Nogues	DEAR GRACE	252
Caryl Pagel	Young Man Afraid of His Horses	243
Kiki Petrosino	Pastoral	22
Peter Ramos	Away from my Dream Desk	60
David Rivard	Excellence	39
Anna Ross	Self-Portrait Before	187
Zach Savich	Demolition Trio	189
Kim Stafford	Benign Indignities	183
Julia Story	The Pain Scale	110

FICTION

Michael Badger	Keepers	61
Anne Bernays	X-Ray	160
Dwight Livingstone Curtis	Five-Finger Discount	227
Mitchell Grabois	Cowardice	48
Julie Monrad	By the Pool	194
Allen M Price	Temptation's Crush	204
Kelly Matthews	The Memorialist	83
Pamela Painter	Empty Summer Houses	8

ESSAYS

Paul Adler	Goodbye Climate Change, Goodbye Poverty?	134
Greta Austin	Living with Pain	143
Carol Band	The Living Dead	184
Harvey Blume	Allen Ginsberg: An Encounter	96
Suzzane Bouffard	In the Pocket	52
Alfredo Corchado	An End to Impunity in Mexico?	248
Alex Green	Losing Translation	244
Kalpana Jain	City of Widows	17
Eric LeMay	In Praise of Nothing	140
Timothy McCarthy	Coming of AIDS	23
Effie-Michelle Metallidis	Interlude: Yemen	238
Carmen Nobel	David Sedaris is Sick of Himself	74
Christina Porter	The Tonic of Wildness	112
JD Scrimgeour	High Street Park: The Kindness of Boys	41
Sebastian Stockman	Licensed Outlaws	216
Tom Zygiel	Holy Family Holds the Line	118